A
Child
of Her Own

A
Child
of Her Own

Lindsay T. Wyatt

TATE PUBLISHING
AND ENTERPRISES, LLC

Published by Tate Publishing & Enterprises, LLC
127 E. Trade Center Terrace | Mustang, Oklahoma 73064 USA
1.888.361.9473 | www.tatepublishing.com

Tate Publishing is committed to excellence in the publishing industry. The company reflects the philosophy established by the founders, based on Psalm 68:11,
"The Lord gave the word and great was the company of those who published it."

Published in the United States of America

ISBN: 978-1-62994-414-2
1. Fiction / Medical
2. Fiction / Family Life
14.01.29

Dedication

Dedicated to my mother, Trina, who taught me to love uncon-
ditionally, and my children Kevin, Kayla, and Jordan, who have
inspired me beyond what words can convey.

In Memory of Edith Farmer, Carolyn "Caddy" Washington,
and Betty J. Nealy.

Tonya

"Our parents died when we were nine." I hate opening a conversation that way, but it has been the opening for quite a few of them. This line is used when I am trying to protect my little sister, to explain the wrong she has done. Even though we were only separated by five minutes, she has always been, and will always be, my little sister. It is amazing what those five minutes changed between us. I often wonder if everything would have been different had she come first. Five minutes. That is all that separated us from the womb and the outside world. But for me, those few minutes somehow contained a lifetime of worries and burdens that eluded her.

I was the protector, the responsible one. My father had often joked that "Toya does everything in her own timing. She has since birth, and only God himself can change that about her." That statement was always followed by a smile, one that was never reserved for me. Considering she was their miracle baby, even though there were two of us born that day, we all treated her as just that. Mom's umbilical cord had wrapped around her neck, and she was breached. My mother, who was a strict Southern

Baptist, always believed that the devil tried to "snuff" her baby out. Therefore it was our job to discover that gift he was trying to hide from the world. Discovering her gifts left little time to explore mine.

It is true, my sister is gifted; everything always comes so easy for her. It would seem that God himself has made it so in exchange for such a hard birth. Even though we are identical on the outside, she is the prettier twin—there is such a thing— and she's the smarter one as well. That wouldn't have pissed me off as much if it weren't so effortless for her. Growing up, my grades were almost as good; however, it took countless nights of cramming to be almost as good.

She had a way with numbers, words, and men. Honestly, there was nothing she tried that she was not positively wonderful at; that is because she never tried to be sensitive to anyone else's needs and she never had to be caring, understanding, or in the least bit sympathetic. Those are the things she'd never be able to master. The saddest part of all for me is realizing that she has become a lost cause. My throat turns dry, as if my body is once again betraying me. This is just the beginning; there will be more revelations to come. My throat is doing the one thing I never allowed my heart to do: closing.

I wish I could disappear, crawl up into a ball, and vanish, leaving behind not one single trace of my existence. After all, if my sister, whom I had shared a womb, a childhood, and my life with, could not bring herself to, for just once, see me for who I am, how can I expect anyone else too? What is the point in remaining? There is nothing left of me to give, and as is the norm when I am drowning, she somehow manages to float.

I remember when Aunt Lynette told us that our parents would not be coming home; in my innocence I thought maybe they had decided to stay an extra night. I knew that meant we could stay up late and watch movies we weren't allowed to, eat the cake we weren't supposed to, and most importantly jump up and down on the bed and giggle until we fell asleep. It never occurred to me then that "not coming home" meant never coming home. It was my little sister that explained it to me as only she could. "No, stupid, they are dead. It's a shame." She continued standing in front of me while I laid in the grass surrounded by chocolates my parents would never have approved off, making me suddenly aware that she was blocking out my sun. In that moment, it seemed she was larger than life, and in my mind, it became clear that she had the ability to take even the sun away from me.

The announcement of our parent's death did little to diminish her presence. I hated her and loved her deeper that day. It was not the first time or the last that I would be jealous of her. It is befitting to this conversation that I remember that day. Even with loss at my door, I still find it easy, almost impossible not, to be envious of her, but once again I will swallow it. I have swallowed a thousand cups of bitterness, tasted resentment, and digested both as if they were sustenance. Today would be no different from yesterday or the days before.

"We're exactly nine years, eight months, and twelve days old today, and our parents are gone. I'll have to write this in my memoirs." Then she burst into tears as if on cue. She was nothing short of mesmerizing, and every performance outdid the last. She certainly had a gift, one for the theatrics. I didn't allow myself to grieve that day or since. Instead, I held my little sister until her shoulders stopped shaking. It's funny to me now, her memoirs. What a story she'd have to tell, and I am certain that I would at least earn a footnote, if not an honorable mention, even though it is I who allows her to live her story. I am the glue that holds her together; no credit is given of course, and most times, I do not ask for it. But today, damn it, I demand it.

My auntie raised us, and she tried her best, but Toya was a handful. When she was sixteen, she decided she wanted to be a doctor; the news shocked us all. We assumed she would want something in the spotlight. It suited her more to play the role of doctor on the big screen. I couldn't picture her dirtying her nails with blood or her blouses with tears from a grieving family. She had done little to offer comfort to her own broken home. Those things we set aside since Toya had declared what she wanted. I pretended to forget my dreams of being a nurse. I knew we'd never be able to afford medical school despite my aunt's savings and my parent's life insurance. I was not bitter about it, not then. Instead, I thought about what I would have to do to make it possible.

I took the easy way out; some may not understand the logic, but it was easier to allow her to succeed than to allow myself the chance to fail. I would have felt inadequate with her having MD next to her name and RN next to mine. I acquiesced, though sometimes I would get angry at my sister for never putting me first; I wanted her to be as sensitive to my needs as I was to hers, even if I never voiced them. I convinced myself that I was just putting my dreams on hold and doing the right thing by our auntie who had given up so much for us. Aunt Lynette wanted us to do something amazing to make our parents proud; we were her baby sister's little girls, and that was a burden I understood even then. We all agreed there would be nothing more amazing then having LaToya Garrett, MD, in our family. I gave her all the insurance money, and I got a job to help with the rest. I was supposed to save for myself. That never happened—the taking-care-of-myself part. Somewhere along the line, she became so much a part of me that I was not complete until she was happy. We shared every accomplishment, or I gave the pretense of doing so. When she made the dean's list, we laughed, stating that she was doing this for all of us—our parents, our auntie, and especially me because I had been there every single day. I swallowed those little pieces of anger, hoping that I did not choke on them.

The magnitude of this moment sinks in. The things that I try to avoid saying are right at the tip of my tongue burning their way out. Suddenly the massive room seems smaller than a shoe box. I really need a cigarette. Once I decided it was time to start a family, I quit smoking. I knew the risk of smoking during pregnancy and after, but today, I need to feel the smoke in my lungs, the burn it brings, along with the sweet dizziness a cigarette will provide. I begin to tap my fingers on the arm of the chair. Lance grabs my hand; he is my quiet during a storm. I love him, though lately I am reminded that he too is a hand-me-down from my little sister. He saw her first and wanted her, but he chose to settle down with me. Settle for me; the jury is still out on that one, eighteen years later.

We had more in common. He said I gave him all the things that no other woman—meaning my sister—could. After our first kiss, he knew I was the one. I believed him because I needed to. It didn't hurt that he was the most beautiful man I had ever seen. Standing an even six foot tall, 220 pounds, with skin the color of bronze bathed in sun light, Lance is the epitome of what a man should be. Naturally, when he kissed me I pictured a house full of pretty babies that looked like him—good hair, a perfect white smile, and wide eyes with lashes a mile and a half long.

His kiss changed my life, changed how I felt about me, because if he had picked me, then I had to be worthy of more than what I had been settling for. There was more passion in his lips than I had ever read about, let alone experienced. It was a far stretch from my first, and admittedly my last kiss with Evan, a childhood friend. Evan too had loved my sister more than me, but I had settled and became a poor man's version of my twin, something I promised myself I would never do again. When Lance kissed me, I thought I would never have to.

I was shocked, and the only thing that seemed right at the time was to invite him in. I toyed with ideas on how he met me; I knew his face was not one I could have forgotten. It delighted me thinking of where he could have spotted me. Never did it cross my mind that he had the wrong girl. I just assumed he wanted me; I envisioned him seeing me at the library or watching me walk through the park on my way home from work. I had mustered up a romantic epic before we reached the dining room.

I was thrilled the most in the knowledge that I would once again be first. No man would dare kiss a woman that way on her door step, making them both speechless, unless he had come prepared with grand plans. That was the way it worked in my romance novels. I would be the first to fall in love. I always wanted the same for twin, it seemed harder for her to form any attachment to someone who did not share a blood relation. I never thought it would happen to me, especially not first.

Then LaToya walked down the steps, and I could see that he knew he had made a mistake. His eyes said more in that second than his lips had moments before. There was a longing there. I went to introduce them, but she already knew his name apparently, and he sparkled at the knowledge that she had remembered.

"Lance Lawson." So much for introductions, I didn't even know his name. "You sit a few seats behind me in women's studies. Isn't Mr. Boatwright the best? I'm not just saying that because he's fine either." She winked and sauntered back up the steps. She never asked what he was doing there. She didn't care because he wasn't her type.

She never liked competition in her relationship. Whoever LaToya dealt with had to be less driven, less attractive, and therefore less desirable. Lance was everything she didn't want, making him more attractive to me. If she had fought for him, I would have lost; sadly she would have discarded him almost as suddenly as she discovered him. His kiss told me he needed something. I would save him from her, keeping him from heartbreak that was as inevitable as the earth spinning.

We sat down on the overstuffed sofa, and I told him I knew he had come for her and he could wait with me if he wanted because I was sure her boyfriend would be leaving soon. I am not certain if he stayed just to see if I was bluffing, but less than fifteen minutes later, Toya walked out the door with one of her "what's his names?" That's what I called them.

Lance asked a few questions about her, and I pretended we were just making conversation as I threw her under the bus. I advised him that What's His Name was one of many, and my sister was as liberal with her bed as she was with her mind. It was true. I would never lie on her; however, I wouldn't have volunteered that information to anyone else either.

My aunt said everyone grieved differently and that she was just looking for her version of love. I was grieving too, but I knew I wouldn't find it in the next condom wrapper. Lance would say that I had him at the first kiss; I knew it was that conversation on the pastel-flowered couch that won him over. How could we disprove him now? Would it be necessary? Would I want to know the truth, if it were different from the one I have allowed myself to believe? Though everything we built may be based on a lie, it doesn't negate the hard work. Our foundation may not be as strong, but the picture is still pretty. Why tear the house down when it is easier to keep adding on to it, making additions instead of repairs? The knowledge that a force beyond our control could come at any time and reduce your life to rubble is always there. The possibility of a huge mess being left in the wake of disaster may seem like a small sacrifice compared to the trouble of starting over. Trying to rebuild what you have lost would be ludicrous, damn near impossible. No matter what, you'll find that you missed the imperfections and there are cracks that you've just painted over and ignored. Women use kisses as love's plaster; we kiss away what we don't want to see, hiding the cracks behind our lipstick stains.

Even still, he is mine and has been since that first day. I wanted a family, needed to plant roots, and start off where my parents left off. There was nothing short of amazing about being a mother. We all want to leave our legacy behind to feel that we have contributed something, changed the world in some way that will be remembered long after we're gone, ensuring we will never be forgotten. There will always be a link on a family tree that says your name. To have that name carried on so that we continue to live even after we have ceased to exist, children fill that void. But I would not be the one to give this to him.

"I'm sorry, Arnold." He looked sympathetic. I have always thought that about him since we met at the firm's Christmas party years ago. He seemed to be just as nervous as I was despite having been with the firm for almost twenty years now. He nods to let me know that he is listening, and even though we are not paying him for his time, he will treat us with the same courtesy as any other client.

"I just don't know where to start. Our parents died when we were younger, and as any older sister would do, I coddled LaToya. I gave into every tantrum, want, or need. I became her surrogate mother—well, that's not the word I want to use here, but I am sure you get the point." *When I leave here, I am buying myself cigarettes, strawberry ice cream, and a few Kit Kats.*

"We tried so long to have a family. I think we only touched each other when we thought it would lead to making a baby." That was my fault. I made excuse after excuse; the truth is I cried after we made love every time. It felt like a chore to me, and I am sure he didn't enjoy it either. It was a far cry from what we had enjoyed our first years of marriage. "We got pregnant a few times."

"Six times. We lost them all." Lance tells Arnold who writes this down. He is making a list of failures; little does he know I have compiled them all for him. I could have typed them up and hand-delivered them if he had asked. I have failed as a wife, a sister, a daughter, and a niece. *We should make those two pints of ice cream.* I cannot imagine what else he has written down or what

Lance has shared. The first two miscarriages were not a secret to the firm; they had been really good about it, giving him time off to spend with me as if his presence would make up for the emptiness. When we got pregnant with baby number three, we decided to keep that one a secret. Now we had lost six pregnancies in four years. He always says "we lost," and I fight back the urge to laugh uncontrollably. Laughter is the best medicine, and maybe I have gone slightly mad. Babies are not keys or directions; the term *loss* amuses me. We didn't lose anything. My body rejected them, every single one after a few weeks. I think that is the only time I prayed harder than after we had sex. The funniest part is after the third miscarriage, I had lost my religion and cursed God, blamed him even. But after Lance rolled off me or that line turned blue, I was back on my knees again praying. It amazes me how we never seem to believe in God until we need him.

"We were told to consider adoption." Everyone always asked us why we never thought of it. "Lance was adopted. I'm not sure if you knew that." Arnold shakes his head no. I wonder how he couldn't. Did he somehow miss the picture of the older white couple sitting on my husband's desk? Maybe he assumed they came with the frame. My husband was lucky; he had been adopted into privilege. Maybe he didn't need to know, but it only seems fair.

"We both agreed that we wanted someone who looked like us, someone that shared a genetic link." When a married woman says, "We both agreed," it usually means she made the decision. This was no exception to the rule. "The next step was obviously surrogacy. It sounded perfect at the time. Another woman would be able to..." This is the part I can never own up to admitting that there is something I am unable to do. I helped raise my sister, worked two jobs to put her through school, and dealt with life after losing both parents. Now I volunteer at three shelters, plan fundraisers, teach Sunday school, sing on the church choir, manage a home and distribute bill payments for two households. I cook, clean, and iron for a husband who has one foot out the door. I do all of these things with a smile on my face. But I will not sit here in front of these two men—one who at this point I believe is staying out of some twisted sense of obligation and the other who's a stranger with kind eyes—and admit that I am less than a woman because of some abnormality that my doctors can't explain. Whatever it was, it was something that apparently did not affect my sister. Even if we are identical on the outside—minus the twenty unwarranted pounds I have gained—in the inside, she was pristine. I'd have to tell them that if there is such a thing as justice in this world, it has somehow missed our little space in it.

"The obstetrician tried to fertilize her eggs, and that's when we were told there is a genetic abnormality that stops them from thriving after a few weeks." Again Lance has to finish what I could not. "They are not sure how or why it happens. It's rare. Our doctor has never treated anyone with the particular mutation. There was no way her eggs would be viable." He squeezes my hand again. As if that would somehow soften what he has said. When the doctor said to me that my eggs were not viable, I heard instead that I was not valuable, to my husband or to myself.

Lance says he does not blame me. I think it is because I blame myself enough. He must wonder what would have happened if he kissed the other sister that first day or just simply walked out when he realized his mistake. There are a dozen times when he could have or should have left. Plenty of missed opportunity, and he has done so without a hint of regret. I have to speak before I allow my mind to wander any further.

"The doctor suggested we use Lance's sperm and someone else's eggs. The idea did not sit right with either of us." Once again the "us" I am referring to is me. "We wanted a child with my smile, his nose, and my daddy's eyes. I didn't want to see the face of a stranger when I looked into my—I mean, our child." I fumbled over the word *ours*. I am sure both of them heard me, but they pretend they didn't for the sake of courtesy. "So that is when we considered LaToya." The mention of her name makes Lance unbutton his shirt. I ignore that gesture while making a mental note to remember if it happens again. I continue. "Toya was always selfish. She never wanted children. Her life is just too complicated for a child. She is single and a surgeon to boot. When would she have time for a child? She doesn't remember to feed herself half of the time. I still pay her bills for her. I write them out and send them off." I wait to see if Arnold has copied down that little piece of information. It may not seem as damaging as six miscarriages, but it should earn me a few points. My thirty-seven-year-old sister still behaves like she is a child outside of that hospital. "She'd come home to no lights and a foreclosure sign on her home if it were not for me." Toya being selfish is not breaking news; it is a reoccurring story. "I tried to believe she would not deny me this one thing after watching us suffer as much as we have." I reached for a tissue off the oversized desk. I am not crying because of what has to be told but because I regret it all.

I regret sitting back and allowing my sister to have everything. She is so accustomed to me curbing my needs to fit her wants that she doesn't see anything wrong with what she is doing to me.

I could have been the one who went to medical school, and then I could have found a way to fix what is broken inside of me. Instead, I sit at home waiting to hold a child that may never come.

"We asked her to carry a child for us. We would have to use her eggs, which was fine because there would be no way to tell genetically that the baby was not mine. We used Lance's sperm. It worked for her right away. Everything was normal. She moved in with us so I could keep an eye on her, make sure she ate the way I would have, took the vitamins, and was never alone." I resist the urge to tell Arnold the real reason she came to stay with us. I don't want to hang her dirty laundry in this office. "It was good to have her back under the same roof. I got up in the middle of the night and answered her craving calls. Lance offered, but this was my way to experience the pregnancy with her. I even ate the things she did—egg sandwiches with applesauce in the middle of the night. Sometimes I even slept with her. We did so often as children, but I would stay until the baby fell asleep inside her. We would lay facing each other stomach to stomach, and it felt like I was carrying the baby. I could feel it move against my skin, and I'd cry silent tears into my pillow. She'd smooth them away almost as suddenly as they appeared. When I cried, we did not speak because we didn't have to, like we were kids again, and she knew everything I had to say without me saying them. When I stopped crying, we'd talk, watching her stomach stretch and roll. We'd guess if it was a hand or a foot. All of it was amazing. She glowed, pregnancy became her. I can't remember a time when we were closer or when I loved or appreciated her more." Despite myself, I smile at those memories. They now seem so bittersweet. The pain I feel is real, as real as if someone had amputated my limbs without any medication. I could not go through that again if we were to lose. I could never again watch another child grow through images on an ultrasound or the stretching of skin across a once firm belly. To think that I would never be able to feel this baby in my arms the way that I need to, the way you hold something that belongs to you, is agony.

"She helped me decorate the nursery. We agreed on yellow since Lance and I did not know the sex of the baby. She did, of course, but respected that fact that we did not want to. I used her old crib instead of mine. It was my way of keeping her presence in my home after she left. It was a gift of sorts. We all agreed that we would never let the child know I had not birthed him or her. But we wanted Toya to be closer than an aunt."

"Five days ago, my sister gave birth to a little girl. We named her McKenzie, and something went wrong, terribly wrong. The doctors couldn't stop the bleeding. My sister almost died, and during those few minutes, I grieved her." The thought still hits my soul like a ton of bricks. The tears are silent but have soaked through my blouse; even now the thought of her not being here cripples me. "I couldn't have pictured my life without her. I wanted my daughter to know her aunt. I wanted to thank her for such an amazing gift, a perfect child. I had never seen a little girl more beautiful in all my life. God couldn't have created a more immaculate child if he worked over time.

"I cried because my daughter would never know her aunt. Then she woke up, and everything changed. At first, they couldn't stop the bleeding, and there was too much damage, so they had to remove her uterus. The doctors advised my sister that she would never be able to have another baby, not that she wanted one anyway, but she decided to keep my child. She told us yesterday, and that's when I told Lance to find someone to fix this."

That was the comfort in having a man like Lance. If I asked him to fix something, he made sure it was done with such efficiency that you often can never tell there was anything wrong to begin with. This situation isn't as easy to fix as a garbage disposal. There will always be something broken inside of me after this. After all I had given up for her, my sister could give me nothing in return. She would never acknowledge me or my sacrifices.

"Biologically I don't have a claim, and I have made my peace with that. But McKenzie is Lance's daughter. He wants his daughter. I want our baby. So what can we do, Arnold? So how do we fix this?"

Lance

We return to the car in silence, something that has become so much a part of our time together, it is hard to remember the time before. I look at her out of the corner of my eye. It is funny how nothing about my wife has changed since the day we met. Time has touched her, but she aged well. There isn't one thing that she has not done well. Her hair remains the same; I told her once how much I like it long, and she hasn't cut it since.

"Familiarity breeds contempt." At times this phrase is more fitting than others. I wished there could be something different. I missed looking at her and trying to figure out what about her had changed. I would of course notice almost immediately, but for a few seconds, there would once again be some mystery about her. Something that would make me "see" her again. I look for anything that is all her own, something that separates her from me, something that doesn't scream Mrs. Lawson.

There was a time when she was all I could think of; the longing for her is what made my heart beat but threatened to stop it all the same. She was my desire, my want, my need, my strength, my weakness.

She would never be considered anything less than breathtaking. She had the type of beauty that is understated and subtle but left a man wanting to do nothing more with his life than make her happy. The kind that your mother warned you about but your father praised you for securing. She is short; honestly she'd have to be taller to be considered short. She's actually about a foot shorter than me. The man that I am demands that I protect her because she seems so delicate, yet she is the strongest woman I know.

Her hair is the deepest black I have ever seen. Now it sweeps across her back, dipping lower than my hands have been in an unbearably long time. It is definitely her crowning glory, and I understand why some religions mandate it be covered. The sway of it as she walks tempts a man, makes him want to wrap his hands up in it like some barbaric ritual and claim what is his. Even that has been denied me—the right to claim what is mine, first my wife and now my child.

Her almond-shaped eyes are hypnotic even when she doesn't mean them to be. They are considered bedroom eyes, and when she is angry—never with me—I find just one look excites me. The eyes are just as dark as her hair, and once they seemed to have something hidden behind them, not in a sinister way but in a teasing way, defying you to guess all her secrets before she reveals them to you herself. But it is her complexion that I adore most. Cinnamon brown, just a shade deeper than mine. When we touch, I love the way our skins complement each other, the sweet dance of caramel covered in cinnamon. I loved and hated her for being so desirable even at her worst. I watch a small bead of sweat roll down the back of her neck, and I want to follow it.

I fight the urge to turn on the air conditioning. She hated it, and I remembered her telling me how much she enjoys that stifling feeling of a car during midsummer almost two decades ago. It was one of those things that made her unique. This small thing was one of the many that made me want to know everything else about her. She considered herself an open book, and then there had always been something new to learn. Even after all this time, I find that I want to explore her. I wait for a reason to do so.

I continue to examine her; it is a little game I play. I watch her as if I don't know her, judge as if she was any other woman and I any other man. I always wonder if she would still affect me in the same way if she did not belong to me. There is nothing a man values more than his possessions. I look twice at her, but even when I try my hardest, I see more than just the physical. I know the toll time has taken; I know the smile she used to have, and I see that, instead of the forced one she often wears now. I remember her before the frown lines formed on her forehead, before she was this familiar stranger that shares my last name. We reside in the same home and, at one point, shared our lives together. Physically she is the same woman from four years ago, before we started this road to build a family, but mentally and emotionally she is alien to me.

She's put on some weight, filling her out in all the right places. Her hips are a little wider; her bottom, a little bigger, giving her a new walk, a sway that wasn't there before. I find myself watching her more as she walks into or out of a room. I've noticed how other men watch her too. Everything about her seems so much softer. She complains about it; I find her more attractive like this. Part of me likes that this was the one thing she hasn't planned— to gain a few pounds and not be able to lose them. This is the one thing she can't control or hasn't found the will power to do so. That fact within itself makes her more attractive. She doesn't have to be a superhero for me.

Her top button came undone a few times throughout the day. I doubt she noticed the way men watched hoping at least one other button would lose the fight as well and just give up holding on. She is alluring simply because she is so unaware of how alluring she is. I do not consider myself a jealous man; I enjoy watching the way other men stare at her. Each time I see someone looking, I find myself staring at the same exact place on her body they are admiring, and I remember that I am the only man who has and will ever know exactly what is hidden there. Then the pain resurfaces, and I realize it has been such a long time since I have known her in that way. I know that she will ignore their stares if she even noticed them just as she will ignore me. It is hard to compliment someone when they no longer believe what you are saying is even possible. I can't tell my wife just how beautiful she is because she won't allow herself to believe it. I do not blame her for this since I have broken so many promises; I promised her everything would be all right, that I would always protect her, and that she would never have to know loneliness as long as my heart still beats. Spending so much time in her little sister's shadow has left her with little regard for herself. I wish I could change this. We've grown in so many ways, but she has managed to shrink, and that is not something that I wanted for her.

We take the expressway home; there is little traffic this time in the afternoon. I continue to watch her, stealing glances out the side of my eyes or in the side view mirror since she has been looking out the car window the whole time. She had told Arnold our story, and I watched as it tore her apart. If she was torn, my soul was shredded. When we walked past the mirrored elevators in the lobby, I didn't recognize myself. The pain was etched across my face. I wanted to kill her sister for what she put us through, but in the same token, I knew I never could destroy the person who had given me such a gift. I struggled within myself because Lord knows I wanted to hate her, to feel anger for the hurt my wife felt. I wanted to kill someone, but it couldn't be Toya. I detested myself for not being able to hate her. I knew my wife didn't truly hate her either, but she was not my blood. I should be able to despise this woman, to vow to never want to see her face again, but I knew I would every single day, if I had to for the rest of my life, if it meant spending time with my daughter. I frown at my reflection in the rearview. I felt joy in my heart, but my mind wrestled with that emotion. And my eyes showed it all.

One couldn't tell that a few minutes ago Tonya was in pain. That is an ability she has acquired. She can mask her feelings. At first I admired this about her. She never argued. She just simply put on her smile and went about whatever task needed completing. Now, it is nothing short of an annoyance.

As a husband, it is my job to provide, to protect, and to fix things whenever my wife commands, and this is not a job I take lightly. But how can I know what needs to be fixed if she pretends there is nothing wrong? It is not that I don't love my wife, because I do. I know she doesn't believe that right now; I am uncertain if she has ever truly believed it no matter how I have tried to show her. For the past few years, I have grown to love her more as a partner than as a spouse, but it's still love, and I try to find a reason every single day to fall back in love with her. I blame her for the way things have changed between us. I am not sure that it's the right thing to do, but it is the only thing that I can do. Sometimes I feel as though once we were married, the thrill for her was gone, but for me, it had just begun. She had won me away from her sister, even though I knew that first day I was not even considered an option by Toya. So I was the stuffed animal that was put on the shelf, taken out only for show.

There is always a competition between the two of them; anyone could see it, and LaTonya is always the one who gives in first. It isn't because she's not as strong or driven; it is because she does anything to avoid conflict. When I came along, she knew I wanted her sister, and I was finally the thing that she did not have to compete for. I often wondered if she would have even made the attempt to fight for me. Would she just simply have walked away? It scares me to think that even after all this time, even if there was a way to know then what we would become, she may not have fought for me. I am unsure if she would try now. If I simply came home and announced I no longer loved her or wanted her anymore, I am certain she would politely pack my bags. There would be no fuss, no argument, no begging or pleading. This hurts more than the thought of not having her. It is not that she doesn't love me, because she does—this I know—but because she doesn't have any fight left in her. Or maybe it is simply because she is so accustomed to losing that she expects nothing more than that.

The problem in our relationship now is that I am her life. In my twenties, I thought it was endearing. In my thirties, I thought it was sad; and as I approach forty, I'm certain I will find it depressing. I never wanted to be her "one thing." That's too much responsibility for one person. It equals a greater risk of disappointment, a greater risk of loss.

Once our relationship progressed to a stall, I thought starting a family would be the best thing. It was something that we both needed, and finally she'd be happy again. It would bring us closer in a healthier, more balanced way. There would be someone else to fill her time, her constant need to mother. It didn't matter to me how we did it either. Just that we did. But that dream has somehow become the reason for so many nightmares, and up to a few days ago, I would have considered adoption. I am a product of it myself. I felt blessed to have been chosen by someone. They chose to love me. It made me feel pretty damn special, and it changed the way I looked at the world. I never asked why my biological parents didn't keep me. It wouldn't have mattered. I knew that there were other children who weren't loved nearly as much by the woman who carried them as I was by the one who chose me. If that were to have been my legacy, to love like that just because I could, I would have died a proud man.

But after I saw how perfect my daughter was, everything changed. I could never turn my back on her. When she took her first breath, she became the reason why I breathed. McKenzie. Even her name makes me want to be a bigger man. It's amazing that once you finally have a child, you wonder what the hell you were doing with your life up until that point. You could argue that you were preparing for the job, but there is nothing that can prepare you for it. No one can explain just how much the experience will change your life or how much this unknown person will unravel you in ways you didn't think possible but at the same time fit everything perfectly together. She was a blessing; what was missing, she was everything to me more than my wife, and I had only known her for these few days. It scared me to think what the next day would bring. How much more could I possibly love this little girl? But I knew in my heart there was the infinite possibility that if I lived every single day of the rest of my life trying to show her the love I felt, it would somehow seem inadequate. My daughter is, as plainly put as possible, the love of my existence. There is still a chance that I will not have the every day with her that I need. Most fathers dread the day they have to send their daughters away to college or, worse yet, give them away at the altar. But these fathers have an advantage over me. They've had time to prepare for the departure. I was given no notice. As soon as she was placed in my arms, she was torn away from me.

There is no way to explain loss, no way to contain grief in a sentence. Even though she is only a few miles away in the hospital, I still want nothing more than to have her in my home, to feed her in the middle of the night while I tell her all the secrets of life I have learned, what to look for in a mate, why she shouldn't eat paste, what colleges she should consider, and why she shouldn't roller-skate in the house. There were a million things that I wanted to tell her, to show her, teach her. But I was most excited about the things she would teach me.

I know that legally there is no way the judge would keep a child away from their biological father. However; being a weekend dad was not enough for me. My father made me breakfast every morning while my mother packed my lunch. I need to be the man he raised me to be. I would make them proud and show them that their love has been kept inside of me for all these years just so that I could add to it and give it away.

I want to say something, to break this silence, to put things in perspective. I have become the villain in these past few days. Who the hell am I kidding these past few months after her second trimester when Twin, the name they used for each other, came to live with us and I was pushed out. I was never formally invited to the doctors' visits even though I went to them all. My opinion was never asked; Tonya didn't want to know what we were having, so that meant I didn't want to know either. They agreed on the name and that the last would be hyphenated in homage to Twin and their parents. They chose the color of the nursery and the items that filled it. The one thing I was responsible for was putting it all together. But I didn't complain. I always believed the end would make it worthwhile.

The silence is killing me, and we are only a few blocks from home. I know once we get there she'll find a way to avoid me. She'll sneak into one of the many rooms we don't need and find something that needs to be dusted for the fifth time today or make a grocery list and one of us will have to go—anything that prevents us from speaking or being alone for too long. I guess she feels as though talking about it will somehow make the pain less manageable. I am hoping that that is what it is; my fear is that she feels she is alone, that she doesn't know that I am willing to carry her piggy back through this hell if I have to. I need to hear her voice. I need her to acknowledge something I have said and thus acknowledge me. I need her to know that I will fight for her, for our family, that I will give ninety percent when she only has ten to give, that there is nothing I wouldn't do to make this right. But first I need to reach her. It kills me to think that I may not only lose my daughter but also my wife. That is unbearable now. It is hard to grieve alone. I give up and say the first thing that comes to mind.

"I think that went well. I'm sure Arnold is working on filing all the necessary paperwork. We should hear something shortly."

I wait for her to say something to me. Instead she just nods as if what I said made absolutely no sense. I could have told her our dry cleaning was ready, and she would have reacted with the same amount of enthusiasm.

I want to scream at her anything to make her say something. She shared more with my partner than she had with me in quite some time. I haven't seen her cry since our first loss. I knew she wept. It was hard to hide her red eyes from me. But it was always in secret, in the bathroom, in the nursery. At night when she thought I was asleep, I'd feel the soul-wrenching sobs that shook her body. She never let me hold her or console her. Even though I am certain I wouldn't be able to do the latter, I held out hope that we could comfort each other. I want to hold her in my arms right now and shield her from the pain she won't allow me to know she is carrying. I want to be her husband in every sense of the word.

You can only push someone away for so long before they walk away on their own. I don't want to leave her, it would be unfair to leave her so broken.

"Do you want to grab something for lunch? We could go downtown and walk around. And it's beautiful out here!" Again I am trying for something, and I am ignored.

This time I turn to her. She was sitting in the passenger seat looking as if she wants the world to swallow her up, or at least expects it too. In the brief second that it takes to turn, another car speeds out in front of me. I see her reaction before I even notice the car. She reaches her arm across me as if that alone would be enough to shield me from the impact if there is one. I brake immediately, and nothing happens. But that one moment of contact changes something between us. The part of her that she has tried to bury in these past few days, for fear she may not have the chance to use it, has emerged, the mother, the protector.

She finally looks at me, and I know what is coming. I know what she needs. I pull the car over to the side of the road. Normally I would rant and rave about the stupidity of Philadelphia drivers. I would complain that most likely the person in front of me isn't in a rush to do anything but be an asshole. But this time, I don't have the words. I give up trying to get her to talk to me. Instead I unbuckle my seatbelt first, then hers.

I pull her over to me, ignoring the way the arm rest is pressing into my side. I kiss her with force, hoping to crush all her restraint. Claiming her. *She is yours*, I tell myself repeatedly. I let my mouth tell her the things I haven't been able to in so long. I tell her with my tongue that I desire her. I use my kisses to promise her that I will not leave, that if she can allow me to win her, then I know there is nothing else that could be unattainable. The kiss slows now to a rhythm we are both familiar with. The comfortable, we've-done-this-a-million-times-but-could-never-get-bored-with way. The way I used to kiss her when I returned home. I allow her to feel the way I have missed her. I allow her to know the ways I want her and the ways that I need her. Briefly I consider taking her there in my car, but I know she would never allow it. We've never had sex outside of our bedroom—well, not since our honeymoon. Part of me wants to demand that she gives in while the other part hopes that I don't have to.

It only takes a few more seconds before she pulls away from me, and I am sure that the kiss was in vain. I am sure that she has not understood anything I tried to explain without uncomfortable words. We will go back to the hours of silence. Maybe she'll say, "Excuse me," if we bump into each other in the hall. Maybe she'll ask me to pass the salt at dinner.

Then she looks at me, and I can see that there is something there. Not quite a fire but a flicker. "Let's just go home. I'm sure we'll find something to do." That is her way of saying she wants me to make love to her. Sex is not something she is completely comfortable talking about or initiating. This is the closest we will ever come to her asking for me. It takes a half of a second for me to place the car back into drive and pull out of the makeshift parking space. I am now the idiot as the cars behind me beep their horns, but I do not care. I cannot hold my daughter, but I will hold my wife as long as she allows me to do so. I will hold her as we fit our broken pieces together.

Toya

I look at my reflection in the tiny hospital bathroom mirror. I don't know exactly what I am looking for, but I expected a difference. I am looking for some outward sign of an inward change, something that noted my new responsibilities in life. It reminds me of our sixteenth birthday; my sister and I both stared into the mirror, hoping to see something different. We searched for anything that may have announced to the world that we were in fact women. I am looking for something that says I am a mother. Nothing seems different. Sure, there are bags under my eyes. They hint toward the past few sleepless nights. But that is nothing abnormal for me. After all, I am a surgeon first and when I have the time, a single woman. Both equal sleepless nights, some more fun than others.

Maybe I should just wear a sign on my back or better yet one of those cheesy T-shirts. My stomach has shrunken some. I guess that is a blessing even though I enjoyed being pregnant. Part of me misses it. If you're lucky, you have ten months to prepare, yet it all seems to end so abruptly. It feels like yesterday I was complaining of never being comfortable or of the constant heart burn. Now I miss those things. I miss the feel of her movements inside of me. I miss knowing that I was taking part in a miracle.

I realize I am just trying to occupy my time. I have never been much of a procrastinator; there were only twenty-four hours in a day, and I often need twenty-six. Today my feet were dragging before I ever placed them on the cold hospital floor. I am not running from my responsibilities; I am looking forward to them. What I am running from is my conscience.

Even though I have pushed my family away, it hurts not to have any visitors. I feel abandoned. As a doctor, I know the correlation between patients who have support and those that don't. One group has a higher survival rate. I guess it's a good thing; I am on the road to recovery physically, but mentally, I am walking a fine line.

I also notice the way people treat patients with no family. You get one of two treatments: either they treat you like shit because hey, if your family doesn't care, why should we, or they're overly compassionate, which in my opinion makes the patient feel worse. It's like saying no one else gives a shit, so we'll try to give a damn. I wonder what category I would fall into if I didn't already work here. Would the nurses and doctors whisper behind my back, wondering what my infraction was? At this time, there are still whispers. I would be a moron to assume there weren't, but there is no wondering. Everyone knows exactly what I have done.

I guess I don't really have a reason to feel abandoned. Lynnette is busy buying me all the things that I would need to take McKenzie home. The thought sends me into a mini panic attack. I haven't had one in years. I know this is something that I want to do, but I am not sure if I know how to do it. I laugh for a brief second. Who would have ever thought I'd be taking a baby home? Certainly not me. Me, a mother, which meant I was accountable to someone other than myself. I never wanted that much responsibility. I have never cared that much for someone.

Afraid that I may fall and hit my head on the sink, I return to the room and sit back down on the bed. I count back from one hundred; with each number, I am picturing the flawlessness that is my child, waiting for me a few feet away. She is what calms me; the thought of her brings tranquility, and it gives me hope.

Statistically speaking, the child should be better off in my care. I spent the whole of my adult life learning how the human body works. I know that I am rationalizing, but that does not stop me. I could bandage a boo-boo just as well as my sister. Better perhaps. She's never had to stitch someone in a way that would leave no scars. I'd know when a cold was just that or when it was something major. I know when you should be alarmed and when you shouldn't. I have all the mechanics worked out. I am if nothing else a hell of a doctor. But the little things scare me. Even though I could, God forbid if needed, stitch my daughter perfectly, would I know what to say while I was doing so or how to comfort her? My bedside manner leaves much to be desired. Would it come as naturally to me as everything else had? This is the first time I have ever doubted myself or my abilities. Ironically, it is the doubt that makes me certain I should be doing this. The fact that I am horrified means that I care.

I stare around the room, amazed by the things I never noticed about the hospital until I became a patient—like these hideous lights that never seem to go out completely. There is no such thing as complete darkness here, or privacy for that matter. The rooms smell different when you are confined to them; the hospital staff looks more tired than you remembered. The doctors whom you work with, and have never had a reason to question before, now become uncertain of the answers. It's true, it is much harder to treat a doctor than a "civilian" if you will. Most patients want you to dumb things down for them, but a doctor expects full disclosure, and that is something that most of us do not like to give. We are just as uncomfortable giving our diagnoses as our patients are with hearing them.

The IV has been removed. I am ashamed to admit I miss the morphine, it clouded my mind and allowed me to feel no pain, even the pain that wasn't physical. I didn't have to think about my decision. I didn't have to think about how I was hurting my family or the disappointment that they felt. I am disappointed in myself. I would give anything for just one more push of that button, the sweet release of oblivion. That would be taking the easy way out.

I am who I have always been. Selfish and needy. I thank my sister for her hope that I could someday change. I am hoping as well. This is just not the right situation to expect anything different. I'm sure she is surprised I did not come to this decision sooner. I didn't wake up and decide that I wanted to betray my sister. It just happened. It's not necessarily that I wanted to be a mother, but when someone tells you you'd never be able to do it again, well, it puts things in to perspective. To know that my body was shared for ten months with an angel who knew only me and be asked to give her up without the hope of a consolation prize in the future, since that is what any other child would feel like, was unfair to me. I wish she'd understand that. I wish Tonya would see this from my point of view. But my point of view is something Twin is never willing to see. She'd always give in just because I was stubborn or because we both expected her to. She never understood me. That has always been the one crack in our foundation. I refuse to go down that road alone.

I reach for my peach robe with matching slippers. Tonya had picked it out and packed it in my bag a few months ago. She is detailed. I hadn't even thought of what to put inside the bag. She seemed to know everything that was needed for the trip she would never take. The thought causes me to pause. It is not that I don't feel for her because I do even more so now. I understand exactly what she is going through. This alone should bring us closer together.

I continue to search my bag; she remembered my favorite body wash and toothbrush. She packed three robes with matching slippers, so I'd have some variety, even the god-awful pregnancy underwear that I had refused to wear while I carried. I can tell that some of these things are just recently added. I remember we discussed nursing. She said it would be better for the baby if I nursed while we were in the hospital but pumped once we returned home. I knew all the medical benefits but refused. She still held out hope; I found two nursing pajama tops buried under the regular ones.

I push aside Tonya from my thoughts. I was certain I was on her mind but in a more unflattering way. I head back to the bathroom once the dizziness passes and brush my teeth. I am unsure if McKenzie would be offended by the morning breath, but I decide the nurses may be. I knew my daughter would be one of the few babies in there. Most new mothers wanted their child by their side at all times. But I feel as though I owe my sister and Lance something. In the nursery, they can visit without having to see me, without having to address the elephant in the room. But no points will be earned for this unselfish act. I am sure my sister just concluded that I wanted to get more sleep, and as long as McKenzie was there, the nurses would do the feedings and changing. She didn't know that one of the nurses brings her to me after my sister has left. On the contrary, her being in that nursery did not allow me to sleep better at all. I tossed and turned wondering what I was missing, expecting my daughter to change overnight and not recognize me in the morning.

Tonya did not know that after five days, I almost have the changing of diapers down. I wished she could see how hard I am trying. I want her to be proud of me.

I dress and begin to walk toward the nursery. The energy in the hall is different from the one in my room. This floor always seems to be the happiest in any hospital. I try not to make eye contact with anyone as I keep walking toward McKenzie. I haven't been on this floor since I did my rotation in obstetrics during my residency. It is amazing how even then I didn't truly understand the miracles that occurred here. Sure, I've seen babies and mothers come out of situations that were considered impossible. I've seen the miracles that the doctors made happen, or that's who I gave the credit to at the time, but giving birth myself compelled me to believe that there is something greater than just me out there. Those few hours did more for the conviction of my soul than the years forced to attend church with my family. There are lessons learned here that were not taught in Sunday school.

I understand the physical part of it all—the way the sperm and egg meet and how one cell divides to become millions. I understand the concept of the heart and the brain's development. I can explain the how, the why, but who can explain the miracle of it all? Who can explain the hows and the whys? It is the one thing that happens every minute of every day that will still be considered a miracle for as long as humans procreate.

I look into the window of the nursery, and I don't need to read the names to find mine. I tear up momentarily. Mine. Yes, she belongs to me. I place my hand on my empty stomach, and it is weird to feel how empty it is. Just a few days ago, I felt her every movement, and now she is a separate person from me all together, which means her needs extend beyond me. That is a bit frightening.

I walk into the nursery, and I can tell I have confused the nurse; she must have been here last night and met my twin. It's funny how people always do a double take when they see us separately. My hair is shorter than Tonya's. I'm also smaller than her. I gained more weight than she has, but mine was all stomach as they say. I am sure the nurse is trying to figure out how I'd managed to lose weight and get a new hair cut in less than a few hours. Not to mention the difference in height. We are exactly five feet, but for some reason, I was always considered the taller one. That annoyed Twin and amused me. Tonya tried to stand straighter when we were together. Before the day is over, someone will fill her in; that is the nature of situations like these. There are no secrets in a hospital. There are charts and bracelets and questions that need answers, and mostly it is for your own good that you confess any wrongdoing.

"Can I hold her?" I ask more so out of courtesy, but part of me is still waiting for someone to tell me no or ask what I think I am doing or acknowledge that I am in over my head and that it takes more than giving birth to make someone a mother. I am uncertain if I would even disagree or if I would simply tell them that they are right and ask if someone could please give my sister a call and have her come pick her baby up. But if no one else has confronted me about my choice, then maybe I have made the right one.

Honestly, I don't know if there is such a thing as mother's intuition or if it has kicked in. To me, this feels more like possessiveness. I know all the basic things that any mother should, like I would live for her and in the same token die for her. Still I don't know if I am the best thing for her. But I am certain she is the best thing for me.

I hesitate, trying to remember exactly how I watched the nurses pick her up before. It is amazing how unnatural this feels to me. I know that I wouldn't crush her, but part of me can't help but notice how fragile she seems. One misplaced hand and there would be nothing more to fight about. I manage to get her out, into my arms, and both of us into the rocking chair without causing a commotion or loss of one of her limbs. It is a small victory for me. I calculate that in a few more days, I should be a pro at all of this—the changing, the holding, and the feeding. After that everything will fall into place.

Once again, I find myself counting all her fingers and toes "She's flawless." I whisper to no one in particular. It is hard to believe that I could deserve anything this perfect, and I am afraid that something will go wrong. I wrap McKenzie back up in her blanket, and I begin to hum a song that I picked up somewhere along the way. I am no good at it, and she becomes a little agitated. I continue to hum anyway after shifting her in my arms. She finds comfort and begins to sleep. Continuing with the song, I remember where I heard it before. It was the song my sister sung to me when I couldn't sleep after our parents died. She has the most amazing voice; the only time I make it to church is to hear Tonya sing a solo. Her voice rocks, soothes, and caresses the soul.

I wish I could call her and ask her the words or if I am doing something as small as holding my baby right. I wanted to ask her for advice and most importantly if she could hold my hand through this all, but I cannot. I miss her. She was always the more domestic one; before, it was never meant as a compliment. We'd joke when we were younger about how I would touch the world. How I'd be extraordinary in some way. But her dreams never extended beyond someone's house with a bunch of pretty babies.

I could be just as good as my twin. It hurts me that she doesn't see that. She doesn't want to give me the time to grow into this, the time I needed to find my way. I even offered to do it as a fifty-fifty thing. We could find a way to make it work. She refused, claiming McKenzie was hers. We picked the name out together one night while we were lying next to each other. I would lie on my side and she would too with both of our bellies touching. It was my idea. That way she could feel the baby's movements as if she too were carrying. She said she would name him Lance Junior, even though it's not what Lance wanted. She said juniors seemed more stable to her, and there was somehow a bond that was sealed with name sharing. She had somehow convinced herself that I was carrying a boy. "But what if it's a girl?" I do admit now I pushed her, only because I didn't want her to not have another option if I left it up to Tonya she'd have named our daughter Lance Junior as well. I was the only one who knew she was a girl, and I could not allow her to have a name we'd all hate. We must have considered a dozen names before we came up with McKenzie. And I have never met a child who fit their name more perfectly. I miss the closeness we shared for these past few months. This is the longest we've gone without speaking after a disagreement. She's always called first to admit that I may be right, never that she's wrong because she never is. This could be the time lightning strikes, and this could just be my moment, the time that I make the best decision, the time that my selfishness doesn't backfire on me.

McKenzie's eyes flutter open. It's amazing how she can look so much like her father at only a few days old. But it is my sister's eyes that I see looking at me, and I wish that she would just close them so they don't cause me pain. Then I could focus only on what I am gaining—this perfect gift, which is an extension of myself—not on what I would be losing—my best friend, the best part of myself.

That is exactly what Tonya is. It seems that when our cells divided, we were split right down the middle. She is everything that I am not, everything that I never wanted to be until now. She is better than me, so much more than I think I ever could be.

Lynette

I wonder if they know that I am technically not supposed to be here. Praying in the house of God no matter what the little differences are must count for something. It doesn't hurt to cover all your bases. But I doubt that meant praying to our God in a Catholic church. That is one of the things I always respected about them: they never close the doors. There's always someone here to hear whatever you need to confess. Though I admire this, I'd rather take my concerns to the Lord myself.

We're all Christians, they say, so I don't think I'll be judged for sitting in this pew. Especially since my pleas are far from selfish. What greater gift to give someone than your prayers? That is the one thing I have bestowed upon my girls every day of their lives. I prayed they were kept blessed and prosperous. I asked God to meet their needs before they even knew what they were and especially before I ever addressed any of my own.

I wish I could be in more familiar surroundings. Beggars can't be choosers, and that is what I am doing, begging for forgiveness, mercy, and most of all, strength. I feel foolish now; I am certain that my pastor would have opened the doors of the church for me if I called her. Embarrassment is what stopped me. I'd have to explain that I let down all my girls—my sister, bless her soul, and our babies. Yes, they are my babies. Technically I raised them longer than their mother had the chance to do, and I often find that I am still raising them. I loved them as if they were mine, more so I'd like to believe.

I cherished them from birth, even helped during their delivery. I gave them everything I could afford, and there was never a time I didn't want to give them more. I have spent every Christmas and birthday with them; I even bought gifts for Easter. That memory sticks with me even when they sometimes forget who they are. I remember them as the little girls with overstuffed baskets, chocolate-covered fingers, and sticky kisses. That is the way we all remember our children. We want to see them as the innocent child they were and not the person they have become. It is through no fault of their own, and even when you are the most proud of them, part of you still wishes to bring back those days of endless sticky kisses. I'd like to believe it is simply because of how short the time of innocence lasted for them. It seemed one moment they were my sweet, innocent nieces and then the next, orphaned by fate and forced to face an uncertain world. I ache for them still. They didn't deserve to know such pain at their age, nor did I deserve to know such joy. I often chide myself; it is sacrilege to believe I have the power to change anything. Certainly I would bring my sister back. I love her still, she is in my thoughts daily.

When my sister died, I thought it would destroy me. I focused on being the mother that they needed. I took the love that my sister could not take with her and gave it to those little girls. My life without them would be empty, shadows of what it has been up until this point. I am certain I would have been included in all the things that they have done. I would have played my role as the supporting aunt, who would give anything. Knowing the sweetness of motherhood, the knowledge that it is only your touch or words that can soothe your child, is rewarding beyond any form of explanation.

Now I am wondering if I did it all wrong. Obviously I gave too much or not enough. Ironically I feel more like a mother now than ever before. I doubt there is someone out there that can understand what I am going through or the way my girls have driven a wedge right down the center of my heart and my soul. I am burning from the inside out because I know the pain they have both suffered. There are secrets that I have only shared with my Savior and that's only because you can't hide anything from Him even if you want to. How do you watch your child walk straight up to a speeding train without being able to stop them? You feel paralyzed, broken by their heartbreak. I refuse to pick sides. I think that is what's best for both of them, but it doesn't matter. I understand where they are both coming from, and I am not certain what the right answer is. It's not hard to understand both of their longing and desire to fill a void, I can't say that one of their desires outweighs the other's.

I know that God is everywhere, so I tell him the things I cannot tell my girls. I argue both sides before I give it all to him, hoping that come Judgment Day he will remember the way I pleaded. This is going to get ugly, uglier than either of them realize, uglier even than I am prepared for. They will both be scarred behind all this mess.

For the second time since my sister's passing, I cry tears of sorrow. The happiness my girls have provided often led to tears of joy. My nieces were the light of my life, and I have always been proud of them both. At this time, it is hard to see those little girls who shared so much and loved each other so hard break their bond this way. What kills me the most is I cannot comfort either of them the way they want me to or the way I need to because the other would take it as disloyalty. It is hard to be Switzerland in your own home, even if that home is figurative. I would give Toya my last breath and Tonya my last heartbeat if either asked. I love them both equally, but for different reasons and in different ways. That is why I blame myself for this.

I was harder on Tonya because she needed me to be. She wasn't a difficult child; if anything, she was a blessing to me, more of a comfort than I think I was to her. But she floundered if she didn't have rules to obey. She always needed someone to tell her what decisions were the right ones. Without direction, she would just sit still.

So I pushed my older daughter forward. I asked more of her because I knew she would never disappoint. I believed when she didn't believe in herself; that was my way of showing my love. Maybe if I didn't require so much, she wouldn't think she had so much to prove. Maybe if I allowed her to be selfish just once and a while, she'd have more to show for herself. Everything that girl is was based upon what she thinks others want her to be. Nothing is done just for her. I wish she'd learned how to fight sooner, how to stand up for herself earlier. I will admit that I am proud of her for doing it now. But I hope she has not bitten off more than she can chew. If she does not win her first fight, she'll be afraid to fight ever again. I am afraid she will cower off into a corner somewhere and lose what little of herself she has left.

I knew the way her miscarriages destroyed her. I saw the change in her eyes, her posture, and her voice. When Tonya sung now in the church choir, I could hear the doubt in her voice. She didn't believe the words she sang; instead, she questioned the Savior she was singing about. Her conviction had been lost; Tonya has become a shell of what she used to be.

I wished Lance had been stronger and pushed adoption. There's no way they would have been turned down. Too many black children are in need of adoption; no agency would turn their back on a prominent attorney and his stay-at-home wife. They were the pinnacle of what any family should be—two college graduates with more love to give than anyone I know and enough money to provide more than just comfort.

Now she would be hurt again. I envision the train hurling toward her with only two options: it would kill her or damage her in ways that could never be repaired. So I would lose my little girl. I still see her that way, even after all these years, as the little girl who knew too much for her own good, but not enough to save herself. She still wanted to storm the tracks full speed toward the train that would mangle her and leave me without enough pieces to put back together. Leaving fragments of my wonderful girl, the girl I would give anything if she only asked.

The saddest part of all is she has not come to me. After Toya made her decision, Tonya shut me out. I know she expects me to be on her twin's side since it is something I've always done. When they fought, I would always ask Tonya to give in before her sister threw a tantrum. Now in the aftermath, she sees me as the enemy. She believes that I loved her twin more just because I gave her more. But that was not it at all; you never know what it's like to be a parent until you are one. This is something that she may never know. She can judge my decisions because she has not had to experience them for herself. I said no to her because I assumed she was strong enough to understand. I was wrong. I asked her to be stronger than any child should be required. I tried to raise her to be unselfish. I didn't want her to believe she didn't deserve as much as others. I had always assumed I did a wonderful job. They had been my proof. But now as everything comes crashing down, I realize I could have done better. I should have done better by both of them.

I was the only one she allowed to see her cry when she lost all her babies. She came to my house and sobbed until her body hurt from the effort. She asked me why God had done this to her, showed her a glimpse of what could be then took everything away. She needed to know how I could trust a God that was so unfair. Each time I convinced her to hold on just a little while longer, to believe beyond her circumstances, to have faith. But look where it's gotten us all. She had faith in the wrong people. She expected a doctor to heal her and a husband to love her even when she didn't know how to love herself. She had faith that I would always protect her, even though I can't this time. Worst of all is she had faith that her little sister would stop being selfish, even though she's never had to put someone else first and that this would be the one time everything worked out for her. Now she has nothing to believe in.

You always vow to protect your child, but every parent's worst nightmare is the day that they actually have to, not for fear that you won't be able to, but the knowledge that someone had the audacity to hurt them. This vow is never spoken aloud. It is never an oath that you have to take, but when you think of these things, it's always the stranger lurking in the background. The man with the candy in the van, the lady who claims that her dog is missing—those were the dangers we wait for. I remember telling them when they left the house, "No one has lost a dog, and if they ask you to help them find one, advise them they're free at the local shelter and run like hell." I would always send them out with their own piece of candy, letting them know that no one could offer them something if they already had their own. It's so easy to plan for the outside attack. You watch them while they play outside or check on them as they grow older, making sure they are where they said they'd be. You fight, you argue, you yell. They stomp their feet and slam doors. They may even claim they hate you; it hurts you to hear it, but you know you're doing things right. I treated the outside world as if it were waiting to personally attack my girls. A parent is always on guard, always looking for any reason to pounce, anything out of the ordinary that signals an attack. I didn't see this coming. Even in all the fights as children, I could never believe that they would hurt each other this way. No matter how Toya behaved, I believed there was some good in her. I want to bite my tongue for saying that. I would never pick sides.

Toya would do as she pleased. Always has. When she was younger, it killed me to be stern with her. She wasn't a bad child; she just wanted to experience things in her own way. I once told her she should learn from other people's mistakes. "But what's the fun in that?" was her reply, and I couldn't do anything but laugh. The girl was serious. I made sure life was fun for her and made it so easy. I led her to believe that everything in this world should be handed to a woman like her. She was brilliant, and that is not an understatement, beautiful by anyone's standards, and most of all, she was fearless. I never met anyone who could stand in her way or anyone who would even dare to do so.

But she has suffered her share of setbacks. Things her sister never knew and would never begin to understand. Toya believed the world owed her something because of what had been taken from her. She resisted any need to be tied down. I knew it was fear. She was afraid that pretty pictures didn't last forever; she had firsthand knowledge of the ways that the colors faded, the way the perspectives change. She didn't believe that anything lasted forever, and she learned all of these things at too young of an age.

In my best effort to change this about her, I gave her anything she could ask for. I wanted her to see that true love changed every single day, but only for the better. I didn't want her to be hurt or be the one to do so. I tried to make up for things that were not my fault or hers either. People say, "God knows my heart." My response is always the same. "People only know your actions." Therefore, I let my actions speak to Toya. Whatever she asked, I did. Whatever she wanted, I gave. Whatever she needed, I did my best to provide.

Even now as I walk myself out of this church, I am headed to prove myself to her. I am going to buy yet another outfit to send the baby home with. It is a tradition in our family that the grandmother always buys the baby's first outfit, and that is the role I will play in this child's life, no matter who wins. I will spoil her rotten. It is my job; it is not only expected, but required of me. But when I look into the face of this wonderful child, my emotions are clouded. I can see why neither of them wants to give her up. All I want to do is protect her just like I would my girls. I wish I could shield her from this as well. She may not end up with two mothers, but she will have two of everything else. Toya left specific instructions, to copy everything that was on her sister's registry.

So McKenzie, the little girl who had started a war before being given a middle or last name, will have the best of everything times two. Organic toys, sheets, bottles, etc. The only thing that I was required to pick out was a crib. I didn't bother to ask where all of these things would go. Instead I have supervised the cleaning out of one of Toya's spare rooms. Most of the furniture has been delivered and assembled. The scariest part is that it is an exact replica of the room sixteen blocks away. Even the pastel walls have been painted the same color.

She was trying to mimic her twin in the hopes that she will get this right. That part scares me as well. What if she were to fail at this? Would she shut down and refuse to love anyone else for the right reasons again? She doesn't know how to handle failure or how to catalogue disappointment. To say I am equally afraid for them both is an understatement.

Birth is supposed to bring everyone closer, to build bridges where walls have been knocked down. Instead, it has managed to create the opposite effect in our family. I hope that after all of this, they will still refer to each other as family again.

Tonya

For so long I have pushed my husband away that it feels strange to wake up in his arms. We attacked each other; all the pain that we were both carrying surfaced from a place that I wasn't sure existed. I wasn't submissive at all, not this time. I hoped that the passion I felt would choke me until I either pass out or succumb to it. I didn't want to feel anything but him. I wanted to live in the moment while pushing all my disappointments to the side, ignore the feeling of my sinking soul, and use my husband as my floatation device. I needed to hold onto him; for fear that I would drown in my pain.

But once my eyes open again and I can see the sun still out, everything comes rushing back. I hadn't made it through another day; the distress has set in, and I begin to panic. There are still hours left for me to hold on and try and repress my need to hurt someone or myself. I have to fight through another day of agony. That is the way I look at every single day, every hour, and every minute. It takes so much to fight for each second, to hold on, hoping that the next breath will be easier instead of crippling. I hold out hope that the next minute will carry just a lighter load. I am hoping that the next hour my heart may just piece itself back together again. But as the sun streams into my bay windows and I know that there are no more distractions, I want to crumble under the weight of it all.

Having sex with Lance was easy. I could close my eyes and not see him—not that I would ever want any other man. But it was easier for me not to look directly at him; then I could pretend that the beautiful baby being denied to me did not look exactly like my husband. I could pretend that my daughter was asleep down the hall. I could pretend that I'd have her in my arms in just a few minutes and that this was just a spur-of-the moment decision. My husband and I had snuck off, as new parents often do, for some adult time. But as the light reveals all that I am trying to hide, I don't think I have it in me to pretend anymore.

I try to sneak out of bed as he pulls me a little closer. I hate to break our connection this way, but I need to hide my shame from him. I feel so much regret, as if I had awakened next to a stranger. I regret letting him distract me. It was easier to live through the pain constantly. The hard part is putting it down and then picking it back up again because the pain becomes more unbearable, the weight greater. You wonder how you held onto it for this long without collapsing. Then you consider the reason you haven't fallen down is because the pain has become so much a part of you that the weight of it keeps you balanced. It's like the lady with a hundred-pound tumor growing on her back. Everyone watches. Some disgusted, others fascinated, wondering how she has lived with this cancer strapped to her for so long. The answer is simple. She's too afraid to let it go because cutting out what has hurt her for so long may leave her with a version of herself that is unrecognizable or even worse, the realization that if things are severed at the wrong spot, the end result will be death.

I try to count to one hundred to see just how long I could endure his arms around me. I make it to twenty-seven before I find it hard not to burst into tears. He is forgiving, and that is the cruelest thing of all. I hate him for loving me when I wanted him to punish me and needed him to leave to justify what I feel about myself. He cares when I despise myself. I hate myself more and more every day because I could not be what he wanted, needed, or expected me to be. His love is a hurtful reminder; he had held up his end of the bargain, and I had failed miserably at mine, but he does not see it, and there are no words to explain it to him. Lance provided more than I could ever want, yet I could not give him the one simple thing I knew he lived for: family. I resented him for not resenting me. Never have I thought of him as foolish until now.

His breathing has changed, no doubt based upon my movements. If I know my husband at all, he will want to talk. Lance will ask me questions that I can't bring myself to answer. Maybe I will get lucky, and he will pretend as if nothing has changed. We will go about the rest of the day as the countless ones before. I am not sure what reaction would push me further over the edge. If nothing is different for him, I have wasted myself, and finally it would seem I have lost my hold on my husband, the one thing that I thought I could count on. I am not prepared for that, and I want to rewind time. I shouldn't have let him kiss me.

Funny how all it has ever taken between the two of us is a kiss. I am reminded how I fell for him after the first kiss that altered my life, and this experience may have done that for him. He will expect me to feel the same. I'd have to disappoint him again. He'll take it in stride because that is what he does, and I'd hate myself a little more. I would never ask for his forgiveness. He has always given it so freely. I know, just as I know my heart could stop at any moment, that I need him. More importantly, he certainly does not need me. There is the unbalance, just as the world is tilted on an axis, one side greater than the other, and our love somehow manages to continue to go on.

I find the nerve and the strength to run from him and the comfort that he wants to provide. He does not understand that the pain is necessary; it is what is driving me at this point, reminding me that I am still alive. Only the dead know no pain. The fight is mandatory. It is for his own good, a defense mechanism, because I know he'll see it soon and realize that I am his handicap. That is when he'll leave and when I will finally lose it. I love him enough to push him away before he has to witness my emptiness. I'd rather believe that I had forced him out than know that he finally realized I was not enough.

"Please, don't go." I don't have to turn around to know that he is not looking at me. It has been too long since we actually looked at each other straight on, afraid of what may be revealed. I want to erase the abandonment in his voice. But I cannot do it for him, not now. I can't save him; I have to save everything that I have left for me. I wish he could understand that. Even though I had taken my vows seriously, and I was more than willing to love him through his better or his worse, I could not allow him to love me anymore. It sickens me to think that this is what the pastor meant when he asked us to vow these things. Lance was the better, and I was the worst, I was a fraud, defective incomplete, and those vows are what kept him here. Those simple words, which I am sure he believes are as binding as any contract he has reviewed, have lead us here.

"Unless you want to starve to death, I guess someone should get up." As if on cue my stomach growls. Under different circumstances, I would have been embarrassed. I saw the way he looked at me now, the way he watches me. I didn't want to get this big. I hadn't planned on it. The sad part is I don't have any excuse. No baby to blame for the sudden increase, and that thought alone makes me want to eat an entire cake. Damn, I forgot to get my ice cream.

Nothing else is said; I steal the discarded sheet from the edge of the bed, wrap it around me, and try to make it to the bathroom showing as little skin as possible. Once inside the master bath,

I turn the shower on and climb in. I am certain there will be some aches in the near future; I used muscles I forgot I had while trying to find a way to outrun the other ache I felt.

I crumble finally under the weight of it all. I let the water run over my body as I lay in the fetal position. The water muffles my cries, hides my tears, and soothes my aches. This is the one place I can fall apart. I feel like I failed us both, and every single day that he wakes up next to me, I am reminded of that. I pray that he finally gets fed up and has enough courtesy to sneak out in the middle of the night, leaving behind some note explaining why he had to go, though no explanation would be required. He is the one thing in my life I have ever been selfish about. Even as I place one more brick inside my wall every day that I wake up with him, I also hope that his presence will inspire a change in me as it had all those years ago.

Anticipating a change that may never come drives one mad. It is what leads to anarchy, hatred, and destruction. History has taught us this at every turn. Even now as the water caresses my body, I am praying for something that I know is impossible, even though this prayer is more out of habit than anything else like saying grace at every meal. I pray that this time God will have pity on me that he will find me worthy enough to bless me with a child, a child that I wouldn't have to fight for, one that would be mine, a gift from him. As I had done a hundred times before, I pray that the miracle of life will take place right here and now for me, that my husband's sperm will find the one egg I carry that is not mutated, that I will become that one in a million, that even though I have been overlooked so many times by so many people, just this one time I will be seen and heard.

But as I say this prayer, it is still the pretty little girl a few miles away that I see clearer than myself. I can feel the weight of her in my arms and smell her sweet breath in my nostrils. She is what I want. So I pray that God, the one who makes a way out of no way, will find his way into my home.

Lance

I don't know what I hoped for. I'm not sure if I were being realistic or just being a man. Sex seems to fix everything for us. You fight; then you have sex, which means you make up. I do not know what the protocol is here, and this is not a position I am at all familiar with. There had been a time when I knew my wife, could read her thoughts, finish her sentences, and anticipate when she needed me most. Now I find myself wondering what I should say and how I should act when she is around. Daily there is a reminder that so much has changed between us, and it is the most petrifying feeling I have ever had. She had once been my core, the center of my world. Everything fell second to any of her wants. That is what a husband does. I truly believed then that she knew she was the only thing that mattered to me. I had been wrapped so deeply into the illusion of us that I somehow missed when everything suddenly went out of focus. There is no one incident I can point at, not a single situation where I can say this was the moment I lost my wife. Now there are only glimpses of her, traces of our life, a time when we were happy. I play these images often. They never come as whole scenes just snippets.

I'll remember the way she looked in her wedding dress, the way she cried softly as we said our vows. Subtle memories often touch me at work, like the way she pushes her hair behind her ears right before she tackles something as minute as folding laundry. The way she bites her bottom lip when she needs to ask me for something, as if she is afraid that it will be the first time I will tell her no, stirs something so deep in me that it can't be explained. She does not understand the way that the smallest things about her drive me mad and make me want to hold her in my world forever. Countless nights have been spent trying to find the way to tell her I forgive her for what she thinks she has done. Explaining my love for her would take ten million life times.

I do not know where to start. The beginning is now so fuzzy, and the middle cloudy. The only thing that I can see clearly is the end. Life is cruel, and God has certainly found humor in the smallest of my plans. I planned to love this lady every day for the rest of my life. I planned to build a family with her, and now it may be impossible.

Telling her that I have prayed and cried just as often if not more than she has would never be believed. Tonya assumes that she is the only person who knows the feeling of emptiness or abandonment as if she owns the rights to such emotions. Talking to her has not worked. Holding her has been forbidden. The only thing she has not taken from me is my love for her. I am stubbornly holding on to it, holding it inside and waiting for a time when I can share it freely without fear of hurting her more. It saddens me to know that it is my love for her that hurts her so deeply.

Tonya does not believe that anything can be promised. She has dealt with the realities of life and the certainty in the uncertain, and it is easier to believe that my feelings are temporary, that somehow if I were to stop loving her, it would be easier to accept that she no longer loves herself, if she ever truly had.

It was thoughtless of me to try and force her to stay, to hope that for a few hours I could be more than her spouse. I do not mean to trivialize the word, but I need to be her friend. I need her to be mine. Certainly there should be some sort of manual explaining how I am to react now. She didn't want me to hold her. I needed to feel her next to me just a little longer. I wanted to smell her; there was something about the way the sweat settled on her skin after we had been together that drove me crazy. Her smell was exotic. If I could take it with me everywhere I go, I would. She is the smell of home; she is my home. This was the selfish side of Lance Lawson. It is shameful that I would allow her to torture herself for just a few more moments of my happiness.

Part of me wishes she would have denied me from the beginning. That would have been so much simpler. We could have just gone about our day pretending the other did not exist. There were too many times that I found myself eating dinner she had prepared for me all alone or walking upstairs to find my bedroom door closed. She never had the courage to lock it behind herself, but the gesture said it all. So I'd pretend that I had fallen asleep in the study while working on a case and explain away in the morning why I had not made it to bed before she even asked, partly because I knew she would not.

But now we've been together, and I feel further apart from her than I have in some time. It's been weeks since the last time we made love. My wife is less than twenty feet away from me, separated by a wall that might as well be made of steel, and my soul is crying out for her, but she does not hear it or pretends not to do so, just as I pretend not to hear her real cried those nights the bedroom door is closed.

So much time has passed since she left me alone. I decide to get up and get dressed. I resist the urge to knock down the bathroom door and force her to let me hold her. I jump out of bed. The sound of the shower is making me sick to my stomach.

I can see the steam start to dance its way beneath the door, and I know that the water is too hot to soothe. She is punishing herself.

I picked up the rest of my clothes before they are dampened by the steam, which now reminds me of the fog that always announces the arrival of a villain in one of those cheesy movies, and place them in the dry cleaning hamper. I make sure I separate them accordingly. She would not scold, she never has, but I enjoy knowing that I am making things as easy for her as possible. This may be the only thing I can make easier for her.

I didn't realize how hungry I was until Tonya reminded me; she was good at things like that, reminding me of what I needed before I knew them myself. Once again, I find a smile spread across my face when that is the last thing I want to do. She wanted me even if she couldn't bring herself to say it, even if she would fight her desires before she admitted to them.

Suddenly it hit me, and I wondered if she too had realized, though it was fleeting, that for an hour or more, she allowed herself to feel something beyond pain. This woman knows desire, passion, playfulness, anger, and a few other emotions I could not name. The fact that she felt even those things in that short span of time makes me look forward to what we have to gain. This one afternoon could change her if she let it, if I coaxed her into believing she could. I would give her all the time she needed as long as there was the promise of having her back again.

"French toast and turkey bacon," I said it as if it were a revelation. That's what we usually ate after a night of making love. The fact that it was still daylight meant nothing to me. I would try to keep this as routine as possible. Maybe somewhere along the way she'll remember what we had. She'll remember all the things we wanted, all the things we planned. She'll remember me. Things would line up. We'd fall right back in step into our routine.

I stumble over a shoe on the steps. This brings another smile. One of these days it will be a toy left there, and the house will be filled with laughter, not this, this thing we cannot name. I will not fight or beg her; I've tried to for so long to no avail. Instead I will love her through this; I will surrender to her, but no one else.

I will wait. This is just the first step, and for her it had been a leap. Even if she doesn't know it, she has given me something that has been in short supply as of late. Hope. That is the best gift anyone can give a dying man, and that is exactly how I feel as if she has breathed life into me with just a touch. It is stupid, childish even. Maybe I have reverted back to adolescence where your first crush seems as if it will do just that: crush you. I have always loved her like my first and treated her as my last.

I hear the shower turn off. I know she'll stay in there for a few more minutes. I rush into the kitchen and take the eggs and milk out the fridge. I make a quick call to the office. I advise Christina that I'll be taking the rest of the week off; anything pressing could be faxed to the home office. If I can make every day like today, there's a chance, and I have to believe that Tonya knows it. If she doesn't, she will. The next time—and there will be a next time—I'll hold her a little longer, make love to her a little slower.

Tonya

I can smell the bacon before I make it down the steps, and the scent causes a ripple. This one ran from my head to my toes. It was as if something went off inside me. I fought for so long and forsaken my vows just to suffer alone. It took the smell of overcooked bacon to remind me of just how much I have missed the man that I promised my forever. I knew he would feed me if it meant he had to starve to do so. He was a man who could be rejected for months and just as suddenly fall back into place as if nothing happened.

That's what he did. He made breakfast the mornings after. Well, the Saturday mornings after we made love, he made me breakfast. I didn't have the heart to tell him that his french toast was too soggy and his bacon too hard because it never mattered. And he was always so proud, yet unsure of himself. I would swallow my giggles along with my breakfast because he always made me take the first bite. If it wasn't good enough for me, I knew he'd start over until I found it acceptable. That was the way he lived. Whatever was done was done for my benefit. He never picked out his own tie, not because he couldn't, but because he claimed I was the only person whom he needed to impress.

This man was considered by some to be one of the legal masterminds of his generation. He played golf with the mayor of Philadelphia and knew the answers to questions I didn't have the slightest idea how to ask. He was always looking for validation from me as if his life's work could be dismissed with a minor suggestion from me. This is one of the reasons I love him, and it only takes the smell of breakfast for me to remember this.

It is impossible now to think that I could not love this man. From the moment we took our vows, he lived for me. I feel like an idiot for pushing him away. I don't remember where I lost my way, what turn I took that led me here. At our core, humans want to know love, need to identify, and need companionship. We'd go mad without it. But he had been stronger than I gave him credit for. He had resisted the urge to follow me over the edge; instead, he held onto my hand and tried to pull me back to safety. He could have left me to drown alone. Instead he opted to be my flotation device, despite the urge to push away out of fear. He clung to me, supported me when I rebuked him, held me up when I wanted to fall.

"Something smells good." I ignore the smoke that has filled the enormous kitchen and filtered its way up the steps. He had to be burning something. I stand behind him and turn down the burners while kissing the back of his neck, hoping he didn't notice my first action.

"Thank you. It's the cologne you got me for Christmas." I see his smile as he turns toward me. Had he always been so beautiful? Once in a while he would turn to me in a room full of strangers, and I would have to remind myself to breathe. I find myself drawn closer even though there is nothing between us but my robe and his boxer briefs. I had admonished him for cooking like this more times than I could count, though I never could with a straight face. He was beyond description; no words could explain just what made him so sexy. I love this part, the way I fit perfectly in his arms. He was definitely the Adam to my Eve. It's hard to fathom that I had not been created just for him when he held me this way. This connection is easier than I wanted to remember.

"Well, you do smell very edible, but I was referring to our breakfast-late lunch-early dinner you have going here."

He chuckles as I bury my face into his chest. I can still smell me on him, and I feel the tremors from what we did upstairs in my stomach. I am startled by the need I feel to have him again. I thank God that he is mine, something that I haven't done nearly enough lately. *Always thank God for your blessing, no matter how small,* I hear Lynnette in my head. He is and will always be my blessing, my piece of heaven on this side.

A car drives past with music blaring. *They must not be from around here,* I thought, dismissing them immediately. However, the song was a bit too familiar. Lance begins to sway, and when he does, I can't help but follow. As it was ordained, he is the head of my home; I should have followed him all along, with or without background music. It's comical to me how neither one of us has that much rhythm. We never minded; it was just another sign that we were so compatible. The smoke gets thicker, and I reach around him again to turn the flames completely off. We don't miss a beat—well, the beat we were moving to, and we continue to dance as if time is standing still. Suddenly, there is no stove, no food behind him, and no battle to fight. Suddenly, there is only him and I. That is the most uninhibited feeling in the world.

"Do you miss her? I mean, I know we don't have her or haven't had her really, but do you miss her?" He stops breathing for a second, waiting for me to answer. After a long pause his heart speeds up some, and I can tell he regrets asking me. It is not that I do not want to answer; it is just that I enjoy the rise and fall of his chest. This is the first time we have spoken of our daughter aloud since Toya made her decision. We shared information with

Arnold, but with each other, it was too hard. I don't know if we were waiting for someone to break the barrier, to say her name, even though he did not. I can't look at him while I answer.

"Yes, I miss her to the point where there is physical pain. It's like being hit by a bus, then having it drag you for a few miles. Everything that passes by seems so familiar, and it's your life that's passing by because you have to try to keep living, but you can't get off. You can't stop or catch yourself. Whatever happened after the accident is a blur. Life becomes a blur." We continue to sway, the music is long gone, but his breathing and heart rate have returned to normal. I know he is waiting for me to volunteer more or to ask him how he feels. I am not sure I can handle his answer. Does he feel he has more of a reason to be heartbroken since she is his daughter in the ways that matter?

I tell myself that I have to ask him something more out of courtesy than curiosity. But I will not ask if he misses her because I know the answer. He thinks I am ignoring him, but I am ignoring his pain. It is irresponsible, and it is horrible to admit. I'm not strong enough to carry his hurt too. I was running from him, abandoning him, because it was easier for me.

"Tell me what you miss about her." I think that's the easiest way to ask the question.

"I miss the way she looks in your arms. When you're holding her, Tonya, it's like everything in my world has found its place. I can't explain it the right way. Leave it to you and our daughter to leave me tongue-tied." I want to kiss him, for using a word as trivial as ours. But I hold back. I want him to continue, to keep talking about her, to make her real and not the pain. Every time we leave the hospital, I fought the fear that I would forget her lips or her eyes, the exact color of her hair or the way it curls. I am terrified that her smell will elude me. The only thing that seemed tangible after we have left was the pain. That's the one thing I could never forget. I am holding onto it because I know as long as I can feel this heartbreak, she is real. My love for her is real.

"Please keep going." I'm not ready for him to stop. His words have found their way through me.

"I miss looking into her face and seeing us both. I miss the way your voice makes her eyes flutter. She recognizes it even in her sleep. That made me a little jealous at first." He closes his arms tighter around me. I guess he is so used to me pulling away. I return the gesture, letting him know I am not going anywhere. This makes me feel even smaller. How long had I been this way? Did I really push us this far apart, where he feels he has to guard his words around me? That was the sanctity of marriage at its basis, the ability to be the person you are without being judged, but instead loved for it. Once upon a time, I clung to his words alone, and now he has to siphon them.

"I'm sorry we shut you out. Well, I shut you out. I was jealous too. She will always be yours forever. I just wanted her to know me." I can't admit to my weakness. The thought that somehow she would know she belonged to him, and not me. That after all I have gone through, after all the hurt, she will look at me one day as if I do not matter.

How do I tell him that I am jealous, that I am weak, that I am not who he thinks that I am? I am a shadow of that woman, a fraction of it. It would certainly be the final straw.

"I don't blame you. I don't care about yesterday. It is today that I am concerned with and the rest of our tomorrows." I do not hide my shame as he says these words. It is impossible to stop the tears. He does not need to know the details. I don't expect him to understand that I am crying for us both.

We end up making love on the kitchen floor. This time we are more patient. This time we do not fight each other. I allow him to rediscover me, and we make up for all that we have lost. The bond that was never meant to be broken had been frayed, but not severed. Once again I offer my thanks for him. Afterward, I make the breakfast.

Toya

McKenzie and I spent most of the day in my room. Now I have to return her to the nursery. This is the part I hate. I wonder if she feels abandoned even for such a short period of time. That would be awful; the thought alone makes me want to hold her and never let go. I know the feeling, and that is a pain I would never wish upon anyone, let alone my child.

Tonya and Lance will be here soon, and they'll stay until morning. Part of me wants to wait so that I can snatch just a quick glance at my sister. I could tell just by one look how upset she is when no one else can. I would always play dumb since it was easier to pretend her feelings didn't matter to me because I knew mine mattered so much more to her. When she would smile and say everything was all right, I'd know it wasn't. I just never cared enough to make things right. I am afraid that I may have separated our connection in such a way that I won't be able to read her again.

Reassurance is fleeting though I know it can't be that easy; you can't hate someone you've loved every day for all your life just like that. It's what I need to believe, and I hold on to the fact that her love had always been deep enough for me to float along despite the weight of lies, deception, and manipulations. If I see her, I'll know if things have changed. She is hurting, and I feel her pain more than I have ever allowed myself to do in the past. Tonya has become my phantom limb. I feel the ache though she has been removed from me. I still feel the need to reach for her or worse yet lean on her for support, though somewhere deep inside, I know I will fall. For a while, my sister will convince herself that she hates me, that she does not need me or want me in her life. I will allow her as long as she needs, but forever was not an option for me.

I know I should be walking back to my room, but my legs have become heavy. I try to force my feet to move faster, but they will not. I need to see her to know if the sorrow has settled behind her eyes. As is customary, it will take some time for us to put everything back together. There is nothing routine about this situation, and it is foolish to compare it to a stolen boyfriend, a borrowed blouse, or a misplaced toy. It will take time to earn her forgiveness, maybe even a lifetime, to earn her trust again. I will do almost anything she asks, trying to make myself the sister she has always believed I could be. Never wanting to be the person in her life she couldn't forgive even in our most heated arguments, I never for once believed we couldn't come back from it all.

But common sense gets the better of me. I decide to leave the nursery because I am afraid of what her eyes will reveal. I am not ready to face it just yet; for the time being, I can just act as if her anger had subsided to mere annoyance. I can do so as long as I didn't have to see it in her eyes.

"She's had her bottle, so she won't need to eat for a few more hours," I tell the nurse. I don't announce that my sister will be here soon. I've met this nurse before. She is aware of the situation. If this was one of those reality television shows, I do not think I would earn the most votes. The nurses watch us both, and whether it is intentional or not, notes are always taken and a score is always kept. Some would decide that my sister was better suited and better prepared; still others will root for the underdog, and for the first time ever, I find myself in that spot. Before I leave, I steal a few more kisses from the sleeping beauty. Even though there will be no votes tallied, I make sure the nurse has a perfect view of that little display of affection. Points were meant to be earned.

The walk back to the room is always filled with dread. We have been here less than a week. Time seems to stand still inside this hospital. It has been so long since I found myself this idle. I have a newfound respect and sympathy for my patients. The only thing that matters is the date of departure; anything in between is a punishment.

Leaving McKenzie unnerves me for obvious reasons, but I am mostly afraid that I will have another nightmare. Juvenile, I know, for a woman of my age. It would seem that I would grasp the concept of the surreal and just surrender to them, but I still fight against my subconscious. It's easier to keep my demons at bay when my baby is with me. I always find something new to admire about her, even if it is as simple as watching her sleep. After the morphine was taken away, it seems that every time I close my eyes, my hidden thoughts wreak havoc.

Purgatory is found behind my eyelids; it is my form of torture. Being self-inflicted does not make it any less frightening. I pray for myself, something that I admit I haven't done often over the years, each time I close my eyes asking for a peaceful oblivion that never comes.

Apparently the punishment had not been reserved for my sister alone. Accepting responsibility may ease my conscience, and I have accepted that I might be wrong, but I will not believe that Tonya is right.

After I said those horrible words, I offered to split my daughter with her, and that had not been enough. Nothing was left to say. I had compromised, something never done willingly. It was not enough for Lance or Tonya.

During my nap, I dreamt of Twin, something I haven't done since childhood. Everything seemed so ordinary at first. McKenzie and I wore matching pajamas, and I was staring out of the window, looking at a picturesque sky with no cloud in view, while rocking my daughter to sleep in her pink sleeper. Children could be heard somewhere laughing in the background, and even though I couldn't smell it, I am sure someone somewhere had to be baking something. We both seemed so content with each other, having her to myself and knowing that I was doing the mothering thing right.

I was in the middle of explaining all the mysteries of life. The things I have learned, the mistakes I hoped she'd avoid, even though I'd still love her no matter her choices.

I told her all my secrets as if she were my best friend and not my child. I don't remember all of the things I said, but I do remember at times I laughed and at times I cried. All the while I held her so tight. I knew she wouldn't judge me; she couldn't actually form an opinion as to the right and wrongs of my actions since she was still just a baby. That fact alone left me open to cleanse my soul.

When I got to the last part, the part where her story began, everything changed. At first, my sweet little baby watched me tell her everything with the most curious eyes. It may have been just wishful thinking on my part, but there was adoration there as well. When I told her of the horrible betrayal that had won me the most amazing thing imaginable—her—those eyes became full of resentment, full of sorrow and hurt. They were my sister's eyes again. This time I could not turn away. They were like anchors holding me there.

She wore the same look of horror as Tonya had when I told her McKenzie was staying with me. In the dream, I started to explain, but those eyes would not allow me. Her eyes, my sister's eyes, silenced me and begged for an explanation all at the same time.

As if someone had flipped a switch, the bright day was replaced by the darkest of nights. The children could not be heard anymore, and I wondered for a second if I had imagined them or maybe I was the cause of all the emptiness around me. For the first time since I felt my daughter move, that is exactly what I felt empty and alone. Unexpectedly, the wind picked up and violently blew everything around the room out of place. The sudden change was what allowed me to break our stare. I knew I couldn't panic—mistakes are made when people panic, and some could not be reversed. I put her back in the crib and ran to the window to close it. Before I reached the window, the wind knocked the crib over. I fought against myself turning back and forth between my child on the floor and closing out the vicious storm. What would happen if I left her just for a second and closed the window? What could happen if I picked her up and allowed the intruding winds to continue with their destruction? Panic is horrible; inaction is worse.

Suddenly the room was filled with laughter, not the adorable laugh of a baby. It was the condescending laughter of a grown up. When I turned around, I saw my sister in the nursery with us. I tried to call out to her to explain what had happened over the rage of the storm, but my words seemed to strangle me. The tempest did not affect her at all. She was standing there as calm as a statue, as if she were watching me in a movie. She was obviously amused yet ticked off at the same time. The wind seemed to move everything in the room but her. Her hair stayed in place as pictures fell from the walls. Not an article of her clothing was aroused while my robe tangled itself around me like a snake.

She cradled my daughter, and I wanted to run to them both to check and make sure McKenzie was all right and to assure myself that she had not been harmed in the fall. Most of all I wanted to show my sister that she wasn't the only one who knew how to calm a baby. I needed her to see me as I had been just a few seconds ago, before everything had come undone.

"Did you really think you could do this?" She laughed again, but her eyes held so much pity. I hadn't been pitied since my parents died. That made me angry; now I wanted to run to her, not for the sake of my child, but to unleash my own wrath. How dare she come into my home and question me. I had everything worked out; I was doing it right. This storm was sudden. I hadn't been prepared for it. This was not my fault. But the words wouldn't come to me. Blinded by angry tears that the wind wouldn't allow to fall, I was thankful for her presence but resented it all the same.

"She's a bad mommy, isn't she?" This time she wasn't addressing me. She was looking at the baby in her arms. My eyes searched the bundle for some sort of sign that my child was in there still breathing and unscathed. Then I heard her coo, and it was a thousand knives in my soul. It was as if she enchanted her in the same manner that she was able to control this storm. In her arms, McKenzie was safe. This knowledge caused the knives to twist and turn to create deeper wounds. I should have just held on to her; I would stab myself again just to take that action back.

The storm continued, but Twin acted as if it were nothing more than just a small aggravation. I watched her walk out of the nursery carrying my child, and I was unable to stop her. All I could do was cry as the wind began to die down; the angry tears turned into grief-filled sobs. Suddenly I had the availability of my voice.

"You could have at least let me say good-bye." I called out, speaking to them both. I couldn't just have my child torn away without apologizing for my stupidity. I didn't want my sister to leave without knowing just how much I had tried.

I was unsure if my limbs would work, but the thought of moving is what paralyzed me. The thought of not saying anything was just as frightening as saying the wrong thing. I needed both of them to know, to understand, to accept that this was not my fault.

My dream was interrupted by the phone ringing. Lynnette called to advise that the baby's room was complete and that she'd be here tomorrow to pick us up and take us home. Part of me was relieved that she had called, but the other part wondered if the dream had continued would I have chased after them? Would I fight for my daughter? Or had Tonya been right all along? I needed to look into her eyes to see if the storm brewing there was anything in comparison to the one in my dream. But like a coward, something that was truly unlike me, I sat in my room, and for what I wished was the first time, I cried until I couldn't cry anymore.

I wanted my mother. I have not felt this way in some time. It was not that they weren't missed. My parents have been like guardian angels or so I have pictured them throughout the years, always watching, but never before has the need been so great. I wanted to crawl into her arms and allow her to give me all the reassurance that a mother should.

I wondered now how she felt at the moment when the fear of never seeing or holding us again became a reality, no matter how quick she would have went. I do know now that it was quick and painless, that moment of utter terror would seem to eclipse a lifetime of peace.

I was terrified of what I had done and by the knowledge of what I may do or may have to do. Would I be able to give my sister up? The ache of her loss, even if I wasn't completely sure it would be a permanent one, disturbed me. Nothing seemed right, everything was surreal. How much longer would I survive without her? How much further would I be willing to go to be the one who protected that baby girl from the storm of life? Even though it was selfish, I wanted to be the only one, if not the first, to hear her laugh. I would walk through the storm. I would fight through it. I just could not do those things tonight.

Lance

We held hands the entire car ride and even as we came up in the elevator. This I was most appreciative of. When someone holds your hand, it is as if they are saying I could be doing a million things, but I just want to touch you, and that thrilled me, validated me in ways that she may never understand, and that is the brilliance of marriage, never having to explain why you feel the way that you do, just the acceptance of it all.

I loved the way her hands and feet were always a few degrees lower than the rest of her body temperature, no matter what the season. I guess I loved being the one to balance things out for her. Once my hands were on her, it only took a few seconds for the shift to happen. I don't know if my hands warmed her or hers cooled me. Either way, it all made sense without having to make sense.

We reach the nursery, and even though I cannot wait to hold my daughter, part of me doesn't want to let go of my wife's hand. I don't want to break this bond that has been formed over these past few hours. There was so much time we had lost; we would never get that back, and today felt like a blessing. A rebirth. We were newlyweds again. Everything is novel.

"You take her first." I can't believe I am hearing those words. This was not the usual routine. Normally I was delegated to holding her only when Tonya had to use the bathroom or when I asked. Most of the time I did not. There was a peace in her eyes when she held the baby. I watched, always praying that she would take some of it with her. I was not jealous of their bond; I just wanted to be a link on the chain.

"Are you sure? I know she must miss you." This was evident in the way her eyes flickered under her lids when she heard my wife's voice.

"She misses her daddy too. Just look at her. She's meant to be a daddy's girl. You could never say no to this angel. She knows it. We all do." We both chuckle. And for a moment we look like any other parents in any other hospital in the world visiting their child. We are giddy at the possibilities the future would hold and bound by our commitment to our child.

She hands me our daughter. I cannot think of her as belonging to anyone else. Even after all this time, I still don't trust my ability to pick her up. I guess it's because I've never had to. She has always been handed to me.

I sit in the rocking chair while my wife kneels beside us. She sings a song that's meant to quiet a sleeping child, one of those songs that have been passed down for generations but never gets old. The song gently soothes my daughter back to sleep but makes me more alert. I don't want to miss a thing. If I could live every day like this with McKenzie in my arms and my wife by my side, I wouldn't ask for anything more.

"Do you think she knows who I am?" I have fought the need to ask this question, partly because I learned a long time ago to never ask a question you don't want to know the answer to or to never ask one whose answer you are not prepared for.

"Yes, I think she knows who you are." I can tell my wife is not saying this just to be polite. She answers thoughtfully. "Do you see the way she's turned toward you? See, all of us want to know love, and when we're as innocent as this little one here, we try to wrap ourselves up in it. She doesn't know anything about hurt or loss. She just knows safety, and she feels that with you. I know exactly how she feels. Your arms are safe, they're warm. It's as if the outside world doesn't exist when I'm wrapped in them. Our daughter feels that. I know she does." I look away from McKenzie and stare at my wife as she speaks. It's as if she isn't talking to me but to the baby in my arms. "She may not understand the title of daddy. But she understands that you belong to her and her to you. I know it. I can sense it."

When she looks at me, I can't hide my smile. She returns one of her own, and if it were at all possible, my heart could explode right now. Just like that, I feel like a bigger man. I shift McKenzie in my arms, and I make room for my wife to sit on my lap. She laughs but acquiesces, and I rock them both as she continues to sing. I kiss them and am rewarded for a second time that night as I hear the sound of my wife's laughter. She gently places her hands on my cheeks—they have once again become cold—and tilts my face so that our eyes meet. We are searching each other, trying to figure out all the little things we have missed. I know what she is doing; it is a game that we used to play. We'd look each other in the eyes and say nothing, just stare. There were times when she'd erupt into laughter or times when she'd burst into tears. It didn't matter her reaction because I always knew what she was saying to me without having to wait for her words.

I wish there was a way to tell her how much I missed those little things, explain how much it hurt to be torn away from her thoughts for so long. No one could ever understand just how much my wife means to me. Robbing me of her thoughts and her fears has been the cruelest punishment of all. Does she know how I have craved the feeling of her tiny chilled hands against mine. Tonya could never imagine the hurt I feel behind losing my best friend. There was no one other than her for me. She was my family, the whole of it, my friend, my lover, and those things were taken from me when she walked away emotionally.

A man does not speak of these things; a man does not tell a woman who has been given to him to protect that she is the keeper of him. Wrong it would be to tell her that I know I have let her down and that I would give anything to take it back, but I need to know what I did to deserve what she had done to me. It would be placing blame, but she has been for me the only thing I have needed. She saved me so long ago with a kiss, and then she was gone. I had lost my soul mate, and that shredded me. It would be heart-wrenching now to lose her in those ways again. I will not imagine my world without her; I refuse to picture life without her by my side.

I tell her these things with my silence, even though I know I should not. But I need her to understand that I could drown in sorrow if she left. I want her to know that my heart threatened to stop beating every time she walked past me in a hall without looking at me. Tonya's eyes cloud with tears, and I can feel the single one that has escaped my eyes. She understands what I have said, and I pray that this is the last time I hurt her ever again. This time she kisses me, and I know that she is promising me something. I feel it behind her lips. She is promising me her forever once again. We will start over. I place her head against my shoulder, and once again she starts to hum her song.

That is how we will spend our night, the last night, at the hospital. Who knows what tomorrow will bring. But for tonight, it is just the three of us, and I know that God is still answering prayers.

Lynette

I can't sleep. Instead I watch the clock as it stares back at me. It's 3:37 a.m. Nothing but the devil is up this late. So I prayed. I think I talked to God for an hour and a half straight, but just for the night, I am all prayed out. I usually feel as though I've reached a decision after prayer. I'm no Joan of Arc, but I know that God speaks to me. There's no burning bush or booming voice, but somehow when I am done, I know what to do. These past few days have been different. Before I felt as though I had a personal connection with my Savoir. We had a two-way conversation. But for this past week, I feel like I've been speaking with His voice mail.

I need an answer since in just a few hours I'll have to pick LaToya up and bring her home, entrusting the life of my grandchild to her. If it were Tonya, I wouldn't be this nervous about it. I try to convince myself that the situation is what has me on edge, but I know this river runs much deeper.

She's been doing well. She's just like any other new mother. I've been telling myself this repeatedly. That did not help to dissolve the lump in my throat. In the hospital, there's always someone monitoring her and the baby. Soon that security blanket will be torn away. Will this be one of her grand plans that she'll get bored with, and after a few weeks will she decide that she's had enough? That is a terrible thought, and I curse myself for thinking it. The last time I forced her to complete something, she hadn't wanted to it changed our relationship and her life forever.

Toya is always finding something new to occupy her time. But her interests were diverted soon after they were piqued. This is not something that has changed with age. Her dates for Thanksgiving never make it back for Christmas dinner, and I think she's changed her furniture at least two times in the past year. One minute she's into art deco; the next, a more rustic feel. She's knocked down walls just to replace them. Her home mirrored her life in so many ways. From the outside, it looks so inviting, like everything is so put together. But once you're inside, you realize that it's nothing more than a mirage. As a child, she tried everything from dance to softball to piano lessons. Whenever she dedicated herself, she more than succeeded, she excelled. This could be, just might be, I am praying that it will be, the same as all the others.

Maybe I should have gotten her that puppy she wanted when she was younger; I think that was the only time I told her no. I did it partly for Tonya's sake because we all knew the responsibility would inevitably fall onto her. She wouldn't have minded at all, but she already had so much on her plate, so I decided to say no for her. The thought comforts me a little bit. One day I hope she remembers I had put my other daughter first, at least once. Once is not enough for a lifetime.

It's better to err on the side of caution. I struggle with how to tell her, how to explain that some people were cut out for this and some just weren't. Being a mother isn't something that can be turned on and off. Yes, some grow into it, and they surprise you, but some just let you down. It wouldn't be me that was disappointed;

it would be the child who loses if this were to go bad. This child, who was now the center of all our worlds, deserved the best this life had to offer. I wish I could ensure that for her. I try to push the doubt away.

When you try to not think of anything, everything comes to the surface. The first sleepless night, I spent begging God to forgive my girls for what they were doing. Then I realized they weren't the only ones who needed forgiveness. I have made my mistakes too; I see those mistakes now more clearly than ever. My only salvation is the thought that maybe I am being harder on myself then I need to be. The things you remember are often the ones others forget. Maybe my mistakes won't be held against me, and the wrongs that are too late to right may be forgiven. Or I am fooling myself.

I decide since I am up, I might as well be productive. I walk over to my exercise bike. I hadn't gotten much use out of it. I think God gave a woman hips for a reason, and if he's pleased with it, who am I to say he's wrong. But for my health, I have to try and reduce some of this weight. After Tonya found out her gift was going to waste, she brought me a flat screen television to put next to it. She encouraged me to work out while I watched my soaps.

Tonight I think I'll try something different. Maybe my body will outrun my mind and I'll finally get some sleep. I put on some sweatpants and my sneakers. I stare at the bike for a few seconds. "No weapon formed against me shall prosper." The scripture makes me laugh. Only I would consider exercise equipment as a foe. I will stop being lazy. I want to be here to watch my grandbaby graduate from college, walk down the aisle, and if I'm not asking for too much, to see her bear her own children. Taking care of myself is the first step to ensuring this. So instead of turning on the television—nothing but infomercials will be on—I try to envision her future. I never place a mother there; my mind won't allow me to choose.

I pick my settings. I don't think I am ready for an uphill journey; there was already an uphill battle going on in my life. I'll just cruise along. Entering my weight and age, give or take a few, mostly take, I began to pedal. As soon as I pick up speed and hear the pedals going, I am brought back to another humid night, more than twenty years ago.

He was out of breath by the time he reached my steps. The poor little thing must have pedaled faster than he ever had before. I tried not to laugh in his face. I knew Evan had come to see one of my girls, but they weren't home.

He was the cutest ugly boy I'd ever met. His bucked teeth and big lips seemed to take up half his face. His eyes were too small for his own good, and the bifocal glasses he wore covered the rest. The only saving grace was his perfect nose, smack-dab in the middle of everything else that was wrong with him. But he had to be the sweetest little boy every created. I guess his mother had warned him early enough in life that he wouldn't get girls on his looks so he'd better learn how to play nice.

I wondered who he had come to see. I could usually tell by the way he was dressed. If he had on a nice button-up shirt, no matter the season, he had come to see Toya. She'd never paid that boy any attention; she only played with him when they were younger and that was mostly to get him to do the things she didn't want to—her chores. She'd send him to the corner store for whatever she liked, and it amazed me how she never gave him any money either, but he'd always come back with whatever she asked. Some days he'd bring himself something back, usually just enough for her. I felt bad for him, warned him even, that he was being taken advantage of. I told her she was wrong. His answer was, "Yeah, but she could take advantage of anyone. And she always chooses me." Hers was as simple: "He likes doing things for me. It would be mean to make him stop when it makes him happy, Aunty."

Who could blame him? I knew the things I did just to see her smile. So I allowed her to use him, and I allowed him to be used. Eventually one of them would find someone else. I hoped for his sake sooner than later.

When he came in a regular shirt, he was there for Tonya. She'd took pity on him, even went with him to the freshman dance that year, but she mainly helped him to study. Their relationship was similar in some ways. Tonya was just as pushy, but she pushed him to be better. When he didn't get an answer right, she gave him a look that said how disappointed she was. It was the same look her sister gave when he returned without something on her list. Every time he disappointed one, he'd try harder to make up for it. But when the answer was right, Tonya was truly pleased. He lit up like Christmas morning. She grossly exaggerated his abilities, telling him how he had to be the smartest boy in the neighborhood, but he just didn't apply himself. That was just like her. She could stroke an ego, but never for her own benefit. Never mind the fact that even in the ninth grade he was doing basic math. Tonya made him feel as if he just solved Newton's equation.

He admired my Tonya, but adored my Toya. I wondered if either of them actually considered him if he'd be able to choose one over the other. I doubt he would. No one could. They were just opposite sides of the same coin. Each offered what the other could not. So as he approached my porch I wondered if he came to be praised by one or reprimanded by the other.

"They're not home, baby." I hadn't noticed how dark it had gotten outside. They should have been home by now. The crocheting I had been doing had occupied my time. Dinner wasn't even finished.

I hadn't noticed the sweat that covered his body. I couldn't tell if it covered his face or if they were tears.

"They hurt her."

I didn't know what "her" he was talking about. So I tried to recall where they were. Tonya was at the library with Ranada, and Toya said something about going to the park with Alicia to work on her jump shot, which meant boy watching. She tried really hard at basketball since I refused to let her quit. Even though they were only five feet and I knew she'd never win a basketball scholarship, I wanted her to learn how to work as a team.

So what he was saying did not compute at all. My babies were safe. One was studying a few blocks up the street, and the other was playing basketball a few blocks down it. I didn't comprehend what he was saying.

"They hurt who, baby?" I knew he couldn't have been talking about one of my girls. No one would dare. I ran off the porch. I think I may even have leapt over a few steps. I got to him just before he passed out falling off of his bike and into my arms. The force of his weight caused the wheels to start spinning again.

I knew then it had to be my babies. No one else could have hurt more for them than me or the other. I tried to shake him awake while asking my questions. I smacked him, right across his ugly face. When he woke up, he told me what had happened, and I ran all the way to her. The whole time I relived the loss of my baby sister. I had let her down, had disappointed her. I couldn't cry. I wouldn't cry. I had to see where I was going, and when I got there, they were loading my baby into an ambulance. I didn't recognize her. I couldn't. If she wasn't wearing her third of our best friend's chain, I would have denied it was even her. But I knew right away which one it was. She had the left side, mine was the middle, and her twin had the right. All her jewelry was still there, so I knew what they had taken from her. And that was the day I lost my baby. They took her virginity and took my soul right along with it.

I stepped off the bike. I'll ask for a treadmill next year. I knew I wouldn't sleep tonight. I would see her broken body in front of me every time I close my eyes. The part that haunts me most is when I called her name, she reached for me, even though it must have hurt her like hell. She reached, knowing I had finally made it to her. It was obvious that she had put up a fight, but she shouldn't have done it alone. That bloody and broken hand haunts my darkest moments.

Tonya

Sadly I can't remember a time when I felt like everything was the way it was supposed to be. Blaming it on the "tragedy" of being born a twin, I often believed it was impossible to feel complete. God designed it so that I would be divided. But I know now what peace wholeness provides, the joy it brings, the serenity accompanied by union.

This is what life is all about. It had taken so long for me to unravel the mystery. People spend all their lives searching for something, wanting to know the secret. It is simple. The meaning of life at its core is love. I know it sounds contrite, too simple, and easy even. But that is what it's all about. To know love, feel it, breathe it, live it, be in it, then give it back selflessly. This right here, this moment, this family, this peace in his arms and her in mine, is love.

Where everyone seems to get lost is they look for perfection; there is no such thing. Nothing in life is free, not even love. It's not something that can be paid for, but it will cost you every time. You misplace some of yourself and replace some of your dreams.

Love allows you to find what was missing all along. You give up your dreams because they change and become ours.

Finding love isn't what makes life worth living; it's when you learn what you are willing to pay, what you are willing to give, lose, replace, change, to have it for just one second more. Once you have found a love that makes you say, "I would give it all for just one more minute of this," you've begun to live. Even though the "this" you're referring to may be flawed or may not be what you had expected, you find that it is perfectly flawed. And that it is not what you expected because in the tiny recesses of your mind, a love like that could never be expected. This is what poems were meant to inspire and what songs tried to capture.

I would give my life if it meant saving the one I was becoming accustomed to. I know I cannot go back to emptiness, not after having my fill of her. I could not go back to loneliness, not after finding my way back to Lance. There was no way I could make it without either of them. If one were missing, all the pieces would fall apart. They were the center of my puzzle, the part that completed the picture. Without them, my life would just be corners, fragments of sky, grass, and lakes. Yes, smack-dab in the middle of the hospital, I had unraveled not just the mysteries of life, but the enigma of myself.

Tonya

Last night had been no exception to the previous ones. It went by way too fast; it will be our last night here in the hospital. It is time to say our good-byes, but this one stings just a little more and opens the wound a little wider. Lance had made arrangements through Lynnette for our visitations, which sounds like such a dirty word. Prisoners were allowed visitation. Bad parents after their children had been taken away were granted visitation. We had committed no crime. Last time I checked, coveting was a sin. We are being punished; there is no other way for me to look at it.

My husband asks that I keep an open heart since Toya could have said no. Legally, no one has custody until it is established by the courts. So it is not mandatory for her to allow us to see McKenzie. Lance says these things as if they should make me feel better. He thanked God for small favors when I was waiting for the enormous miracle. I will try to see things his way and be grateful for what we are given. A few minutes holding her would be better than never having her again. The thought of sneaking in my sister's back door while she walked out the front makes me feel dirty as if I have done something unspeakable. I want to be as thankful as Lance, but I cannot find it in my heart. He wants me to show gratitude to my sister for this small thing as if it negated all the wrong.

My consolation is the knowledge that Arnold has pulled a few strings, and our court date should be coming sooner than expected. Yesterday was not soon enough for me. I want to put all of this behind us. Start the life I pictured. Fill the empty albums with inconsequential pictures that showcased the absolute nothingness that made up everything, the moments that could never be relived and would be etched in a memory, never to be forgotten because there was proof, evidence that I had shared in those moments.

There will be pictures missing—I have come to except that now—but how far would the gap extend? The only pictures that occupied the album were her sonograms and the pictures taken right after her birth since I hadn't the heart to take any more for fear that they would be the last pages in the album that would hold its place on our shelf.

There will be no section of "baby coming home." There would be no pictures of proud daddy opening car doors. It is amazing what people take for granted. Nothing was guaranteed. I am fighting against the invisible current.

McKenzie will be leaving the hospital today, and I refuse to think about what will happen once they drive away. Will the peace I found last night somehow evaporate once exposed to the outside world? Or will the connection break due to the distance placed between us, like the toy walkie-talkies I played with as a kid.

"Just five more minutes please," I ask Lance. He thinks it will be better if he delivers McKenzie to Toya himself as a goodwill gesture, to show her that we would be cordial during our visitation. I ask him for five minutes as a child would who wasn't ready to put down their favorite toy. I can't bring myself to give her back to the now impatient nurse. She couldn't be more than a child herself. I wonder if she's still asking someone for more time throughout her day. I hated her the moment I saw her in those cartoon scrubs. I know she's just doing her job. I am doing the same, being a mother. Part of me wants to make a run for it, but I wouldn't want to give anyone more ammunition.

"She needs her bottle, and it's now 8:17," the cartoon wearing nurse advises me.

This time, I fight away the thought of smacking her. What she wants to tell me is my time is up, that it is now my sister's turn to play mother, her turn with McKenzie. As if I wasn't aware of the schedule.

"We'll feed her. Dr. Garrett is waiting for me to bring the baby to her anyway." Even if she wanted to question him, she would not. That was the beauty of a man like Lance. He could make a statement that sounded like a command and a question all at once. And people often, if not always, gave him exactly what he wanted, even though they thought they were being asked.

"Sure," she says in a voice much different from the one she had reserved for me. She doesn't realize that she's being handled; even if she did, I doubt she'd mind. I haven't met a woman who wouldn't want to be handled by Lance.

Once the nurse walks away, I lay our baby in her crib and begin to undress her. Lance stands above me, looking over my shoulder. I know he is curious as to what I am doing but will not ask. I pull out the outfit that Lynette had purchased weeks ago. I wasn't sure if she knew the sex. If she had, she played along, purchasing one blue and one pink.

I place the pink dress on her, complete with little pink bloomers. She is adorable. Amazingly, it fits perfectly. "Where's her headband?" I ask Lance more accusatorily than I meant to be. "It's part of her outfit."

I could tell he had no idea what I was talking about. Asking him for her headband was the equivalent of asking him where Jimmy Hoffa was buried. He has no idea, and worse yet, the look on his face hurts me more. The world is shifting, and the static can now be heard on the line. We have not left the hospital yet, but the distance between us has already started to grow. I want him to look into me like he did last night. I don't want to have to explain, never again how and what I feel. I just want him to know. I expect him to remember us even though I am the one who has caused his memory lapse. I want him to forget these past few years where I pushed him away. I need him to be the old Lance, the one who could just with one look know I was falling apart and glue me back together.

I can tell he is confused as to why a simple headband would mean so much to me. It is not the headband because that would be too simple. It is the fact that not even this moment can be perfect or go off without a hitch that destroys me.

Will he understand that my biggest fear is that these may be the only pictures in our album while she still belonged to us? Well sort of. Those pictures will be missing something. Maybe no one will notice, but I would always know and feel it in my heart that I had somehow done this all wrong, and the possibility of not being able to correct that mistake makes me start to hyperventilate. Life was not a dress rehearsal; there will be no do-overs. Not for us anyway.

Before I know it, he has his arms around me. He nods at the nurse who now comes and picks up the baby. I am irritated at myself for allowing the nurse to see me this way. My husband whispers things in my ear that calm me but are forgotten right after he speaks them. Now it is my turn to be handled.

"I'm fine," I tell him. "I said I am fine." This time I say it with more conviction. He is now watching me as someone would an accident about to happen.

"Excuse me." This time I address the nurse. I can tell that she is now bored with all our antics. That brightens my mood a little more. "Can you take pictures of us please?" I poured sugar over my words. She wants to say no—I can see it in her eyes—and I think she's concerned about handing over a baby to a woman who was panicking less than a minute ago over something as trivial as a hair accessory.

"Thank you," Lance interjects, not giving her the chance to deny me. She entertains us and takes the pictures, never once asking if we were ready before she snaps them or asking for smiles. I don't know if I am able to muster one up anyway.

She hands the camera to Lance, and I begin to undress McKenzie again. She has slept through it all; that I am thankful for. I hand her to her father once she is dressed, and he kisses me. He tells me he'll be right back or something of the sort. I am numb now, allowing nothing in or out. I kiss our daughter, praying that she will remember me for one more day as the woman who held her while she slept and loves her every second with every breath and every moment in between.

I wait patiently by the elevator, not sure of how much time has passed. It could be seconds or hours—it would not surprise me. The elevator had returned to the floor three times already. Each time, I get in, press G, and get right out. My tears are steady since my head is hung so low. They do not reach my shirt, but I am certain they have created a puddle on the floor. For some reason, I cannot bring myself to lift my head. The teddy bears that adorn the walls now seem as if they are mocking me instead of smiling. I find the pictures that tell stories of happy families intimidating. So instead, I concentrate on the nondescript blue and white tiles. They appear on any floor in this hospital; that somehow comforts me, making it easier to wait. I hear a man's voice in my head. It is not my husband's.

"He never gives us more than we can handle. He sees all, and I'll pray for you in your time of loss." Just like that, and he walks away. I look up just in time to see that it is a priest.

"I haven't lost anything yet, Father," I whisper to myself as he walks away. I know how I must look—crying while holding the tiny dress in my hand. Anyone would be confused by this.

Lance returns. We enter the elevator in silence, both reaching for the ground floor button together; I pull my hand away as if he shocked me when we touched. There is no reaction at all from him as we walk to the car. This time, the silence is not uncomfortable. I don't know what he is thinking, and I'd rather not know. My thoughts are enough to occupy a lifetime.

He opens my car door, always the gentleman. I sit and look behind me. The emptiness of the back seat screams at me. There should be a car seat there. I don't bother to ask him when he removed it. I guess he knew it was for the best. I turn quickly to put my seatbelt on. I am certain that he will have me committed after the scene in the nursery if I break down now over a missing car seat. In the crevice between the seat and the armrests, I find her pretty pink head band. I hold it in my hand, hiding it from him; I don't know why I feel the need to do so.

"Can you hold me?" He reaches over to unbuckle my seat belt. I stop him. "I meant after." He understands and pulls the car out as slowly as if there were a little one in the back. The speedometer has not reached higher than thirty-five. He is not in a rush, and I do not take this as an insult. I know that he needs me as much as I need him. He is giving us both the time to put our thoughts in order, to find the missing pieces, before we become one again.

He would never give me half of him; I am guilty of doing so for quite some time. He has learned from my mistakes. This time he will be gentle. I can tell by the way he tenderly caresses my thigh the whole ride home. This time, I will pray that it lasts forever.

Lynette

I am hiding in the waiting room, trying to avoid being seen. I know this is childish, and some might even say petty, but walk in my shoes and then tell me which route to take. From here I could see directly into the nursery, so I saw the panic in her eyes. I wanted to run to her to ask how I could fix it for her, but the better part of me decided against it. My presence alone may cause her to fly off the handle. I don't know if I could blame her.

They say you shouldn't shoot the messenger, but I was more than that. I guess I am the constant bearer of bad news. There are no rules about shooting them. I refuse to be the cause of a scene. I've always prided myself in never being a public spectacle, and I made sure my girls lived by the same rules. After all that has been done, I can't put anything past either of them. Tonya could be happy to see me or pretend I did not exist.

This day has finally arrived, and even though it seems like yesterday, everything changed. It feels as if the night before was unbelievably long and a sleepless one. Toya will be taking my granddaughter home today. I refuse to designate McKenzie as being either one of their daughters since she belongs to both of them in every way that could possibly matter. I will assume that I will still have the privilege of being called Nana or Grammy one day.

In my haste to get here, I arrived well before the right time. If I walked past the nursery, there would be no way that Tonya would miss me. I didn't want to make things any more uncomfortable for her or myself. Last night, I came to the decision to make today as wonderful as possible. I thought it would be best for me if I just enjoyed every possible moment of it. I ignored the fact that it was already ninety degrees before I opened my eyes, one of the downfalls of Philadelphia summers, or that the traffic getting here was horrendous. The expressway was anything but express this time of morning. Instead, I concentrated on the delightfulness of the day.

I was not at all prepared to see Tonya or Lance this early. I thought I'd have time to prepare myself for them tonight when the unofficial visitations would start. By then, I could compartmentalize my feelings. By then I could hide my smiles and frowns until either was the appropriate emotion to show at the time. This morning, I was giddy at the thought of bringing my first and, as far as is foreseeable, my only grandchild home. This morning, I didn't think of the heat, only the sun. I couldn't be upset about the traffic; maybe the drivers were headed to find their own source of joy. This morning seemed so far away as I looked into that nursery window.

I watched Tonya as she dressed McKenzie a few minutes ago. The fact that she did place her in the dress I picked out was encouraging. I hadn't been completely written off. She has no idea how much I want this for her. But I saw the way her lips curved more so to the right when she smiled, which meant it was a fake one. She was using the forced smile, which I hated to see on her face.

Then suddenly the smile was gone, and a look of horror, was there. The mother in me demanded that I respond, the same way I would've when she fell off her bike as a child. As a matter of fact, that is the same look she wore on her face. It was if her security had been swept from underneath of her, and she now found herself on the ground hurting with no explanation as to how she got there. As a parent, we see the whole thing. It plays more slowly for us. We know we will not reach them in time. We know that the damage will not be as bad as the child first assumes. So we wait in the wings for their reaction. Will he or she simply dust themselves off, pick up the bike, and start over, or will the shock of it all be too damaging?

Lance saw me as I rushed to her. His eyes stopped me. He was taking his place; he was the one who was now entrusted to comfort her, to make the boo-boos disappear even if they were imaginary. We had never allowed him to do this for her before. I was afraid that my place would be lost. I am uncertain of what she feared. I was always the one to make things better for her, to soothe the pain invisible or otherwise. Except something in his eyes made me stall. They held me right there between the waiting room door and the nursery. I was accustomed to being in limbo these past few days; somehow this was different. By the time I made up my mind to go anyway, I was not needed. Her smile had balanced itself out. It was not the perfect one I missed, but it was no longer slanted.

My little girl did not need me today. She may not need me tomorrow. She had found someone to steady things for her, to make right the wrongs, to soothe the hurts. And I was left hiding behind a waiting room door, doing just that, waiting. Confused more now than ever, I felt like one of those old ladies who are always looking for something but never quite remembered what it was they were searching for. I wished she would look up and see me, and then I'll know just how far the wedge is between us. Or maybe I was waiting for her to leave so I can have my time of joy. However brief it may be. I continued to watch her.

She undressed McKenzie after a few awkward pictures are snapped by the nurse. Then she reluctantly placed her back in Lance's arms. She stole a few kisses from my granddaughter, then whispered even fewer words. I wonder what she had said, what she could possibly say. She waited by the elevator, afraid to lift her head or her eyes. I know she is trying to hold herself together. I've seen this stance more times than I care to admit. Her shoulders stooped in defeat, her back still ram straight to the point where it looked as if it hurt. Her feet pigeon toed even though she is not. Her head held down as if she were waiting for the perfect time to collapse. She often reminds me of a puppet when she stands like that. There is always someone else pulling her strings. Curtain call never comes fast enough, and before the illusion is completely etched in your mind, before you start to see each puppet as having their very own personality or identity, the puppet master allows you this glimpse; you remember that the character has done nothing on their own.

"Would you like to take this walk with me?" Lance appears in front of me. I know he is not asking me. He's assuming that I will because it is what he wants, and he knows it is what I need. To be close to Lance is almost the same as being near my child.

"How is she doing? Have you given her my messages?" I don't need to hear his response to know that he has. Not only is Lance impartial, he is honest, sometimes more brutal than discretion should allow. That is the benefit of family. He doesn't answer because he knows it will hurt me to know the truth that my daughter has ignored me, shunned me, and thrown me away. She chose to abandon me before I had the chance to do it to her, not that I would.

"Are you taking good care of her?" This question he will answer simply because I need to be reassured. A few years ago, I wouldn't have dared to question him, and he knows this is through no fault of his own. I am asking if she is allowing him to take care of her. I need to make sure my baby has someone to be there during the times she will not allow me to be.

"Things are better." There's hope in his voice, something that hasn't been there in so long. He is not the only one wishing for a better outcome. There is something very different about him. He was always a handsome man, but now it seems as if his soul is glowing in the midst of all murkiness. He has the nerve to be smiling. Looks to me as if he would break out and dance if he could. That is what I told my girl to fight for, to search for. Everyone needs someone who makes you wanna dance so much on the inside you can't hide it on the outside. I wondered who had given him this thrill, my daughter or my granddaughter. I don't pry or ask for all the details. After all, everyone is entitled to their own secrets. It is not a far walk to Toya's room. She is sitting there patiently waiting for us.

She lights up when she sees the bundle in Lance's arms. The smile stings because I know the joy that she feels right now is the cause of her sister's pain, of all of our heartache. She drives me crazy. I want to run to her and hold her while scolding her at the same time. I have waited for years to see that type of joy in her eyes. It is what all mothers hope for: to see their child feel this way. This moment should be filled with joy of my own, but I cannot find it. Instead, I find that I can only feel the hurt of my other child. I turn to Lance expecting that he too will see all that I am carrying, hoping that I will not have to restrain him from wiping that smile off her face.

My question from the hall is answered as Lance's face glows just as bright as hers. Suddenly their eyes lock, and Toya is smiling back at him. They look like any happy family, but that is not the right picture. Am I in the wrong room or a bad movie? I feel dirty as if I have walked in on a husband and wife while they were undressing. I blink repeatedly hoping to erase the image from my mind. This is all wrong.

I could kill them both. I could erupt right here and now if I thought it would do any good, but a mother knows her child, both of them, and I know it will not. Toya will deny, and Tonya will resent. She was selfish, spoiled, and a brat. (Lord, forgive me for calling her that.) She has already laid claim to the one thing her sister wants; now she has crossed the line. This I won't be able to forgive.

Lance

I don't know what happened. Honestly, I am not that man who, on some subconscious level, is still pining away for his wife's sister. Those feelings had been put aside years ago, swallowed the day I met Tonya, or so I assumed. Now I am wondering if they were put behind me or buried.

Nothing that I say can rationalize that, for me—since I will not speak for LaToya—there was something there. The scariest part is the not knowing what that something was. I am praying for the past tense. I am praying that it was just one of those fluke things that we never repeat. I am praying for a lost cause like praying for a hurricane in the desert.

I could blame it on emotions, lack of sleep, or any number of things. The fact that I need to rationalize this makes me feel worse. I am looking to excuse my behavior, to justify what I have done.

For some strange inexplicable reason, everything felt right… with the wrong woman. Now I am questioning what makes things wrong or what makes something right for that matter. Is it normal for a man to feel some connection with the mother of his child? We will always share a link because there is a reminder that we breathed, lived, and loved, and that reminder is the sweetest thing I've ever known.

It had not been done for me; it had been done for her sister, the beautiful woman who is just starting to put the pieces back together, the one that I promised to love, not just years ago inside of a church, but every single day of my life. Today had been no different. Every morning at the first moment of clarity, before I even open my eyes, I pray that God makes me a better man, more patient, humble, and understanding than I was the day before. I pray that my actions reflect the man he created me to be. I pray that my life has not been in vain up until this point. The final thing that I pray is that if today was to be my last, my wife would have no doubts that she was loved unreasonably by a seemly reasonable man who adored her. I prayed for these things even when I didn't necessarily feel them. I asked God to help me love her even when she pushed me away, even when she made me feel inept, less than because she obviously couldn't or wouldn't love me back. I prayed that I could love her better, or the right way. This morning, however, when I prayed for these things, sitting in a hospital rocking chair, I thought I meant them.

There could be no greater betrayal, in her eyes or anyone else's for that matter.

What was worse is that Lynette witnessed whatever it was. Her face made me want to stop my heart from beating right there on the spot. Part of me wished she would have done it for me. Even still I could not pull myself away from my daughter and her mother; I had been caught but refused to pull my hand out of the cookie jar.

My poker face had been left at home, or in the courtroom, because nothing was hidden. The longing oozed from every single pore; it was palpable, as if it encircled everyone in the room.

I couldn't imagine what Tonya would have thought. No, I know exactly what she would have thought because it's what I thought ever so briefly. It's what I am repenting for now.

Just for a second, my heart wondered what could have been, my mind thought about what should have been. My soul knew they both were wrong.

I would never act on any desire. That is not the word I am looking for because it sounds filthy, but there was nothing sexual there. I realize as distance is placed between me and the room, where the world seemed to shift, I did not desire Toya in the way that my wife or even her aunt may assume. I did not yearn to have her in that way. Instead what I want from her is the one thing that seems to elude me—every day with my child.

My fault was placing another woman in the same perspective as my wife. Since the day she gave me her hand to hold, I knew I would do anything to keep her safe and near to me. It wasn't a conscious decision at all. That was my role as man in her life, and for a brief second, I had thought about taking that place in her sister's.

So I am indeed a fiend. A liar. I vowed to forsake all others, and now I know that I cannot keep that promise. I would never see my sister-in-law without, because of what she has done and in spite of what she is about to do.

I reach Tonya at the elevator, and I want her to look me in my eyes and see what I have thought and condemn me for my desires. I wish she would punish me for wanting someone other than her again.

Instead she takes my hand into hers and squeezes ever so gently. Once again, her hand has lost its warmth, and I thank God that nothing about her has changed. I brush my lips across her delicate knuckles, thinking that if there was anything in this world she could provide, she would and also understanding that if things went wrong, I would never feel her close again.

If everything we have gone through means that I get to love and be loved by her for the rest of our lives, I wouldn't change a thing. That is what I know now, but that is not what I felt minutes ago. Sadly I cannot promise her or myself that in my weakness, it will never happen again.

Toya

Sometimes you have to use what you've got to get what you want. The one thing I have plenty of are acquaintances who don't mind being used by the right person for the right price.

I made a few calls and found out a few things—some my sister may have known, some she did not. This is her fault because she buries her head in the sand when it comes to the ones she loves. I am uncertain of how Lance will react, and for some reason, I am more concerned about that than I am about my sister's feelings, maybe because it is her fault that I have to resort to these measures or because on some level, Lance and I share a connection. That is what I told myself on the way here. It is so much easier now to be angry with her than sympathetic. Anger doesn't afford me the time to miss her or allow me to regret any of my choices.

Now I am sitting in this office, waiting on Lance's past and hoping to secure my future. It is now that my daughter crosses my mind. I know she is safe with Lynette, but part of me wishes I would have thought of her sooner. How easily distracted I can be—out of sight, out of mind. For the future, I will remind myself to think of her more often. I am lost in thought when she appears.

She's taller than I pictured her on the phone. She also has a more earthy look, the one that is often mimicked by others with less style. Her outfit could have easily been something she picked up off the rack at Bloomingdales, but on her, it looked nothing short of couture. The brown suit hugs her body the way a man should. Her champagne chemise hid nothing but left much to be desired.

She wears her hair natural, something that I would consider unmanageable in this weather, and it frames her face perfectly. Her hair is a deep brown with shades of red changed by the sun. It compliments her honey complexion. Her face is distracting, but in a good way; I find myself searching for her best feature, but it is hard to single out one. I continue to stare. Even her jewelry looks as if it has been made just for her. All of this seems effortless, controlled but not contrite. She would be the night to my sister's day.

I watch her cross the lobby to meet me. I'm certain she is the woman I had come to see, but part of me is hoping that she might not be. Something about her made me pause. Considering that I am a beautiful woman myself, that speaks volumes. She has to be at least six feet easily. Every one of her movements seem so fluid. I can tell she is accustomed to the way people stare at her—well, *gawk* is more like it. I saw a few mouths open and prayed that mine had not done the same. She notices the way people are looking at her but does not seem impressed or put off by it. Her hips and breasts are more than what would be appreciated on a model, which makes her every man's dream. Even though I turned a few heads when I walked into the building, I felt like a wallflower next to her. She is a walking, talking, breathing Barbie doll.

"Veronica Thompson, and you must be LaToya Garrett." She extends her arm for a brief handshake, and even that one gesture has to be more graceful than anything I have ever seen in my life. "Everyone calls me Ronnie, but I'm sure you know that." She tries to follow that statement up with a reassuring smile. As I shake her hand, something about her puts me at ease, and just as suddenly, it puts me on guard. There is one thing I know for sure: beautiful women don't trust other beautiful women because we all know deep down exactly what we are capable of. We hold the ability to control others, and it's that ability that leaves less time or desire to control one's self.

She had once been the other woman. My sister's nemesis. Okay, I am being a tad dramatic. She had once competed for the affections of Lance. He claimed nothing happened between them. My sister and aunt believed him. I didn't assume anything. I never really cared either way. Now as I stare into her hazel eyes, I know that Lance is a liar. There is sexual tension surrounding her. It wafts around her like expensive perfume, and everyone around her is affected by it. I don't think any man could be left alone with her for more than a few seconds without considering sleeping with her. There is something about her that tempted a man to try and tame her, though it seemed highly unlikely. She and Lance would have made a very striking couple, and unfortunately for my sister, I am sure I am not the only person who noticed. I wonder what she could have done to lose him, not that my sister is not wonderful in her own right. Veronica was the type of woman who eclipsed other women.

"Should we continue the introductions in my office?" The smile is still there, but I can tell it is now her turn to size me up. Before she allows me to respond, she starts walking back the same way she had come. Addressing her secretary, she says, "Two waters, no ice. Hold my calls. No interruptions. If the building burns down, we'll find our own way out." She says these things without breaking her stride or making eye contact. Her male secretary jumps as if his seat is now on fire. I'm not certain if he is afraid of her or attracted to her. Maybe a mixture of the two.

We make it to her office, and it is not what I expected it to be. I had never been inside of a law firm before, not even my brother-in-law's, but it is not what is depicted on the television shows. The lobby of course was cookie cutter, complete with posh furnishings that intimidated anyone who dared to sit upon it as well as stuffy-looking secretaries. I wonder if they require a master's degree to answer their phones, considering the way the assistants looked down their noses at everyone. I had purposely introduced myself as Dr. Garret when I signed in.

This office however matched her personality. The furnishings were all earth tones, plush, and inviting. Her artwork did not compete for attention; instead they complemented each other as if one were an extension of the previous. The office seems more of a living space than a place of business. I will try to remember to ask for the name of her decorator.

The second thing I notice is there are no pictures of her family. No snapshots of little snot-nosed crumb snatchers or of a distant husband that often comes with the territory of working long nights. Not even an overbearing mother is displayed. She is however wearing a platinum wedding band.

I am hoping her life did not stop with Lance's affection. The story I was given was that she was deeply in love with him. When he finally gave her a chance, after a breakup with my twin, she jumped at it. They dated for a few weeks, but in college terms, it may as well have been years. Once Tonya had cleared her mind and calmed down, she called him. He walked out on Ronnie and didn't look back. Apparently she was still in his room waiting when he would return hours later. He said that he was back with LaTonya, and he walked her back to her dorm. When they made it to her door, she confessed her feelings, told him she had felt that way for years now. He confessed that he could never love someone like he did LaTonya Garrett. That was Lance's version. I wondered how different hers would be.

"Why don't we sit? You can tell me what you think I should know, then I'll ask you what I need to know. Fair enough." She is definitely an attorney. I have often heard Lance use that same tone with others. He is the reason I refused to date any of the lawyers he tried to set me up with. Besides the fact that I never dated anyone who took their careers more seriously than me, their job requires them to stretch facts, find loop holes, and then convince you that they are on the side of right all the time. The purpose of any lawyer is to convince you that their version of the truth is the only truth while simultaneous using, manipulating, and bending the laws that they hold sacred.

There's a reason why only witnesses are required to tell the truth, the whole truth and nothing but the truth. If attorneys were required to hold the same standards, the court house would be empty.

Another thing that my potential attorney and my brother-in-law have in common is the ability to put me at ease; it takes only a few seconds before I began to unload my life story. I feel as though the background is just as important as what has happened in the past week since it has led us here.

"Well, our parents died when we were younger. Nine years old to be exact." I had never told anyone that during a first meeting. "My aunt raised us, and she loved us more than I think was required or expected. I was her favorite, and anyone could see it. It bothered my twin. Still they both gave me anything and everything I asked for. I think Tonya did it as a way to gain approval from my aunt.

"When I was younger, I took advantage of that fact. When I was older, I had just become so accustomed to it that I never thought twice. It was as if they set me up to believe the world owed me something. Now I am thankful for it. I achieved everything I wanted because I believed I was supposed to. I put myself above everyone else because that was the way my family functioned. I don't think I've ever been told no. I only asked for things out of courtesy. It seemed the polite thing to do. We all played a certain role in each other's life." That is no exaggeration. "My sister was the supporting actress, Lynette the director. There was no question that I am and have always been the leading lady. That was a hard pill to swallow. It seemed they thrived on my life. If there was nothing going on with me, then there was nothing for them to do."

I have gone off track a little bit. I am uncertain if this woman is the one I should be discussing my sister with. But again, I have very few options. Most attorneys would salivate at the chance to go against Lance in court, but they were like chihuahuas—all bark, no bite. Everything in their world was political; you never know who you'll need until you know that you need them. So this is my final option. She is my last hope, and even though I may be reaching, I'd like to believe I am hers as well.

"Tonya resented me, partly because I was our parents' favorite. Not many people know what it's like to be hated for something that's beyond your control. Can you imagine how that felt?" Ronnie nods yes. I am sure she understood what I am talking about. I am sure there are women who hated her just for breathing. I continue to tell her my story. I don't know if she needed all the information I gave her, but I was never one for female companionship. It felt good to vent, to tell my side of the story to someone who was on my side. It didn't matter that I was paying her a hefty fee to see things my way. I was given the chance to purge.

That is exactly what I wanted to do—relinquish some of this guilt. In a way, I was apologizing for all my wrongs by admitting to them. I had caused destruction without as much as a hesitation on my part. But that was all that I knew. I have never been expected to do more, so it is not fully my fault.

They were punishing me for being myself. Ronnie made me see just how unfair my family was being.

Ronnie

I will admit that when I first spoke to LaToya, I had mixed emotions. Yes, part of me has been longing for the chance to confront Lance since the night he broke my heart, and I can't believe that it will be just as easy to destroy the woman he left me for. But the other part, the smaller, almost inconsequential portion, would like nothing more than to just walk away, act as if he has not been the silent partner in my marriage, my career, and my life, unbeknownst to him for all of these years, to prove that I do not care enough about him either way.

I would like to pretend that I have grown up, grown into the type of woman who doesn't seek retaliation. I once heard that the best revenge is to just be happy. That is something I have been unable to do, and I have tried.

I made all the right choices. I married my second best option and took a job at the second best firm since the best sought him first. I would have broken down if it meant seeing him every single day. Therefore I lived a second-rate life. Despite having anything I could ask for, I didn't have the one thing I would have. So if revenge would equal my happiness, then deduction would lead me to believe that the second best revenge would be to take away his. I wanted to hurt him in the way that he hurt me. Steal the future he pictured away from him, the way they both stole mine all those years ago.

When I spoke to LaToya on the phone, I didn't want to appear too eager. I would hate for her to take this opportunity away just because she thought I wasn't stable enough to handle it.

After meeting her, I am certain that she is just as hungry for this chance as I am. There is not one word that could sum up LaToya. The lawyer in me didn't care that she was morally wrong; it was my job to shy away from those insignificant facts. I wouldn't classify her as one of my favorite people. I felt somewhat sorry for her sister, but not sorry enough to not play my role in her downfall. That is the saddest part of all. This woman has no idea that her sister and husband will be the cause of her heart break and the reason for it is simple. They chose me. That was the chance she took when she stole him back.

I had checked up on Lance periodically—seven different times over the years to be exact. There have been subtle noticeable changes. In the photos, his smile, like his eyes, had dimmed some. He didn't seem as big in pictures, not necessarily in height but in stature. He seemed defeated, and I will admit that I have wondered why, but this situation was not what I had expected. I am uncertain if I truly wished him unhappiness; that would be heartless. I just didn't want him to be happier than me—well, happier than others thought I should be.

I revel in the knowledge that he has not been. This information makes me smile. My heart race. It gives me optimism, something I had let go of a long time ago.

Lance decided he would leave me for someone who would give him the things I never wanted. I wanted to travel the world while changing it. Changing the world did not leave time for changing diapers. I was a hopeless optimist then.

But I would have given that man anything he asked if he had given me the option. Five or six babies, a house in the suburbs. I'd even drive a minivan; I'd draw the line at bumper stickers though, if he wanted. But he was too good of a man to ask me to give up my dreams. That is the reason it's so hard to let him go. He left me because he thought it was best for me.

Sometimes that gets me through the rough spots. Thinking that he loved me a little more than her, enough to let me go, made it a little easier to smile at the memory of him. I make myself believe that it hurt him just as much to let me go. When I think these things, I feel sorry for us both. Unrequited love is the hardest to live with.

Then I have my seasons of anger. I remember the look in his eyes right before he left me in that room where I waited for hours, hoping for the chance, trying to find the words to make it right. After I figured out the words to say, after I had swallowed my pride enough to promise him everything I knew he wanted in exchange for him, he told me he wanted her.

That was the hardest part of all. It took me just a few hours to decide that what I had planned for most of my life could be given up for a man. I had convinced myself that changing the world by myself was not an option, that if he were not there to share it with me, it was worthless. In short, I pushed myself to the side for Lance. Then that man advised me that in the same few hours it had taken me to make peace with my new future, he had decided that he did not want me in his.

I guess the knowledge of what I was willing to give up for him haunts me. It was so easy for me to conform to his wants and easier still for him to push me to the side. After all that I thought we shared, I meant nothing to him. It hurt more than I fathomed something could.

I was not the woman I thought I was. Instead I was one of the ones I often complained about. I was weak willed. I was lost in a man, albeit a wonderful one, that couldn't bother himself to find me.

He went back to her and got nothing in return. The life that he planned turned out to be just that plans no fruition.

I had convinced myself that I wanted what he did, and since I am not the type to waver about anything, I stuck to those plans. Afraid to ever let someone change me so much again that I would never be able to recognize myself, I became stubborn. I married shortly after graduating. I passed the bar, and once my career was stable enough, I started a family. I have everything that he wants with a man that I don't want them with. He has nothing with the woman he wants everything with.

I tried because that is what I do. I gave all that I was willing to spare to my family, and it is a thankless job to say the least. If my husband knew just how close I come every day to walking away, he'd appreciate me more. That is the wrong choice of words because my husband does adore me; *worship* may be a better expression. I don't know if the fact that his adoration is misplaced annoys or angers me.

I hate my husband because I can't love him through no fault of his own. Adam was perfect. He is by far one of the handsomest men I had ever met—tall, dark, and handsome. The first time I brought him home, my mother joked that I had found my very own Ken doll. That was what he was to me back then, something to play with. I was infatuated with the fact that he was infatuated with me. Things snowballed. Everything moved faster than I thought it would. He was not the first man to claim to love me after Lance, but he was the only one who proved it.

Not only was he handsome, he was also wealthy. I think that would be an understatement. He was a trust-fund baby, who had managed to make his own way in the world. Realistically, my income—and I do very well for myself—was a pittance compared to what he had.

That did not hurt when it came time to accept his proposal, even though I did ask that he wait until I graduated. I was waiting for him to give up on me, or for Lance to give up on Tonya. But he did not. He grew to love me more through that time.

I was the one woman who could and would tell him no. I was not impressed by his money. I could honestly live without it, but it did help. His looks, even though he was gorgeous, had no effect on me. I knew the pain caused by loving a beautiful man, so I had built up immunity. I saw him as a man, just the same as any other, even if his eyes were the greenest I had ever seen and his olive skin always looked kissed by the sun despite the cold east coast weather. He was nothing more to me than an accessory, like a beautiful couture purse. You know that they will last a lifetime and truly never go out of style, but after they are purchased, in your heart you are still waiting for next year's version.

Women fought to be near him, but I barely acknowledged him. The more he chases, the farther I run, and I know he would run to the end of the earth for me. I pitied him for that. I could never love a man I pitied.

There have been countless assistants who have promised me nothing happened between them. Unfortunately, I believe them all since I married a man with character. His father had been a cheater, and he told me before he felt more betrayed than his mother by it. Adam's father, whom I like very much, more so than anyone else in his family, was a ladies' man, whose son did not understand how he could betray his family in such a way. I wondered how he would feel if he knew I have betrayed him the same way in my heart. Emotionally I have given myself to another man, and if given the opportunity to have him, I would never look back.

Adam is a wonderful father to a son that I love even though I am certain that I would have loved him a little more if he were in fact Lance Jr. That is a hard pill to swallow, and I do try. He fell in love with our son the moment I showed him the pregnancy test. He insisted I never lift another finger and hired more staff to tend our home in Villanova. I was also rewarded with another gigantic ring and yet another expensive vacation all because of a plus sign on a stick.

My husband did not see any flaws in our life; it was perfect to him. He wanted more children; I drew the line at our son. I am not a villain, and the thought of leaving behind a house full of children when I find reason enough to leave would be hard for me. I try to be the wife he needs and the mother my son deserves.

That is what annoys me so much about our life together—the fact that I have to try so hard for something that should be so natural, easy, carefree. Try to love my son a little more. Try to be more understanding of my husband. Try not to run away. Try to pretend I am happy. I've tried to try for too long.

Yes, I love my son, but not in the way that I know a mother should. He is never considered first. I would never say that he has been a priority. I do what I must, and he is well taken care of. But something is missing. I hear the way other women speak of their children; my son has never been the highlight of any of my days. His smile does not fill me with contentment. My heart does not burst with pride when he accomplishes things that I consider nothing more than mediocre. He manages to use the potty, and he can recite his ABCs. I hear other parents say these things as if pissing were the equivalent to curing cancer. There is no sense of awe. I never stare at him in amazement. I have reconciled myself to the fact that I will never feel that way about my child.

This will be the turning point. It is kismet, fate perhaps. I'll walk into the courtroom, and Lance will melt. He'll realize what he could have had. Maybe I will get my fairy tale ending, or maybe I should be prepared for the nightmare to continue. Either way I push the thoughts of Lance and I aside and instead concentrate on destroying Lance and Tonya.

I asked Toya if there was anything I should know about her sister or her brother-in-law. She shrugged, trying not to acknowledge that they were in fact the better choice. She implied that she was not certain if they were really happy. Blaming the miscarriages, she admitted that she is unsure if their marriage will survive losing in court.

There has to be more to this story. It seems that marriages don't fall apart overnight. I know, because I've wished upon a few stars for exactly that. Now comes the time where we retrace their steps, find out exactly where they faltered. I call Lauren, my secretary. "Get Martin on the line ASAP. After this call, I'm leaving for the day. Clear everything." I was so use to barking orders at him that I never waited for him to say hello or even acknowledge what I had asked, commanded, or demanded. I hung up the line as usual. Before I can open my bottle of water and reach for my migraine medicine, my phone rings.

"Martin? I need your help on some—"Lauren interrupts me, which is something he only does when he knows I will be angry if he lets me reveal too much.

"I'm sorry, Mrs. Matthews. Just wanted to remind you that AJ's conference is at three p.m. The teacher said you wouldn't be able to reschedule since they are now in the middle of the summer semester, and you've canceled four times already"—his voice drops, and he mumbles the last part of the sentence—"and not shown up twice." This is the way he delivers bad news. The fact that he is studying law at night surprises me. I do not believe he has the backbone for it. I doubt he could tell a lie if his life depended on it.

"Call Adam and see—"

"Mr. Matthews is in New York. He won't be back until this evening. He'll meet you for dinner at seven."The fact that Lauren knows what is going on in my life better than I do makes him indispensable but all the more annoying.

"Get Martin on the line. Call AJ's school. Let someone know that they can discuss whatever they need to with the nanny when she arrives for pick up. If they can't, we'll have to wait for the fall semester."

What did they possibly have to tell me? *Congratulations, your two-year-old knows that he shouldn't eat the finger paint.* What more can they teach him in the two hours a day he is there?

"As for Mr. Matthews"—I never refer to him as my husband. It is either Mr. Matthews or Adam when speaking to friends— "let him know I'll be working late tonight on this new case, so I won't be joining him for dinner. Call. Have something delivered to the house. You know which restaurant is his favorite. The one who delivered for our anniversary." That is the least I can do. "Also call the florist and have them send a bouquet of something to my home."

"What should the card say?" Again he has managed to irritate me. I have lost count at this point.

"Make something up. You're good at it. Apologize for my absence and advise that I'll make up for it. Figure it out. You're a smart boy, aren't you?"

Adam just may get lucky tonight even though I will be making love to another man all together in my head. I dared Lauren to ring me back and hung up. There was no way I would let anything or anyone steal my joy from me, even if those people were my son and his father.

Tonya

He is different. I can't put my finger on it, but a woman knows her husband. Maybe he has changed so much during the time that I paid him no attention that I honestly have no idea who he's become. It's my fault. I pushed for so long, and eventually even the mountain will be moved by the stream.

It started yesterday, around the time that we left the hospital. Maybe he wasn't as prepared to leave McKenzie as he thought. I wouldn't have been able to hand her off as you would dry cleaning. I didn't give him enough credit; it had to be hard. I appreciate that he is trying to hide his hurt, but I am hurt by it also. I thought we'd come further than that in these past few days.

I was even silly enough to think that our lovemaking would change him. It had worked for me, but it was like being with a stranger. Lance was distracted. There was something off about our connection as if we were communicating via satellite. *Delayed* would be the best word to describe it. He did what he was supposed to but a few seconds after I expected or needed it. He kissed me at the wrong times and touched me when it was no longer warranted. If I had not known him, I'd swear he was lost in thoughts of someone else. For years, he always knew when, how, and where to touch me. But yesterday, he fumbled and stumbled over me like I was someone unfamiliar to him. The thought unnerved me. I quickly pushed it away, waited for our lovemaking to be over so I could erase what had actually happened and replace it with a better memory.

Afterward we both went about our day. He was perfectly attentive; he asked if I needed anything. He actually changed the linen after we made love in the afternoon. Dinner had been a production; it was filled with conversations designed to take up time but used little imagination or mental energy. We talked about the weather and about the neighbors moving and wondered who would live there next.

This was the easiest time of the day, even though we both found ourselves sneaking quick glances at the clock, hoping the other had missed it. It seemed like forever since my meltdown in the hospital earlier and eons since we held our daughter. Lance cleared the table after we ate; this was something most women would have begged their husbands to do, even fight about it. I was not like most women.

Again I found it easy to think of what he may have done wrong, I felt like I was betraying him. He was walking through his own personal hell right now. I knew all too well because I myself have taken the scenic route.

The only time he smiled was when we visited McKenzie. I was relieved to see that she had not changed very much in the few hours (fourteen hours, thirty-two minutes) we had been apart, but I wondered what she had heard, learned, or explored while we were away. I hate to think of the things that we missed.

There was little reaction from McKenzie when we arrived. This did not upset me; it was as if we were expected. The transition was smooth; she fit into my arms just as gracefully as she had the night before. She yawned and cradled herself into the small place that had been reserved for her. We both took the time to smell her sweet breath, and everything was right again.

"That girl doesn't stand a chance. She'll be as spoiled as they've ever come," Lynette joked, and it was good to hear the lightheartedness in her voice though I could tell she was anything but.

Lance responded, "My daughter is and will always be a princess. She earns the right to be spoiled simply for being." We laughed at this. I even managed to give Lynette a hug. I refused to allow her to speak about anything that would have ruined the night.

"I want to enjoy our daughter. We'll make it right when the time is right." She accepted that answer. Looking back, I didn't give her much of a choice.

I refused to talk to Auntie, knowing that my sister was just a few feet away from where I was standing. That would have transformed everything from surreal to real in a matter of minutes. I doubt my sister would have eavesdropped, but I am uncertain of what my response would have been. I am positive that no matter what was said, I would feel attacked, standing in the home of the "enemy" nonetheless.

No one commented on the fact that the nursery was identical to the one in my home, which was the cruelest compliment. At first, it angered me; obviously my sister knew that what I had pictured would have been the best thing for our daughter. The bottles, the borders, even the stuffed animals were all the same.

Then I was saddened by it all. If by some chance of fate the judge ordered us to share custody, how would McKenzie know the difference between her real home and the other one?

Admittedly, the evening had not been what I expected. I am not sure what I expected. No cloaks or daggers or awkward handoff. Instead, we were met at the door by Lynette. She looked a bit apprehensive; her face mirrored my thoughts.

She had changed as well, even managed to lose a few pounds. I guess I was the genetic abnormality once again. For every pound that she has lost, I managed to find two more. Her face did not hide the fact that she missed me any more than her arms or her smile did.

I needed to crawl into her lap, like a child, and expected her to make everything right. This time that could not be done, despite knowing that it is indeed what we both wanted.

"I'll leave you three alone. It's time to rest these old bones goodnight, my loves."

I knew she would not be far. Just as when we were kids, she was never more than just a few feet away. But somehow the gap seemed larger as if there were miles between us.

Lance

This is unacceptable, inexcusable, and unforgivable. I have spent most of these past few days making excuses for LaToya as I try to understand or reconcile this thing in my mind. I have tried to be the mediator, partly to expunge myself of my transgressions. I have held the pieces together when it was not just necessary but expected for them to fall apart.

When I thought we could put it back together, knowing it would never be the same as before but maybe somewhere along the way we could mend fences, she pulls this shit.

There would be a conflict of interest. The lawyer in me knows that I should explain it to Arnold. It is only fair that I not allow him to be blindsided in the courtroom. If it were my client, I wouldn't expect or accept anything less. But this is not another case. This is my wife's sanity. I do not know how to explain it to him in a way that he will understand or better yet, in a way that will make this less painful for Tonya.

This I will never forgive Toya for. Being a parent makes you understand the illogical and comprehend what can never be explained. I know the need to protect one's own and to want to be there for every breath, bad dream, and milestone in between.

For that reason alone, I never condemned her for her choice to keep my daughter; instead I justified it in the smallest corners of my mind though I could not accept it. This decision she should and most likely will burn in hell for.

Ronnie.

That name haunted my marriage for the first five years. I saw Tonya's looks of panic every time my pager went off or the way she searched cell phone bills when they later replaced the archaic method of keeping in contact. Tonya would cringe whenever she heard the name, even when it was not in reference to the Veronica we knew. The same name was on the tip of my wife's tongue before and after every single argument all those years ago and some more recently than her sister could ever know. There was always the need to reassure her that I would never regret my decision to be with her. Those moments made it so hard not to walk out of the door. Leaving would have been better than living through the constant accusations that could not be proved or disproved.

Ronnie was once the chip in the corner of our fragile lives even the slightest amount of pressure would have caused destruction. When the phantom could no longer be ignored, we went to counseling and buried the memory of her. Admittedly, I grieved for my old friend, not that I had been in contact with her or ever had the desire to do so. I grieved for the possibility of it all, not of what could have been between me and that woman, but of what could have been for my wife had she never thought to compare herself to another. Tonya had decided that Veronica was a better woman than her and made up her mind to the fact that she had won by default despite my protest that there was never a competition.

The past can only be the past if you leave it there. So we left her there. I even donated my college jersey since there was a picture of Ronnie wearing it in our year book; consequently that same year book is currently residing in our basement in a box marked "Christmas decorations." Her name was not mentioned again, until the third miscarriage.

Tonya insisted that I leave her. She believed that my life would be everything I wanted if I didn't want her in it. She said that I could have Ronnie, who was whole, sane, and could give me the family that I wanted. I tried to explain to her that the word *family* meant nothing to me at all if she were not a part of it and that I'd rather call her my own than pretend to enjoy a life with someone who would never be the one thing I'd always need—her.

I didn't understand how hurt she'd have to be to suggest this, how broken to even consider it. So I patronized my wife, slightly. I am man enough to admit, though never to Tonya, that I have often wondered about what may have or could have been. If I had never answered her call or if I hadn't come running back to her the moment she announced she was ready to have me back.

Would I have fallen in love in another week? Could I have forgotten all about the broken twin who stole my heart in a few months?

Then it seemed so unlikely. Now, I am wiser. I have grown so much, and I realize that as the man changes, so does his perception and his perspective. Then I thought I could never truly live without her, which is still partially true to this day. But after living through her emotional absence, I know that it is possible. That if need be, I would wake up tomorrow, and the earth would still revolve if she were no longer the center of mine.

Now Toya has breathed life into the ghost and has given her not just a pulse but a reason to confront my wife, all under the guise of family court. *Family.* The word we keep coming back to, the ones who should make everything right even when it's not.

The people that make home just that. In the end, that is what we are all fighting for—the right to have the family that we believe is fair. But this is what family can do to you: watch as you fall to pieces, console you while you try to pick them up, and just when you think that you've smoothed the edges, that all the parts are aligned, they grind those pieces into dust. But how can you call the enemy to come sweep out what's left?

That is exactly what Toya has done.

Toya

I made it through another night. It was different than the hospital stays. This time, I heard her when she cried; there weren't a few dozen feet separating us, or other's babies cries, to drown out McKenzie's. I had to fight back the urge to run to her, to cradle my daughter in my arms as we have both become so accustomed too. I knew my sister was there, and she'd handle things, but nothing felt right.

It did not ease me in the least bit knowing that someone else was providing for my child when I was certainly capable of doing so. Would she get confused and look for one of us when she was with the other? Would she somehow think that I was not doing it right or not as well as my sister? We are all great when there's nothing to compare with. Worse yet, will she ever know the feeling of abandonment, the soul-numbing pain of being left behind?

It was a sleepless night. I drifted in and out of dreams. Some I didn't care to remember; it had been that way for the past few days. The settings changed, but there was always a constant Tonya. Sometimes laughing, sometimes crying, but she haunted me just the same. The laughter was always cruel, deranged at times, and her sobs were soul-wrenching; in my dreams, they threatened to tear the house down.

"Tell me about this one," she'd say as she smoothed my bangs back from my sweat covered forehead. I remember one of the dreams, since even then, they never truly varied.

In my worst nightmare, it would be assumed that I would relive my parents' death, that I would find myself in the car with them, or even worse watching and not being able to stop it from happening. That dream would have been hard to cope with but easier than the one I was forced to relive night after night.

In this dream we were being separated. Auntie no longer wanted us, and even though it was never confirmed I knew it was because of something I had done, some minor infraction that had been the straw which broke the camel's back.

It always began the same. She'd do the talking; promising to make sure whatever "we" had done would be corrected, pleading that "we" be given one more chance. Never once did she place the blame on me, even though we both knew that is exactly where it belonged. While she fought for us, I cried. Her body shook with the effort of my tears. There was nothing that I could say, since I was the only one of us who seemed to know what was to happen next.

Then the mysterious men began to pull, the strain on their faces mirrored the horror in ours. She was always so shocked by it all. As they pulled us apart it became apparent that we were connected, in some dreams it was at the hip others we were back to back. They all ended the same. Eventually the men won and Tonya was dragged away with pieces of me. I was always the one who lost something, the metaphoric limb, because she was an extension of me. In her absence I would have been useless.

I would be forced to go through life missing something. The horrible thing is, even then, I knew that she may have been better off without me. She was always the whole one. Nothing was taken from her, nothing left with me.

Missing the arm or leg did not horrify me however. That is not what I cried to have back, instead it was her, always her. In my dreams I resented the fact that she seemed so much taller, brighter, and stronger even, once the connection had been severed. I hated her for it. Part of me needed to have her back, not just for my benefit, but to punish her for thriving so without me even if just for a few seconds.

It amazes me now how once I was sleep and the sun shone on a new day, the dream was forgotten, and we both went back to ourselves, me the selfish spoiled sister who treated her twin as if she were nothing more than a door mat and Tonya the selfless martyr.

She never threw the dreams in my face. That is something that I would have done. She never reminded me that my subconscious knew that I would be nothing without her, emotionally disfigured, in her absence.

She just accepted her role in my life, allowed me to walk over her. Maybe that is why I took so much from twin, as I revert back to my psychology classes. Since I knew that she would eventually leave me and take something away, I coped by taking things from her first. That's something I am certain any psychologist would love to pick apart.

I would exchange anything right now for one of those nights back, that is a lie I doubt I would change anything, it is hard for the well to say I'd rather be dry. But I do miss the warmth of her arms and the coolness of her hands, no matter the season.

In the darkness I would tell her how it hurt me to think of not having her. I'd leave out the part about her taking pieces of me with her; even then I was too stubborn to admit I needed her. I'd also forget to mention how brilliant she looked, how well my absence flattered her. She did not need to know those things.

Instead I'd make myself the heroin and she became the sobbing twin. For some reason no matter how creative I had been with the story, I am sure she knew. When I was done she'd sing me a song, something that she'd make up on the spot, before she made it to the chorus I'd be sound asleep, only to find myself humming something similar the next day.

I sit in the nursery now holding McKenzie as if I had been doing so all along for all my life. There was something so natural now about her and me. She is all of me; everything that I could ever ask for before I even knew what to ask.

I wondered what my sister thought last night as she sat in this same rocking chair. Was she flattered? Probably not. Tonya is not the woman she was for all these years. I could hear the change in her voice. There was a power there, an assertiveness that I had never heard from her before.

McKenzie has been a blessing to us all, in her own special way. She has made me softer and, at the same time, made my twin stronger.

These are the things that make me smile. A little more than a week old, and this beautiful angel has a power over all of us; that could never have been imagined. My daughter is very much a part of me. Still I miss the original piece. I have come too far now. I cannot just simply hand her over and think everything will go back to normal. Tonya will never forgive me, and for that reason alone, I must keep fighting. It's impossible now to have everything. I will instead settle for something, rather than being left with nothing.

Ronnie

Just yesterday I was in a much better mood. The closest to happy I have been in sometime. Martin called sooner than I anticipated with news that assured me a victory. Yes, I was certainly happy at the way things were turning around.

It is amazing how we prepare ourselves, or at least like to believe we do, for the worst, and when it arrives, we feel like the pig with the house made of straw. Exposed.

"You can't take this case. Call Toya and tell her you made a mistake."

It takes me less than a second to recognize the voice I hadn't heard in ages. And as soon as I identify it, my mind races with images of the perfect set of lips that spoke them.

"Well, how are you today, Counselor?" I hope he didn't notice the pauses. Each word had been an effort as if they were a sentence all their own. I tried to sound as professional as possible; I tried to look at it as a practice run. I failed miserably, and there was no time to rebound. This was happening now. He will always be the one to unnerve me.

"Cut the crap, Ronnie. You heard what I said. This is definitely a conflict of interest, and you know it. Do the right thing. Walk away."

The fact that he still refuses to curse in front of a lady makes me smile; however, I do not care much for his tone at all. I have come a long way from the little girl who had thrown herself at him. It has been years since I let a man dictate anything in my life. My husband has to ask permission to make suggestions. No matter what the reason, he had no right to take that tone with me. Not now, not after the past we shared.

"Yes, I do recall now that you equate walking away with doing the right thing. It's a shame that we don't share the same point of view, obviously a vast difference of opinion." I used the voice I reserve for witnesses right before I tear them apart. It is inviting, welcoming, and before they know to fear me it is over and I have already gutted them with a few well placed words.

"Don't make this about us." With that sentence, I pull the phone away from my ear. The fact that he has the audacity to say that to me makes me want to wrap the cord around his neck and hang him from it. He does not realize that everything from the moment I laid eyes on him has been about us.

"How can I make this about us when nothing was ever about us?" The lies burn my lips as they escape and assault my ears as I hear them for myself. "Are you truly that self-centered and delusional that you could believe that I am taking this case just because of some meaningless fling from a lifetime ago?" The one thing Lance is not is delusional. "This case is groundbreaking simply because of the nature of the relationship between the mother and the plaintiff." It's a cheap shot, but I refuse to say her name. Not on our first conversation. Not until it can be used in the past tense. "Toya has every right to change her mind. I would have thought you of all people would have covered all the bases. Where's the contract, Counselor? Not that it would have protected you, but at least it would have offered some sort of leverage. She is the biological mother. I met her for a few minutes, and I was not surprised at all that she changed her mind. How did you not see this coming?" I pause for a second, allowing him to find his fault in this situation. He had been too trusting, and yet again, it bit him in the ass. "Now because of your error in judgment, you want to take an innocent child away from her mother."

He cut me off. Apparently I had hit a nerve. I knew from the moment I was told that there was no contract that it had not been his doing. Lance is smarter than that. Leave it to his wife to once again be the weaker link. She should have known how to protect herself, more importantly him. I want to confront her, yell at her for dropping the ball when it came to Lance. I would have ensured his protection. Once again she has proved that not only does she not deserve him but that she is inferior to me.

"McKenzie is my daughter. There's no court in this country that could say otherwise. She belongs with me. How can you not see that you know how much family means?"

"I am certain that the judge will sympathize with you on some level. Visitation can be arranged. My client is more than open to that as an option. If you'd like, you and your attorney can come in. We'll lay this thing out, and no one will have to go through the ordeal of a trial. It would be what is best for all."

"You know that is not an option."

I knew it wasn't, but I have to keep him talking, I need to hear his voice just a little longer. I am imagining the slant of his perfect nose, as the shadows dance across his eyes. Anger suited him so well.

"It's an option if you make it one. Discuss it with all the parties involved. Let's be mature about this thing." The fact of the matter is at this point, we are beyond any discussions of visitation; I made sure of that before I signed on. It's never about the easy resolution. Easy resolutions aren't discussed at Christmas parties. They do not get you looked at by senior partners, they're not sprawled across newspapers, and most importantly, they are never found in legal journals.

"You do know that I hate to repeat myself. I have little patience for it. So I will say it one more time and only once more. Visitation is not an option."

He was definitely upset. I would have given anything to see the look on his face. He was an impressive man combining beauty, strength, and passion. When he was like this, I found him so hard to resist. I pushed him then, just for the thrill of it all.

As sadistic as it may sound, I loved a man that could be feared. Part of it is evolution, survival of the fittest.

"This will not go in your favor. You know how these things work. It's all about who can paint the prettiest picture. And from where I stand, there are too many shades of gray floating around your home, marriage counseling, emotional abandonment, trust issues. Are you sure this is the best environment for any child? Because I am not as positive." I shuffle a notepad on my desk, for effect alone. I wanted him to believe I had mountains of transcripts when in truth, everything had been committed to memory. I had taped our first meeting, and after listening to it more than once, Toya's voice became too annoying, so I had Lauren spend his free time transcribing them. I had read and reread the parts where she outlined in details the flaws in her sister's marriage, taking too much pleasure in it for my own sanity.

"Despite that, it is my job to at least pretend that I feel this way. I must say I am afraid to be the one that hands that beautiful child over to someone who may not be the best mother for her."

It was completely unprofessional for me to reveal some of my strategy to him. The point of this call was to rattle me; he had done so with the very first word. It was my turn now.

"What the hell did she tell you?"

"Enough to win, and that is putting it rather mildly. I'd hate to do this to you. But you are giving me no other option. Visitation is looking awfully good right about now, isn't it? Tempting? Or at least it should be. By the time I am finished, I will paint your wife out to be the monster. She will be looked at as a jealous sister, an incompetent wife, and worse yet an unfit mother before she's even had the chance to be called one. You run the risk of her losing any type of relationship with this child as well. Who will you choose if a choice has to be made? Walk away from your wife or your daughter?"

"You are the monster." Those words stung. This had gone farther than I expected.

"If I am, it is what you have turned me into." With that said, I have lost the argument. This conversation has turned the corner. I should have hung up ten seconds ago. I should have never taken the call. I was blindsided, told that it was Arnold on the phone. I expected the usually legal bantering. I did not want this. I hate to be unprepared for anything. The years have changed everything between us, and nothing at all, so it would seem. My stomach still turns at the sound of his voice.

"As I said, Veronica, this is not about us. I cared for you, and in some ways, I always will. You were my best friend." At that last statement, I have had enough. I wanted to rip his heart from his chest, crush it like he did mine, like he is doing right now.

"We were best friends? That's quite amusing, Lance, simply because it is far from funny. You can tell her whatever you'd like about us, for all I care, tell her I was like the sister you never had, but don't patronize me. I guess all this time has allowed you to rewrite history, to mistake what actually happened for what makes it easier for you to sleep at night. You loved me. I know that just as much as I know that I love you. So don't you dare call my office again with a list of demands and expect to get your way.

Not this time, not again. I'm in charge here. I am the one holding all the cards."

So he had called my bluff. My strategy of minimizing what we had backfired. When I did it, it was a game. When he did it, it was cruel. He was not the type to miss anything. That is one of the things that separates a good lawyer from the best of lawyers.

We are trained to listen to each word, dissect it, turn it around, and then serve it back to the witness in such a manner that they too are uncertain if what they actually said is congruent to what they actually meant.

I used the present tense of the word. I admitted that I still love him.

"Ronnie, I didn't mean to hurt your feelings. This is not the way I wanted this conversation to go. I planned this, went over it in my head a thousand times, and even wrote things down on a flash card. Then you were on the line. Suddenly it was you, your voice, and I forgot what I wanted to say. I am not the type of man that asks favors. I am not the type of man that begs, partly because I've never had to, mostly because I've never wanted anything as much as I want this. Correction, I need this. I need my daughter. You are taking away my air, do you understand that? I am begging you. Talk to Toya. If you can't convince her, then walk away please. If we were to lose, if my wife has to face you and lose, she'll never recover."

It hurt me even after all of these years; it hurt me to hear the defeat in his voice. The man that I knew was hiding somewhere behind this coward. I want him to fight. I need him too. I need to know that he is the same man I have imagined him to be all of these years. I need to know that if by some miracle he ever returns to me, he will be everything he was—no, honestly more than I ever thought he could be. I expected the years to add strength, polish his character; this was not what I wanted. This is what she has done to him. She turned him into the type of man that would beg. What disgusts me most is that he is begging for her. The Lance I knew would rather lose standing than win groveling.

"I'll see you in court, Lawson. Make sure you prepare her for me, if that is at all possible." I hang up the phone. This time I am the one who ended things.

If I weren't one of those people who refused to break their own things, I'd smash something right now. This vase filled, yet again, with flowers from my husband would be in pieces, similar to my mood.

How does he do this to me? Why do I allow him to? For what I wish I could say was the first time, I want to hate that man. I wish that I could erase every trace of him from my mind to forget that he exists.

This I will have no luck with. Forgetting him would be the same as the earth forgetting the sun or the tides forgetting the moon.

He is the reason why I found it hard to leave Philadelphia when my husband would have preferred New York. He is the reason why I practice law, the reason why I agreed to be a mother when Adam said it was time to start our family. He is my reason. He doesn't even know this. There's no need for him to concern himself with the trivial things, which make up my every day. Would the sun cease to exist without the orbit of the earth or the moon seem less bright without the movement of the tide? The answer is obvious because he is my proof: he will go on without me and live as if he had never known me.

My eyes are now closed, fighting back a migraine as well as tears. I have never been what others would classify as claustrophobic, but now everything seems so tight. Even my clothes seem binding. I know it is my own skin that I want to outrun. He made me feel so comfortable in it once upon a time.

Every man looked at me as if I were something to be had; I was for them a challenge. Lance never saw me that way. He was the first man to ever ignore me. I did not exist to him, all those years ago. I walked up to him one day after class and asked if he wouldn't mind tutoring me. He knew he was first in our class but did not know I was second. He turned me down, twice actually, but our professor was in no way immune to me. It took nothing more than a tight sweater to convince our instructor to ask Lance to tutor me even though we both knew I didn't need it, and Lance reluctantly agreed.

As most women would have, I considered it our first date. I dressed as if we were going to dinner, wearing an all too low and too tight dress. He suggested we meet in the library. I allowed him to believe I did not feel comfortable there; instead it would make more sense to meet inside of my dorm room, which was actually closer to his apartment. Once again he agreed without much enthusiasm.

We spent the whole night debating everything from religion to politics, subjects that most people found off putting or too personal to broach. There was an immediate comfort allowing me to believe nothing was off limits. Lance opened my eyes to a world that I did not know existed, but one I wanted desperately to be a part of.

Eventually we discussed literature, my passion up until him, since I had been destined to write the Great American novel. We discussed everything but what he had come there that night to do. We never cracked a book. That was the first time he saw me. It did not take a low cut pink sweater dress, to attract him. He saw through the makeup, I never wore any around him after that. Everything that I was and everything that I longed to be was left uncovered to him. He was the first man to unwrap me in every sense of the word.

That night I fell in love with Mr. Lawson. Six years of adolescence had come crashing down on me hard. I had never wanted to be near a man as much as him. It was as if on some level my soul craved his. I had never thought twice about a man before, not even my first kiss, which was done more so out of curiosity on my part than any desire. I tripped, stumbled, and fell head over heels for him in a matter of a few hours. There was nothing that meant more to me than his opinion. He was my transition. I had waited for a man like him; I promised myself that he would be my first and only and that I would love him for as long as he looked at me in that way. That I would give him anything he asked. Then I had no idea exactly how much he would ask for.

After a few conversations, he suggested that I change my major from English to prelaw. That was a lifetime ago, something that I will always be thankful to him for. We arranged our class schedules around each other and became unofficial study buddies.

"The law is flawed, simply because it was created years ago by men who could never understand where we as society would end up. Then it is left in the hands of twelve men and women, who do not necessarily understand it either. Everyone wants to be dazzled. It is your job to do just that. Right or wrong, and I doubt I have ever met anyone as charismatic as you," he said to me one night, but it was him who shined. He wasn't just dazzling he was blinding. For that reason alone I took on the role of sidekick, silently praying that he would be mine. It was a childhood fantasy, of which I am aware now. But the day I had prayed for came, suddenly for him, though I had anticipated it. Granted it had not unraveled in the way that I expected.

Tonya had finally had enough, considering he blurred the lines between us often, confusing one of our conversations for one of theirs and vice versa. When he had first done it with me, I was devastated. He laughed it off, calling me one of his favorite girls. Since I was so important to him, it should be understandable that he confused us so easily. I especially hated it when he said "I thought you hated" or "I thought you loved" this or that and he was usually one hundred percent incorrect. After a half dozen slip-ups with choosing the wrong ice cream—I am after all allergic to strawberries, and she hates vanilla—he gave up the idea of surprising either of us.

It got to the point where we knew each other without ever having to meet. He tried to introduce us, she refused, and I was relieved. I didn't want to meet her any more than she wanted to meet me. I was curious of course. I needed to know what exactly she had over me. Eventually curiosity killed the cat; I think she had the idea almost as suddenly as I had. I had to see her, to hear her, to understand what made him go back each and every time after he left me. It had been two years then. Two years of him, and it was more than I'd ever expected a life time to hold.

But I was greedy. Truly I'd rather neither of us have him than to have to share. It seemed unfair to me, him as well. Was it fair for him to divide himself in such a way? Granted I had parts of him that she would never know, I could push his buttons. This I did often when the thought of him being with her became more than I could stand. I'd argue with him about something that he was completely right about, but I'd be persistently and excruciatingly wrong. It would upset him, hurt him to the core, that I could be so naive. So he'd run to her, angry with me about some minor infraction. I am sure that is the way she saw it, and then they'd end up arguing.

I wanted him to be as crippled by the thought of not having me as I was with the thought of him not being there. I wanted him to realize that he could not live without me; I had already decided I would not live without him. He was relationship-challenged back then. He did not understand, or maybe to my credit believe, that it had all been done on purpose. He refused to believe that I was trying to ruin his relationship, no matter how many times she warned him of it.

Tonya knew then, the first night he had come to her upset with me, that I was more than just a friend. No other woman should have the ability to enrage someone else's man. Getting along was easy and in some cases effortless, but in order to be angry or disappointed, there had to be some level of intimacy. That ate away at her in the same way that her very existence ate away at me. Certainly he loved me and just didn't know it because of her.

Would he realize what could be if I remove what he thinks should be?

Tonya

There is a subtle difference between comfortable silence and what is surrounding me now. A passerby would never know the difference. They'd assume that this was just any other day in the lives of a married couple. Some might even stop and stare and remark on how they'd hope to be here someday, in a place where you are so comfortable with life, with your mate, with yourself that nothing needs to be said. In their innocence, they would not understand that more can be shared without words. A million conversations have been held in complete silence.

There will be hell to pay, that is what his eyes are telling me whenever I am offered a passing glance. It is unlike him to avoid eye contact. It has always been one of his most endearing qualities. There could be dozens of people in a room, but once Lance looks at you, it becomes just you and him. Today we might as well be seated in Madison Square Garden with countless of witnesses.

I tried at first to dismiss it and pretend that I had not noticed. I have seen it before, usually in reference to one of his cases. However, I know that he has cleared his work schedule, turned the more pressing cases over to his partners, and instructed his secretary that there were to be no interruptions until further notice. Something had interrupted us, and it was eating him up.

We were doing so well; though some things seemed forced at times, our marriage was better. The therapist would be proud. After I had stormed out on one of our sessions a few months back, I promised Lance we didn't need help. I promised him we would work it out on our own, and we had. No one knew how long it would take, and when I said those words to him, I didn't believe it at all. This was the one promise I was able to keep. We had not climbed our way back to the effortless part of our relationship though progress had been made. I no longer cringed when he touched me or pretended he did not exist when we passed each other in the halls. We spoke during meals and spent countless hours holding hands while we lay together in bed.

So much had happened while I was on hiatus from our marriage; I had missed him, more than I think I realized. Truthfully, we had become strangers, and we were working at falling back in love with each other.

Trusting him had become increasingly hard because I no longer trusted myself. Dr. Philips had been quite clear about this. She had told us countless times that trust had to be the foundation of any relationship.

When I exposed my fears and pains to him completely in these past few days, I thought we were gaining that trust back. No one could understand the damage that my hurting him had caused me. In these past few hours, the small repairs were faltering, and I am afraid that I will lose him again.

I watch him open his mouth and then shut it suddenly. This would not be good. I understood already, and I have prepared myself for it. I need him to get it over with and rip the Band-Aid off.

We had both agreed to leave any pain at my sister's door step and pick it back up when we left. There was no way we would allow McKenzie to feel any discord between us. If I could feel it, I am certain our daughter will as well.

"Tell me." I say it as if I am undefeatable, as if there is nothing that he can say that will break me. I say it, and I hope that he understands. I have braced myself for the unknown, even though that is impossible. With each passing minute, the silence continues as his body stiffens. I wonder if he has yet to take a breath since I last spoke. Even in his stubbornness, he is unforgivably beautiful.

After all this time, I find the need to reach out and touch him to reassure myself that his existence has not been a dream, that this man is real and so has my life been up until this point. He is perfect, and that within its self is scary. Through all the hurt and pain, he has remained. Maybe it is his strength, maybe it is his weakness—I am not sure why, and that is how I know that I love him. But there is something about his stone-hard face that lets me know the love I feel will not be enough, not right now. I do not know what has silenced him, but I know it will wound me.

"Will it hurt?" I ask. He nods his head in agreement. There is sorrow there, like a good husband, he feels my hurt, and I can only imagine how bad he must feel knowing that he will be the one delivering this news to me. Again I find that I am bracing myself, the way you do right before you are in an accident, knowing the bracing is what causes the most damage. He walks over to me and places my hand in his. I take the time to sort things out.

I run through every possible scenario in my mind, considering we have been through more than our share of heartbreak. The possibilities frighten me, and suddenly the room becomes much warmer. Through everything, his nerve has never wavered. Up until recently, I honestly believed that he was not as devastated as I had been. Now I know the truth. He had been strong for me. He had cried a million times, but never in front of me.

His strength was tested, and during his weakest moments, the times when I was supposed to give him all of me, I gave him nothing. Uncle Eugene had told us during our wedding rehearsal that a marriage was never fifty-fifty. The true measure of a marriage was being able to give your spouse 90 percent when they only had 10 percent to give. For so long, I had given him nothing and expected him to give me his all. Now I am willing to put the work in, and I need to believe that it is not too late.

"Is it my sister?" Once again, he nods; then as if on second thought, he shakes his head. What has she done now? Certainly Lynnette would have called if there was something to warrant this response.

"Is it Lynnette? Did something happen to her? Is she okay?" He squeezes my hand and shakes his head no. But he has yet to offer me comfort.

"Are you leaving me?" Ironically, this is the question that hurts the most to ask, the unimaginable. The thought makes my throat close, and I am surprised that I managed to even ask.

"No." That is all that he offers, and that is all I need to hear. I did not need a paragraph of reassurance. Lance is a man of his word even if it is just one. I thank God for him.

"If I have you and Lynette, then there is nothing else that I need to worry about now, is there, so you can just tell me?"

Then it hit me, knocking the air right out of my chest. Gasping for it, I am unable to speak. He leaves me momentarily and returns with a brown paper bag.

He gently pushes my head down between my legs. Rubbing my back, he whispers, telling me to breathe. The rest he speaks in French; even though I have no idea what he is saying, it comforts me in a way that no language I can understand would.

"She's fine. McKenzie is perfect. She's probably still taking her nap. Breathe, baby. Our daughter is fine." The words reach me, and it takes a few minutes to regain myself. Despite the central air, I am still clammy, and my hair is stuck to my face.

I look into his eyes. There are still things we have not forgotten, just as he knew the panic I felt minutes ago could only be in reference to McKenzie. I know our connection has not been lost completely. I see now why he would not look at me before. This won't hurt me, no. This is going to kill me. What could he say? What else is there? I refuse to break our stare; I refuse to let him be silent.

"Ronnie."

It makes no sense at all. I search my mental Rolodex. R. There is only one Ronnie that we are both "acquainted" with, and I cannot fathom the reason why her name would be spoken today and why it would cause such discomfort for us especially now. After everything we have been through—no, after everything, we have made it through. There is no correlation to her and us. Not now.

"Ronnie what?" His eyes are lowered again. But he is still holding my hand, which I suddenly pull away. He grabs it again.

I had not suspected it even though I had honestly not ruled out the idea of him having an affair. I suggested it once upon a time.

"I'm going to be sick," I say as I snatch myself away from him. I know I will not make it to the bathroom, so I vomit into the trash can. My body seems foreign; it has once again betrayed me when I needed it most. I recognize the feeling of him against my skin. That is how I know that I am still in one piece, which saddens me. I need him touching me to convince myself that I still am here, breathing.

He is behind me rubbing my back again. I want to scream at him, *Do not touch me!* and beg him to not let me go all at the same time. I had been wrong and intentionally and unintentionally abusive. I had taken him for granted, spat at him, denied him the one thing he should never have to ask for. Me.

I had pushed him away and he had run to her. *Her.*

"When?" That is all that I can ask as I silently beg my stomach to stop turning. He left my side for a second and returned with paper towels. He cleans up my mess.

"Yesterday," he answers. Just seconds before, I had been racking my mind, trying to figure out when it could have happened. Now the knowing is worse.

My knees buckle. As he always has, he catches me before I fall.

"But you are not leaving me?" This time, I avoid his eyes.

I close my eyes praying that this had been a dream, and I will wake up next to him. I open them almost as quickly. In the split second that it took, I saw them together. My stomach turns again, and I vomit one more time.

"Wait. You don't think that I…?" He doesn't bring himself to finish the sentence. The words will not be said.

"Didn't you?"

"No, never. Never. I made my choice, and I would make the same one a million and one times again." I hear the conviction in his voice. He waits for me to understand to find the truth in his words.

"Your sister hired Ronnie. She will be representing her." He waits for my response. The only thing I can do is laugh. He is certain I have lost it, finally. There is relief in his eyes. How long had he been waiting for this, for me to fall apart?

"Why would she do that?" It is a rhetorical question. Toya would find any way to hurt me at this point.

"She is the best." That is the easiest way for him to put it. Yes, she would most likely be the best. I know he is not saying this to defend Toya or to make me feel any worse or better. He is saying it because it is a fact.

"I need to get something for dinner." I say this as if nothing has happened. That is the way that I cope. We will forget that I accused him of being unfaithful and that I doubted his character.

If I have my way, we will pretend as if the last half an hour had not happened. I will not think of the look in his eye nor the panic of mine reflected in them. I will fail to remember that he had spoken her name before advising me that my sister is the reason behind another piece of my heart breaking.

Ronnie.

That name brings up skeletons that I thought were long buried. I hated her the moment I realized that he did not.

So she has come back. Part of me always knew that she would. It had been made quite clear that she believed Lance belonged to her. I waited for this for years, and then I knew we'd be able to deal with it.

She chooses now to do this. I was far from ready the first time. I was naïve, immature, lost in thoughts of losing him. I had not known what to expect. She was a stranger to me. This time will be different; I am fighting not just for love but for my life. This time she has no idea what is waiting for her. I am no longer timid. I am no longer afraid.

In those hours of not knowing what was upsetting my husband, I had prepared myself for the flood, but instead I am facing a drought.

Lynnette

LaToya's told me what she has done. More like confessed after I confronted her. That is the story of our life. She confesses after a confrontation, and there is never any remorse. Toya is Toya. That's what we always say as if it was some sort of excuse, or better yet a synonym for her antics. You can't blame the snake for biting you anymore than you can blame Toya for doing whatever it is she has done. It is in her nature.

I told her I couldn't stand by her this time. I'd stay, of course, because McKenzie needed me, but that was all I could do. I refused to support her now. It was one thing to knock someone down; it was quite another to kick them while they were there. For the first time, I am seeing that she has the potential to be truly hurtful. It scares me because I see so much of myself in her more than I ever thought possible. I remember the way I felt so many years ago, I knew that I would kill or die for them, even if it meant losing my sister. Thankfully I never had to know just how far I would have gone to keep my girls; unfortunately, I know we will find out just how far my girls will go to hurt each other. Tonya is soft in that way. She always has been.

"I expected more of you." That was the extent of my reprimand. I did not yell—I was never one for it, especially when it came to either of the twins. Tonya would cry at the slightest hint of disappointment. Toya was too stubborn to let me know she was affected in any way. If I had been a yeller, it would have done little good. Toya has made up her mind, and history has shown she will not change.

She was never the one to fight fair; that is an understatement, but this is underhanded. Toya will never admit that she has done anything wrong. She claims that Ronnie is the best, and it would be unfair of me to ask her to rest her fate in the hands of someone who was less capable. This is her way of rationalizing, which has always been her strong suite. I wish I could have called her on her bull. I knew that she has done this for one reason only, and that is to hurt Tonya.

"She started it." And once again I see her as the little girl who always got her way. The one who could talk herself out of trouble because, given enough time, she could and would make you see things her way. No matter if she was the protagonist, she always painted herself out to be the victim.

I had enough. I cannot stand anymore. I want this to be over. I want what is best for them both, and this situation is not it. Washing my hands of it all is not an option, neither is pleading with the sensible side of Toya. There is no sensible side—I know because I am the creator of this monster. Never did I lead her to believe that anything she had done was wrong if the ends justified the means. Placating her was my job, and I had always found a way to justify any of her antics in my mind. Our family denied that there was anything wrong with the dynamic; we pretended that everything was fine.

Abusive is what anyone else would refer to her actions as. The younger twin had been emotionally and verbally abusive to her sister for so long that it has become expected of her.

Always waiting with a backhanded compliment or a derogatory statement. It had long since passed the stage of sibling rivalry and turned the corner to cruelty.

The floors must be worn with my pacing. I want to call Lance—since I cannot bring myself to speak to his wife just yet—and ask if I needed to be here tonight to let them in. I knew my daughter well enough to know that she will not let this come between her time with McKenzie. She will smile at me as if her heart had not been broken again. I am sure Lance has told her by now. I advised him to do so immediately after he told me. She needed time to prepare herself for this. She could not walk into this thing and be blindsided. I knew what he did not; I knew what she carried with her for all these years.

The need to be near Tonya grows stronger until I find myself at the door. A mother knows when her child is in need, it doesn't have to be announced, or stated aloud for that matter. The tug in your heart is firm no matter how faint the cry.

I decide to take Toya's car. It is immature of me, in my old age, but I enjoy the thrill of the speed. On second thought, if Tonya saw her sister's car in the drive, she may shoot first and ask questions last. Locating my purse and keys by the stand near the door, I check my reflection in the hanging mirror. I look my age. Time had once been kind; now it appears that I have had too little sleep and not enough cover-up.

Before I can open the door, I hear the bell. *Lord, please give me the strength.* It takes one second for my eyes to adjust to the brightness; against the back drop of the afternoon sun, she looks murderous. It is understandable, yet frightening. The thought that she has been pushed to this point leaves me teetering on the edge of my own sanity. Even without words, I know there is a rage inside of her that I would not wish to be unleashed on my worst enemy.

"I need you." That is all I want to hear. I have been waiting for it for too long. She is in my arms, and before I know it, I am walking her away. This is my way of shielding her. Maybe I am wrong; maybe I should allow her sister to witness the pain she has caused. To see where we are headed, but now is not the time for this.

"How did you get here?" I did not hear a car, but I was preoccupied with my own thoughts.

"I walked. I didn't know where I was headed at first, and then I was here." She sounded so detached from reality. "I sat in front of the house asking myself why. Why did I come here? I was ready to…" This sentence she does not complete, and I am thankful for that. I do not need to know the harms she wishes toward her twin, even if it is deserved. "You opened the door, and I knew I was in the right place." Without warning, she is in tears.

I can tell this was not the first time she has cried today. No matter how many times you witness the tears of your child, it is something you cannot get used to. Her eyes are swollen; lost is the light that had emerged for all too short of a time.

"I don't know why she did this. I just can't wrap my mind around it all." I know what she means because I have been struggling with the same questions. Part of me wants to defend LaToya; she doesn't understand the intensity behind the history of Tonya and Veronica. But I know it is the wrong time, if there would ever be a right one, to defend her for this or ever again.

"I hate her. I hate her. Sisters don't do this to each other." She sounds juvenile. Once again, I find myself flashing back to childhood arguments. I can't bring myself to say the things I know I should, the things I would have said twenty years ago, because this time I know she means those words no matter how strong they are.

"Did she tell you before she did it?" It hurt me that my child thinks I would have any part in her undoing, but I know why she feels the need to ask.

"You know she didn't. I would have talked her out of it." I need her to believe me. I have done little to shelter her in the past few weeks, but this I would have shielded her from. I would have promised Toya anything she asked if I could have changed her mind.

"You would have tried. No one can talk my sister out of anything. Thank you. I'm sorry for thinking you had anything to do with it." She tries to smile, but I know it must hurt her to do so. She reminds me of a character from one of those stupid comics my students used to read. The smile does not suit her face.

"Lance told you, didn't he?" I simply nod. "I should have known he would tell you before telling me. You two were always close. He regards you as a mother too since his is gone." I needed to hear that in my weakness, she still thinks of me as her mom.

"How is he taking it? He was more concerned with your feelings when we spoke. I don't think he's processed his own." Lance reminds me so much of Eugene in this way; he would store his hurt and anger until he has found a way to make sure my daughter is fine.

"That is what I think I am mostly afraid of. He doesn't know how he feels yet, but I know he still loves her."

This is her shame. I know she will never be able to admit it to him.

"He loved her, even though he still denies it. She knew it. She told me herself, and I tried to deny it. She knew then that he'd be better off with her. It kills me. I knew that she was right but I wanted him so badly. I made him come back. She was right, and I was willing to risk his happiness for the sake of my own. Now she knows."

I search my purse for a tissue. Even though we are supposed to be stronger than our children, I am not. I have never claimed to be.

"Now she knows. She knows that I cannot give him the one thing we both knew he wanted. It was the reason he chose me. The reason why he did the first time and again the second time, and I failed him. I promised him a future that I could not give. Every day I have to live with what I stole from him. I have to think about what he gave up for me, and I want to hurt myself. I love this man more than I have ever loved myself. I know you always told us never to do that, but I couldn't help it. I still can't help myself. I am Mrs. Lawson. That is my identity, that is who I am. What would I be without him? I have always known I am nothing without him."

I want to interrupt to tell her all the things I should have told her all her life. So often I wished I could hold a mirror up and allow her to see what I see when I look at her. "I could live with me knowing this and him pretending not to see it. But now she will be there in court, and she will know. I can't live with that." She would be exposed in front of the woman who had caused her nothing but pain and had haunted her for years after.

"Lance came back because he loves you. Not because of what you promised him or what he thought you would give him. That man loves you for you. And that is the reason why he never left. That man loved you enough to fight for you, even when it meant doing nothing at all."

She dismisses what I am saying, and once again, I am hurt for her. I should explain the reasons why I did nothing for so many years. I was always assuming there would be another opportunity to put her first; another situation would present itself and allow me to choose her over her sister.

I am confronted now by my deepest fears. I see in her eyes that I have not given her the strength that her sister was born with. My job was to prepare her for the world, no matter how cruel and unforgiving it could be. My job was to make sure she knew her worth, to find her center without needing someone else to define it for her. For years, I pretended she was just sensitive to others, that she was in fact sweet and caring. It has never dawned on me that she was not just these things but that she was oblivious to how wonderful she is.

Lance had been that for her, a mirror. Now the picture has become smudged, by the dirt of the past.

Tonya

I have never told anyone the whole story. Auntie is the only one I have ever shared most of the details with, but I could never bring myself to tell her everything. Lance knew I met Ronnie; he thought it was just a random encounter. He never knew what was said nor did he know that our meeting was the cause of him and I breaking up.

To him, it had been something minute, it was inevitable that we should meet, and he was pleased that it had been done with little interruption in his routine with either of us. Considering he had been trying to accomplish just that, our meeting, he was happy that it had been done. We both spared his feelings, even though it was something we had not discussed. Neither of us bad-mouthed the other. We acknowledged each other's attributes, ignored the flaws, at least for his sake, and always feigned some sort of excuse as to why we would or could not meet again.

Her words cut me; it damaged me in ways that I didn't think possible up until then. I had run into a few bullies, most ignored me, simply because of who my sister was. Toya was not frightening; she was always the most popular girl wherever we went. Popularity breeds contempt, but never disloyalty. Therefore I had been shielded from childhood cruelties and spared having my insecurities pointed out. I had managed to slide through life, not knowing the feeling of having your soul crushed by someone intentionally. I never considered my sister's actions as intentional, just consequential. Up until that day, the only person who had ever hurt my feelings was my twin. I looked at Toya's actions as kind and welcomed her slighting me because she did not do these things to be mean, it was because she did not know any better.

Back then, I toyed with the thoughts of unleashing her onto Ronnie. Toya would have been a better-suited match. My sister had a sharper tongue and a quicker wit, but I had grown tired of allowing her to fight my battles. I loved Lance enough to do it myself, loved him enough to risk embarrassment. I needed to fight for him to prove to myself that I had it in me.

It was unseasonably warm that day; it had to be one of the hottest days on record for November. The leaves were the most beautiful I had ever seen them. The oranges, yellows, and deep reds had managed to give me a sense of peace; I took it as an omen. A foreshadowing of what was to come. I had been right. There would be a change, as the leaves predicted.

I thought the beauty of the day, the lovely leaves, and the warm weather would somehow make things easier. They would mirror my mood—light, colorful, and vibrant. But that had not been the case. Instead they reflected my relationship, dying, and I was too dazzled by the pretty picture to see it.

Just before Lance was to start his break, he told me that Ronnie wouldn't be going home for the holidays. He thought of inviting her to his parents so she wouldn't be alone. That, coupled with his need for us to meet, was reason enough for him.

I knew he hadn't said it to be mean, and I think that was the part that hurt me the most, knowing that this man would never intentionally hurt me but would continue to do so without realizing it. I knew if I said something, he would make a choice. He has always been honorable and never one for games. I am almost certain he would have chosen me because that was the right thing to do. I couldn't bring myself to ask him to make the choice, to seem that weak, that pathetic. He had promised without being prompted that she was just a friend. The sister he always wanted even though he did enjoy being an only child. Even in my certainty, there was room for doubt. It hurt me more, knowing that I allowed him to hurt me. It does not make sense even now, so much of my life had been bent to the will of others; it seemed a minor sacrifice to allow him to bruise my heart little by little instead of breaking it all at once.

The silence causes Lynette to squeeze my hand. I had forgotten she was even sitting next to me. I smile at her, letting her know that I am fine, even though I am far from it. I know she is wondering where my mind has retreated, the look in her eyes lets me know she is afraid that she has lost me for good. I have to do this here, with her, even though she has no idea what has caused my silence. I refuse to go home and remember. I refuse to carry these memories across my threshold. Even though I chose to stay here in her arms while remembering the past, I refuse to share it with her. I know she will listen, and I know she will try to offer me all the comfort she possibly can, but it will only make her angrier.

We were punished as children for speaking negatively about ourselves or each other more so than we were for speaking ill of others. It was not that my aunt raised us to be careless of someone else's feelings; she wanted to instill a sense of self that could not be shaken by anyone else. I love her for this, and I hope that I am able to do the same for my little girl.

I have fought the memory of that night for so long.

"I was wondering when we'd do this," Veronica said as if we had an appointment, to which I had been late, or old friends meeting over drinks, instead of two women who were obviously in love with the same man that belonged to both of them. He was mine. I had the majority, or so I believed.

I wanted to run. She was so striking. I felt underdressed in my jeans and blouse, even though she was wearing a pair of jeans herself. I had changed my clothes countless times, but nothing seemed right. I had no idea what to wear to confront the other woman. I regretted my decision before she had even had the chance to size me up. She looked as if she just stepped off a magazine cover. Her cat eyes taunted me as if waiting for my move. She had initiated this even though I was the one who made the trip. I wondered how many people she had manipulated into doing her bidding without the slightest hint that they were in fact doing what she wanted. She obviously knew I would come; she had goaded me before we met, and now she was flaunting their relationship in my face.

Suddenly I was angry again. The weather did not warrant a jacket at all. She was obviously wearing it just because it was his. I wondered if anyone else noticed, it was hard not to tell, that it was too big for her. When she placed the book to her side, the sleeves hung below her hands; even though she was almost as tall as him, she looked so tiny behind his coat. I wondered then whether Lance had given her his jacket or simply left it. I was uncomfortable with either idea. It would have been just as incriminating for both if I had caught her in a pair of his boxers.

"Is there something you wanted to say?" Again she was talking to me like an old acquaintance. She, the smug girlfriend, the one who always talked down to the other, the one who made you rethink everything you were about to say or do or wear. I am sure that in some circle, she had always been and would always be the queen bee. Unbeknownst to me, I had become her flunky; the inflection in her tone made it perfectly clear that she did not consider me an equal.

"I want you to leave Lance alone." That was the reason I had come. I had forgotten the speech I meant to give, even though I practiced it a thousand times, not just the dozen on the way over, but ever since he said her name and smiled before he could even tell me why he had brought her up. This time, I had not said it with as much resolve as I had mustered in my bedroom mirror. I had adapted quite well to my role as flunky, it was not new to me. Living my whole life in the shadow of another beautiful woman was my comfort zone, the backseat, it was all too familiar.

"No." Still standing there in front of me, the smug smile had been removed. Instead in its place was a look of pure confusion. She appeared to have no idea how I could have the audacity to even ask this of her. I knew she meant what she said, that there would be no changing her mind. I hadn't expected it to be easy; no one could simply ask me to walk away from him either and expect compliance, but she was rude, blatantly so.

"Lance loves me, and I am not letting him go. You need to walk away." I said this as convincingly as possible. I wished I had brought along the girl who said these things in the mirror, but she was nowhere to be found. I held on to the one thing I was certain of since it was no longer myself: he did in fact love me.

"I know that he loves you, I am just not sure why." As she said this, she looked me up and down again as if a second inspection would reveal the answer. "I doubt he knows either. But you're not here because Lance loves you. Are you?" She paused, giving me time to think. I was uncertain of what my reaction should have been. Once again, I wanted to run away, the thought first crossed my mind when I laid eyes on her. "You're here because you know that Lance loves me too." I tried to control my facial expressions. I had learned all my life that when there was nothing left to do you smile as if you were okay with it all. It took too long for the smile to appear. She had slowed me, not just mentally, but physically, as if her presence alone was a sedative. I was dull in comparison. She knew now that she definitely had the upper hand. "You want to know if I feel the same?" She was now controlling this conversation. I had lost before it begun. I lost the first night they spent together "studying." She continued to wait as if it would only take me a few seconds to catch up with her. I was waiting as well for her to answer her own question. We both know she already had, with her refusal to leave him alone, but I needed to hear her say it as much as she needed to say it to me.

"Do you love him?" I asked, bracing myself for the answer. I knew she would be brash about it, but I needed the pain to be swift. She had to say it, to prove that I wasn't completely insecure or jealous. If she said yes, she loved him, it would vindicate my feelings. I'd be able to tell him with a clean conscience that he could no longer see her.

"I thought I did the first time I saw him. I believed I could the first time I heard him speak. Now, yes, I know that I love him." And just like that, my world cracked right down the middle. Once again, we took on the role of old friends. She seemed to gush about the new love she had found. A smile spread across her face as she told me those things. And despite the weather, I am certain that we both had goose bumps. In another world, I would have congratulated her.

"If you love him, you'll walk away. Let him be happy." Now I had been reduced to begging. I sounded like a spoiled child begging to keep the puppy that followed her home, knowing she could not give it anything but love, knowing that she could not possibly take care of it the way it would need, but begging for a chance to prove herself. I looked into her eyes, despite the height difference.

Never trust a woman with eyes like a cat. They are just as sneaky and harder to put down. I hear my mother's voice in my head as I stare at this stranger who is familiar in so many different ways. She is no longer Veronica or Lance's Ronnie. She instead became the faceless woman that represents all the "other women." The lady who always had sugar-coated words for our daddy after church service, causing my parents to argue for hours and my sister and I to hide under our bed. She was the woman who stole Mr. Morton from his wife a few years ago when she cried on Auntie's shoulder as if she had lost something she would never be able to replace. She was the woman who had run away with Lynette's high school sweetheart, causing her to wrap herself up into two little girls afraid to love a man again.

"I can say the same to you, if you love him, which you must for obvious reasons, you'd let him go." Unlike the Sunday morning lady who wanted my dad, she did not coat her words in sugar. They were covered in venom. She circled around me, looking for the easiest point of attack. All I could do was stand there, waiting for her to sink her teeth into me, to have her poison spread through my system to my heart, where it seems they have already taken root.

She stopped at my right side before she had come full circle. She whispered in my ear, "I am sick of waiting for him to tire of you. My patience has worn way too thin. You do understand how hard he tries to be the best, and still you hold on to him. It's only fair to Lance that he has the best." She then stood in front of me. This was tactical; she was displaying herself to me, waiting for me to accept the fact that she was the better woman. If there were checks and balances and life was in anyway fair, she'd be right.

"I'm not saying you're not a nice girl, pretty even." That was a backhanded compliment if I had ever heard one. "I will admit there is something about you. I didn't see it at first. It's subtle, easily missed." Another pause, as if she is trying to put words to what it is that makes me "pretty even." Once she found the answer, she continued, "There's brokenness, vulnerability about you, like a broken-winged bird, and I know the type of man that he is. He has dreams of saving the world, so of course he would want to rescue you. Standing here, I want to rescue you also. But not at the risk of sacrificing myself, and that is what you are asking him to do. Those things that make you endearing also make you a liability. I know you. I grew up with girls like you, and I see more of them every single day. You'll catch a man, a great one even, like Lance, and he'll realize, as they always do, that you can't be fixed, that you are and will always be broken, weak, and needy. When he realizes it, how much time will pass. I have yet to see him give up on anything. Years later, you'll have a few children, and he will wake up one morning resenting you and them. I've seen it. I've felt it. Lived it. I was one of those resented children myself.

"It wouldn't be fair to disappoint him in that way, to lose him years from now surrounded by children with no way to explain why Daddy could not stick around. Walk away now because it will benefit you in the long run. I can smell the desperation on you. You won't survive it when he leaves. I won't tell you what to do. That would be stupid of me to presume you'd listen, almost as silly as it was for you to make this trip hoping I'd listen to what you had to say.

"Lance is the type of man that needs to be wanted. You are the type of woman who will always need him. Let him go. I promise to take care of him in the ways you'd never know how to."

I couldn't say anything. I was paralyzed by her words. They stung. She was right. I had no way to defend myself against the truth; I had not come prepared for this. The only fact I wanted to argue was that Lance and I loved each other. Yes, I needed him, and there was nothing wrong with that. I needed a man who did not need me; it was scary to have someone else point it out.

"I can't." The tears surfaced, and I was not bold enough to wipe them away, afraid that with any movement, she would pounce on me. Part of me wanted her to pity me, to see just how much he meant to me. I was willing to win by default.

"There lies the difference between the two of us. You can't leave him, and I won't." With that said, she walked away from me. There was nothing more that she could say, or I for that matter either. I had failed, she won. She was right.

I was too weak to walk away; she was too strong to let him go. That was years ago. That was before I had known the bitterness of betrayal, and the despair of too many losses. I have never fought for anything, not even Lance, for fear that I would lose not just the battle but myself somewhere among the rubble.

She knew exactly who I was then when it seemed I had no idea. Now I am someone altogether different. At first glance, I may look the same, but if one would look closely, one can see the scars and trace the lines that once weakened me but have now became the source of strength.

Lance

Webster's dictionary defines *mediation* as an intervention between conflicting parties to promote reconciliation, settlement, or compromise. With that in mind, I have no idea why we are here. There is nothing I am willing to compromise on; that has been settled. Therefore, reconciliation is out of the question. Arnold knows this, and I know he is the best man for the job. I am trusting him to make the right decisions, and this meeting had not been up to him though he acknowledged the need for it.

This is what needs to be done, and it will be. The thought leaves a bitter taste in my mouth. The knowledge that nothing will be changed amplifies my hostility. I would have preferred a different approach; maybe with more time, I could plead with Toya's sensibility. I could help her to see things our way, the right way. That cause has been lost; there is no going back. I knew it the moment she hired Ronnie. In my infinite belief in the goodness of man, I believed that Toya would eventually come to her senses. Now, I am admittedly jaded. She has colored my perception; it took one person and a few weeks to undo what my parents had instilled in me over my lifetime.

Tonya has been gracious about all of it since the first day when I told her about Ronnie's involvement. I did not ask where she went; she did not volunteer any information, so I didn't push. She was, however, a new woman, when she returned. She has found some measure of strength that I did not know she had. I watch her, wondering where she hid it, how she allowed it to lay dormant for so long. At every turn, when I expect her to fall apart, she doesn't. Once again, I do not question her; instead I am thankful. I find myself falling in love with her over and over again.

She is no longer the little girl who needs me or the woman who could not do without me. I know that she has found her strength simply because it is necessary to keep our family together, even when I think that it may be impossible.

I wonder if she knows now what she should have known all along. Tonya is a brilliant woman, and I do not understand how a man like me earns the privilege to call her my own. I wondered before, and somewhere along the marriage, I had forgotten who she was, shortly after she had forgotten herself, and now she is all that consumes me.

When she asked me if I was leaving her, it broke me into pieces. I had thought of it more times than I'd care to admit. Surely any man would have, had he been pushed aside like I have been. It scared me to think that even in the midst of all this, she'd assume I'd betray her, and we both knew she'd somehow find a way to survive it all. So maybe part of me wants to still be her everything and the reason for her smile.

I think of this as I watch her. It took her twice as long to dress today. There is nothing to wear for an occasion such as this. She has never been one of those women who complained about not having anything to wear, simply because she looked good in everything.

She had never taken more than ten minutes to dress, but today was different, and we both knew it. So I was not offended when she asked how something looked and then changed clothes immediately regardless of my insistence that she looked amazing, beautiful, or perfect. I was patient since it is something that I reserve for my home life alone; I have it in abundance when it comes to her. Eventually she returned to her third choice (Or was it her fifth?). But I saw that she regretted that decision as she pulled, straightened, and then smoothed imaginary wrinkles from her skirt.

We rode here without speaking. It wasn't that I didn't have anything to say; it was that I couldn't find the words to say them. It seemed that the ride had left me speechless and her silent. It seemed we only had the ability to articulate when we were with Arnold, who had met us here.

That is a decision I now regret. It would have been customary for us to come with him, showing some form of solidarity, also giving him time to address any questions or concerns. I wanted my wife all to myself. I wanted to be the one to offer words of comfort, to be the one she relied on to offer the answers to her questions. I have failed her once again.

I promised that I would never disappoint her; now I wonder how often I have done just that. I asked her for forgiveness this week for doing so, and she laughed. She told me I was being absurd and that I had never disappointed her and never could. I wished I could understand the way that she loves me. On second thought, I am glad I do not. Great love can never be put into words, even though we often try to do just that. I know that I love her simply because the thought of having her or losing her makes me speechless. The only person in this world that I could ever love more is my child. McKenzie—she's the reason why this battle must be fought, why I would fight it a thousand times more. Just like that. I too am a new man.

I need to speak to Tonya before I am no longer the voice that she hears, before everything is turned upside down and she is hurt by words that will never be forgotten.

"It is a scare tactic," I remind her. Arnold and I reassured her of this over and over again when she asked why this meeting was necessary. The fact that we both felt the need to reassure her, more than once, left me anything but.

The thought of this amuses me now while I am sitting here. They are attempting to scare a man who is afraid of nothing. I have faced my darkest fears and beat them back; I have come to the realization that there is nothing I am unwilling to do to assure that my family is whole mentally, physically, and emotionally.

So I am fighting more for her than myself. She needs to find her redemption, and I would walk through hell to give it to her.

"Is this another scare tactic?" Tonya asks me, and I am not sure if she really expects me to respond since she did not look at me when she asked. It appears that she has ironed out all of the invisible wrinkles and has now occupied herself with her watch.

As are most things in life, this is a power struggle. Not only do they—since Toya and Ronnie have now become synonymous with the thorn in my side—have almost every advantage going in, they have chosen to take the home court advantage. If I were not sitting on the opposite side of this table, I would consider it a move well played.

Tonya has now found something about the table that interest her, or maybe it is a tactic all her own. She is using it as a way to avoid looking at me. I know she is expecting me to fix this, or at least she had been, but so much has shifted in these past few days. She has become aware slowly that I am not the superhero she has built me up to be. I am partly relieved and ashamed. I cannot let her down; it is something that I never thought I'd have to face.

We have been waiting for twenty-two minutes. Now I know I am being toyed with; that is not something I am at all used to or comfortable with. I am used to everything being done around me; my schedule is always considered first.

I am afraid for Arnold. I am sure that he has done his research, as any good attorney would. Veronica is the best and has rightfully earned her reputation. I wonder if he is frightened; if not, he is a fool.

As if they were there the whole time, Toya and Ronnie appear. I wanted to say something to Tonya first; now I am regretting not using my time spent waiting more wisely. It is hard not to stare at them both. They are exquisite, and I can tell that this has not escaped my wife either. The wrinkles have returned, and the table has lost its appeal. She is doing anything possible to avoid eye contact. I had briefed her on these things—on what can be taken as a sign of weakness.

Her gaze was supposed to be strong and indifferent, while mine intimidating. We have both failed at our assignments. Her sister is now the strong and indifferent one, and Ronnie has definitely taken the reins on intimidating.

If this were any other day and I had the time to reflect, I could consider myself a lucky man. I have loved and been loved by each of these women at some point in my life, in one variation or another. They have changed me, and mostly for the better.

"Shall we begin?" Three words is all it takes, and my heart falls from my chest. Now it has been replaced by rage and adrenaline. The table does not seem as strong a divider as I need. My primal urge to destroy has taken over, and I am certain that if I open my mouth to speak, nothing but a growl will escape.

Toya

This I am not ready for, no matter how many times I try to convince myself I am. Something just isn't right; as a matter of fact, everything is so very wrong. Ronnie has coached me, some things have even been scripted, but here in this room with the two people that I know best in life sitting across from me, I feel like a stranger. Not just to them, but to myself. My voice does not belong to me, my gestures not my own. Even what I am seeing seems slightly clouded as if I am watching through someone else's glasses. I want to stop the room from spinning and question all parties involved; maybe someone here can confirm who I have become. Introductions are in order.

I am lost inside of myself; that is the scariest feeling I have ever known. I have no idea how I got here exactly. Where did I take the wrong turn? Is it possible for me to back track, to set right this path? That is ridiculous. The damage has been done, and feelings have been hurt, hearts broken, and trust shattered. Someone might say that it is at hand, others say that I was forced here, pushed into this corner. I have never been the type to blame someone for my choices, but now I understand; that is because I have never questioned my decisions before.

I lived life just as one is supposed to. I prepared for tomorrow by living as if there was only today. I have regretted only a few things—this will be one of them. How absurd does that sound, yet how often does it occur? You ignore your gut when it tells you that your choices will bring nothing but regret, hurt, disappointment and shame. I believe it is part of the human experience throwing caution to the wind and jumping even when broken bones are certain to be the end result.

How funny is it that I think of broken bones now? Despite all the crazy things I have done pre- and post-adolescence, I have only had the "pleasure" of breaking a bone once. When we were ten, our friend Evan dared me to climb the tree behind his house. Tonya told me not to—actually *begged* was more like it. Even then she tried to plead with my common sense. It never worked. I was always the hardheaded daredevil who wanted to learn and experience things on her own.

"Evan said you can see clear across the park from the top of the tree." This was my answer to her pleas. I would not acknowledge that she had a valid point. Doing so would only add another few minutes to her tirade. My mind had been made up. I wanted to spare her the time wasted trying to change it.

The air felt, smelled, and tasted of summer, even though the break had yet to begin. It was one of those days that tempted you, made you forget about things such as homework, or school days. All that made sense were the late nights, which in this case means staying out until the street lights came on, water ice, soft pretzels and fire flies. Thoughts of the beach whispered us to sleep, promises of amusement parks and vacations were our lullabies. Twin and I had no idea what the summer would hold since it was our first as "orphans."

No one said it, because there was no need to address the fact that we were becoming the people we were going to be, but our parents' death had changed us both. For some reason it made us polar opposites, the different side of the same coin. Whereas I had lost all restraint, my twin had gained the self-control of a parishioner.

I was by all indications a bright child, but much more active than anyone else I played with. Why walk somewhere when you could run? Why just swing when you could jump off at the top? What was the point of looking both ways when crossing the street, after all when it is your time; it is your time right? So I pushed the envelope a little farther every day.

Tonya was more extreme in her "safety" as well as mine. She blessed her food twice; mine three times because she was certain I forgot when I snacked. Crossed at the corner but only after checking and rechecking that not only were there no cars coming but no one was pulling out of their drive ways either.

It had been less than a year since we lost them, I knew that Tonya would freak out at the thought of me climbing the tree, I expected her too. I counted on her response to make everyone more excited. She was my personal front man. Her pleads to think about what I was doing, followed by her warnings of what could go wrong, always the same warnings, "You could break your neck, blind yourself, go deaf." Never was she without a slew of consequences for something as routine as being a child.

It is miraculous that any of us made it out unscathed, according to my sister walking while chewing gum could lead to death, or if you were lucky just serious bodily injury. It didn't matter that traffic was always slow on our street, and that all the neighbors knew to beep their horns as soon as they turned on the block to alert us. She yelled her warnings at all the children some older most younger from the safety of our porch. Always advising what dangers were included in our childhood games. Whenever something did happen the injured child would make their way to her to be bandaged, then sent home, the lucky ones were allowed to stay and yell along with her, until they forgot just how serious their condition had been and returned to continue their games.

We had been fixtures on this street since we learned to walk, now we were here to stay, it wasn't just a visit this would be our residence. I had to usurp the throne, mark my territory. I was after all the prettiest girl, it didn't hurt that I could not only run quicker, climb higher, throw harder, spit farther, swim faster, and curse better than every boy in a three block radius.

"How hard could it be?" I asked her. "The tree isn't as tall as you think. Remember, you are looking up, so it distorts the image. We've watched Evan do it dozens—no, hundreds of times." *He was after all half blind and a boy.* That part I left out because no one likes an ungracious winner. There was never a challenge I shied away from. They both knew this. Everyone did. I prided myself on being able to do anything my male counterparts could as they looked on envious and amazed, especially since I knew it was my looks that made them watch in the first place.

I was nervous, my palms were sweaty, and my heart raced faster than my mind, just like now. I scaled the tree in my head and pictured myself sitting on top of the highest branch. Not only did I have to climb it faster and make it higher than Evan, even though that was not part of the dare, I also had to make it look effortless.

It took me less time then I assumed to climb the tree. The other children were not impressed instead intimidated. It was obvious that none of them would be able to beat my time.

I saw the branch, Evan's favorite. I decided to keep going. It was then that the murmurs stopped. Everyone hushed, except for my sister, who was praying for me while I was doing something extremely stupid. I remembered one of the phrases she borrowed from Auntie then and used quite often. "God protects babies and fools, and you haven't been in Pampers for quite some time now." So maybe I was a fool; either way we both knew she loved me all the same.

After threatening to run home and tell, after promising to leave me because I was doing something that she deemed both stupid and irresponsible, she stayed. Not to cheer, not to reprimand, but to offer the only support she could, and the only thing I wanted or needed was her presence.

I wanted to look down at her. Considering she was afraid of heights, I knew her eyes would be closed, so she would not be able to see my look of reassurance or see me plummet to my death, as she so dramatically put it.

That was the comfort of Tonya. She was loyal, whether I was right or wrong, she would stay with me regardless of the outcome. I wish now that I could have been just as loyal, I had been given the opportunity plenty of times before. Yet, I always believed there would be a next time.

I planned to say her name as soon as I made it to the top, speak only to her as I described just how far I could see. But something went wrong. Before I could catch myself, just as I was about to call to her, I lost my grip. Even though I had made it to the top in record time, it was nothing compared to how fast I hit the ground.

I broke my leg that day. Amid all the panic, she remained calm. She took charge and advised the children there to run and get our aunt. She told Evan, who had begun to cry before I had even realized I slipped, to go inside to wake his mother and tell her to call 911.

I wasn't yelled at. Auntie would never do that, even if it was making dumb decisions that lead to my broken bone. That was not my concern. Broken things can be fixed, but my ego had been shattered. She praised Tonya, advised her that if she hadn't thought to pray, things could have been a lot worse. She told my twin, as I lay on the hospital bed fighting away tears of pain, that she was lucky that at least one of her girls was responsible.

That is when I began to cry; she assumed it was from the pain and walked to the nurses' station to get me something for it. Evan, who had made the trip with us, promised that he would come over every day and sit with me if I liked. He'd skip the pool as well. Tonya was the one who understood that it was the comparison that hurt my heart.

Never before had she called me the bad twin even though I knew that was what I was, for her to acknowledge it made my heart heavy.

"She was trying to say that I am just not a daredevil like you." Tonya offered. Those were her words of comfort.

"You have to be more careful. You could have killed yourself, and you do know that?"

"Not from that height. I'm not stupid. Maybe paralyzed but not dead. She didn't give me credit for that, did she? Nope, she probably thinks I jumped."

"Even you aren't that crazy." We both laughed.

I waited for Evan to walk off to the vending machine before I said, "I wish I were more like you." He had sensed the girlie moment and made his exit.

"Everyone's always watching to see what I'll do next. It's hard sometimes. Now they'll be watching me sit on the porch. All alone." This time I refused to cry.

"You won't be alone. I'll be there. We'll laugh at the neighbors. I'm sure Mrs. Huff will have plenty of visitors we can talk about." Again we shared a laugh. When we returned home, Tonya was forced to go out and play. I was indeed, expected to learn a lesson, and I would not be able to do so if I were having fun. I cried the first two nights. I was definitely being punished. I did not, in my young age, understand why. So I pushed my twin away and told her to make all the new friends she wanted. "I'd rather be dead than bored and lonely." She knew I meant it as I cried into my pillow that night. I refused to talk to her that day, no matter how many times she snuck back into the house to tell me what was going on outside.

I don't know if it was my threat or the silent treatment, but the next day Tonya returned home from school in a cast as well. She had broken her arm by jumping from the jungle gym at school. Auntie didn't ask if it were done on purpose because anyone who knew Tonya knew the answer. I still remember what our aunt said to me the day she returned from the emergency room with my twin: "That girl would give her right arm for you, and she just proved it." At that age I didn't know how to process my feelings. I resented her for being self-sacrificing; I loved her for loving me but hated her for loving me that much. It was a suffocating feeling.

Her love was my burden to carry. I understood that even as a child. I wanted to love as easily. To give myself to the feeling completely, but I could not. I couldn't trust that it would not consume me, that it would not allow the flood gates to open, and every other emotion would come just as easily. If I could love like her, I was afraid that I would be able to hate just as fiercely.

That is what I was running from; even then, I understood it. The rush of adrenaline prevented me from processing everything else. I wouldn't feel pain, abandonment, and all of the things I knew were there when my brain was processing only the next thrill. So I spent my whole life thinking of only myself to avoid thinking of what I have lost.

What we all lost. Yes, we lost our parents and our innocence. We lost ourselves or what we should have been. Even now as I sit across from the woman whom has proven time and time again that she would give me anything I asked and most importantly the things I would never have to ask for, I am reminded once again that I cannot love her the same, that I cannot put her above me even when that is the right thing to do.

Tonya will not look at me. I am not sure if I honestly expected her to or what I thought I would gain from it. The bond has been lost and replaced with something that I will not name. Hate I could live with, because that never seems permanent. Like love, it is easy to fall in or out of. Hate and love consume too much of your time and demand too much attention. It is a constant breathing thing. I have to remind myself, often, as to why I feel the way that I do.

That is why our relationship has been not just the longest but the most stable in my life. There is not a day that goes by that I am not reminded of just how much my sister loved me. Just how much she sacrificed and for those reasons alone I adore her.

You never forget your first love, and if I am truthful, that is what she is to me. We knew each other before anyone else had the pleasure. People often wonder why the connection between twins is so strong; my answer has always been a simple one. Before there was the identity of self, there was always the knowledge of us. I learned her heart beat before I was able to distinguish my own.

For years, I looked at her and was unable to separate where one of us ended and the other began, not because we were so much alike, but because we were in fact so different. She was the answer to my flaws, and I the same for her.

She was my harmony, what glued the pieces together. Certainly I will fall apart, shatter like broken glass. These things I blame on her. It is unacceptable for her to love that way for so long and then snatch it away. Where are her prayers now, her admonishments, and her praise? This is not a tree in someone's back yard I am climbing here. This is my life, my daughter's future, and the one person in this world who has loved me through it all, who has carried me when I couldn't crawl, and bandaged me when I was broken is nowhere to be found. She was my best friend and had been more to me than I could have asked of anyone else. She was and has been the only constant in my life. How dare my sister decide that she cannot be bothered when I need her most?

Ronnie

So it was difficult—that's putting it mildly—not for the reasons one would suspect. We were crucified, and it is not an easy pill to swallow, especially considering we went into this holding the upper hand. If I remain rational, which is getting harder to do minute by minute, it's easier to see how things fell apart. Toya was not ready for this, and I can only fight but so much for her. I search my bag for my migraine medicine, wishing that I had something strong to wash it down with. My husband was upset when they were prescribed; leave it up to him to do the research on what I put into my body. It reminded me that he knew I belonged to him, and he was as invested in my health as I was. That irritated me to no end. I swallow an extra pill dry at the memory. Seeing his last name on my prescription bottle makes me want to down all of them.

I was prepared to spend a night filled with meaningless sex with my husband in celebration of destroying the life of the man I wished he was. I had planned to pick my son up early and pretend to enjoy time with my family, not because I appreciated it, but because in the event that things went my way, I wanted to leave Adam with memories. I'd have Lance, and he'd have the family that he wanted. We'd fit perfectly together, a son for him and a daughter for him as well. It is the dissolution of this dream that is causing my headache.

Any case will have its hang-ups. Nothing is a slam dunk despite what primetime television tells you. Toya faltered, wasting a lot of my time and energy. Though I am upset, I am not surprised. Well, that is not true; I am a little taken aback. I wanted to ask her where the woman I met a few weeks ago was. Had she disappeared altogether? Her fight was gone; her determination had wavered. It was silly of me to think that anyone could hold on to that much resentment simply because I had managed to do so for all these years. I am, after all, exceptional, and I am not saying it to brag. I am an exceptional liar, manipulator, and lawyer. I have never given my all to anything that did not benefit me. That is not the whole truth. I have only been disappointed when it came to the two of them, now the three—Toya, Tonya, and Lance—have become a constant headache. I am still trying to remain rational and failing miserably at it.

Everything that we rehearsed was forgotten. She stumbled when she should have been assertive and cracked when I needed her to be firm. These things I expected, but that does not make it easier to live with. I played the waiting game for too long. Now that this opportunity has presented itself, she will not take it from me. I'd rather for her to have sat there silently than to have spoken and sounded as if she doubted herself. Better to be thought incompetent than to prove yourself to be just that. Even though she never formally stated she was not the right choice, she had cast doubt. Every attorney knows that doubt can make or break any case. It is such a finicky word, a dirty one at times, but a saving grace at others.

This will not be a jury trial, thankfully. Despite her obvious appeal, I am certain, beyond a reasonable doubt, that Toya would be her own undoing if today's appearance was in anyway an indicator. No one would be able to see past her flaws unless she made it easy for them. Today it was impossible to do so. Nothing about this meeting was easy; that did not give her the right to make it harder than it had to be.

It wasn't so much what she said; it is the things she did not. Unlike her sister, she did not become indignant when shots were thrown at her. This was in fact a shooting match, and she hadn't even bothered to come prepared with a knife. I was her weapon of choice and honestly the best choice she has made so far, but that does not mean that I won't need something to work with. She should have given me more. I prepared her for the fact that nothing would be won today. All parties came in knowing that nothing would be decided. It was quite cut and dry; both were fighting for sole custody, and unless someone was willing to give up their claim, we'd see each other in court.

I would have suggested this meeting either way, even if the judge had not ordered it. I needed to be in the same room as them. To see him and smell him, even if it were from a few feet away. I needed to see for myself if she is still who he wanted to be with. I could only imagine the tolls taken by all their disappointments. I hoped for a clue, something subtle from the man I once knew better than I knew myself that would tell me how easy it would be to slip myself into the cracks that were starting to form in his life.

Once upon a time, there were fireworks that bounced between us. No one could stand to be in the same room Lance and I occupied for fear that they would have to witness that uncomfortable feeling of intruding on two lovers. We were something magical, and it was never just in my head, despite the uncertainty these years have cast.

I needed to know if it were still possible to be near someone and feel that tug of hopeless, desperate need. I had forgotten how it felt to want someone until every single cell in your body ached. The years did not erase the knowledge of a want so deep, it was unbearably hard to pull your eyes away but increasingly hard to keep staring.

It is childish, sounds too much like a crush. But there is no other man that I had ever felt these feelings for, and time has done little but to play tricks on me. I wonder if I had made those feelings up because surely it is impossible to love that way, that fiercely. Then suddenly, he was there, and I knew that nothing has changed.

The pull was there; unmistakably my soul was drawn to him, and I needed nothing more than to curl up next to him, touch him, reassure myself that he had not been a figment of my imagination. He is real, and so are the feelings. It took me a few seconds to enter the room completely. I waited for him to turn to look at me, to see the aftermath of what he had done. He didn't. Then she saw me, and for a second, there was the smug smile of victory sprawled across her lips, the same lips that kissed him every night and whispered the words that I was never allowed to say. I hated her more now than I had believed before.

Tonya, of course, played her part perfectly. Thankfully, there was no one there to witness it; she'd definitely win over any crowd. The sad eyes, defeated posture…it was sickening.

I am not sure who to credit with her performance; she has, after all, always been a manipulator. I am sure Lance coached her, or maybe it was Arnold, who, I must admit, had a few surprises all his own. Either way it was a job well done. She had proven herself to be stronger than I think anyone expected.

There were tears when appropriate. She refused to address her sister or me directly. I think that is what hurt Toya the most, and that is what cracked her facade. She was not the only one hurting in there. It pained me that Lance would not acknowledge me. Even when I asked him a question, he would never answer me directly; instead, he'd pass his answer down to Arnold as if we were playing whisper down the lane. Never did any of his answers vary. They all began with "Tonya and I have decided" or "Tonya and I have come to the conclusion." He would not separate himself from her. That, coupled with his inability to look at me, hurt me more than I had anticipated.

I hope I was able to shield my irritation and hide the fact that every time I saw her lips move closer to his ear, I wanted to move my hands closer to her neck. She offered him comfort even though it was always short lived. It took one sentence from me, and there it was again, his anger festering until it boiled over. I knew the signs all too well. The anger started in his eyes, moved to his jaw, which would suddenly become so rigid. His body would tense and then just as fast as it had happened, he would relax, always in such control of what he allowed others to see. If I had not known him so well, it would have been missed or just dismissed.

But I have known him, loved him, held him, wanted him, and felt him, and for all of those reasons, I want to erase this afternoon from my mind, just as much as I want to replay every moment of it.

The look of his mouth when he speaks, the ever so elegant gestures of his hands when he wants to emphasize something, the crescendo of his chest when his mood changes—I had remembered it all so vividly, at least I assumed so, but today I realized that what I had remembered was nothing more than a faded version of the real thing. My memory was a black-and-white photo. He was radiant, and I had done him no justice.

He had chosen to rewrite our history. Lance would forever remain the greatest chapter in my life, but I was just a footnote in his.

Tonya

I did not die even though I wanted to. It is sad that this revelation is the highlight of my day, my week even. I wonder how detrimental to my mental stability this will be when I allow myself to feel all the things I am fighting not to feel now, but I will deal with it when the time comes. For now, I will do just as I have always done: push aside my hurt. This time, it is not for others. This time I am doing this for me.

If I were not afraid to appear completely delusional, I would burst into song right here inside this huge lobby, something completely inappropriate for the moment or even my age bracket. I am sure Arnold is not prepared for any of my Lady Gaga renditions even if the acoustics would be perfect. So I hold my tongue and enjoy the fact that I could sing right now or dance if I wanted to. It feels as if I have a secret that I know I should share but refuse to. I'm keeping it to myself, for now, even though it is trying to work its way out. I want someone to notice, someone to ask where this joy came from. I know they will not. Arnold is busy on his cell barking orders to someone; it is amazing to see that I am not the only one who's found their stride. Lance is lost inside his own thoughts, and that is fine with me; it took so long for me to find myself that I am not willing to look for someone else, not just yet. I'll let him stay there; he has earned the right to this moment, and this is his time for reflection.

He had lost his temper a few times; I was shocked, frightened, and a bit turned on all at once. This is who he is. I have never known this side of him, and I want to. Once again I learned what power I hold over my husband, and that is something that never gets old. It took one word from me to quiet him and one shed tear of mine to enrage him. I know him well enough to know he thinks he has failed me; he could not be further from the truth.

He needed to be my protector, but there are some fights that must be won alone. For the sake of his pride, I will allow him to believe that I need to lean on him a little longer. I'll give him exactly what he wants. I will fall apart—not today because I will not let anything spoil what I feel now, not even his ego, but someday soon I will fall into his arms the way he needs me to.

I look at him and wonder where his mind is now; I am waiting for him to realize that I am not defeated. It amazes me how he can be so intuitive at times and completely naïve at others. I should be thankful considering he was unaware of the way Ronnie looked at him, the way her eyes begged him to make contact. At first, the thought of the two of them sitting in the same room together drove me crazy. I wondered how he would react to her. There was the overwhelming knowledge of what could have been if he had made a different choice that surrounded us. I have spent my marriage in the shadow of what they shared so long ago.

I was jealous of her; she had everything that I had hoped for—mostly a solid marriage, a successful career, and above all else a family that belonged to her. Those are the things that I should covet, but it is not the reason why, and I would be lying to myself to claim those are the things that make me envy her.

I resent the way she knew him even after all these years. The way she loved him makes me want to vomit, but not before clawing her eyes out.

I doubt even Arnold was immune to the energy that passed between the three of us. She flinched every time we touched. It was subtle, but she could not hide it. I took advantage; I touched him when it was not necessary, whispered things in his ear that could have been said aloud, referred to him as my husband when it could have simply been Lance or Mr. Lawson.

The pain was unmistakable; I could not be cruel even when it was necessary. I wanted to explain it to her, to apologize for it all in a way that one does after someone has suffered a loss. The apology changes nothing but means everything all the same. I will not apologize for being his choice, nor will I for fighting to have him, but I wanted to offer her my condolences. It was only fair to let her know that I, after all, know exactly what she is feeling—the overwhelming need to have him, the thoughts that bordered on obsession.

The ache was still there for her; it was not hidden behind her smile or her eyes. She was just as desperate as I had been, maybe more so. She will always have the advantage because I would never be able to fight dirty. This is something she is more than comfortable with, and I am sure time has only sharpened this ability. I push those thoughts aside. I am certain that this is just the beginning. There will be more to come. That is a fight for another day.

The pure bliss of knowing that I have survived the first battle overwhelms me. No, not unscathed. There will be bandages, but I am walking away from something that I thought would cripple me.

My husband is still holding my hand, which reminds me that I am still loved. I squeeze his hand, and as if by reflex, he squeezes back. That small gesture is all the reassurance I need. No matter what hell I am facing, there will always be someone there to squeeze my hand, to hold me through it all. For the briefest of seconds at that table, when I wished that it would stop, my heart continued to beat, reminding me that I have something to fight for, a reason to live. Even if for now it continues only for the little girl who knows my heartbeat as her own personal lullaby or for the man who holds my heart as firmly as he is holding my hand right now, I will fight until my heart beats its last.

When I pushed myself away from that table, I imagined that I was doing the same with my old life, a metaphorical pushing aside of the weight I had carried, dragged, or succumb to since I can remember.

Despite the tears I cried silently and despite the hurt that I felt going in and coming out, I know something is healing. It has to hurt first; that is something I've learned over the years. We all run from pain, avoid it at every measure, shy away when it is exactly what we need. We learn from it; we don't know the true power of fire until we are burned. You can't enjoy the miracle of love until you've had your heart broken.

I wish I would have learned these things earlier because that is exactly what I have deprived my sister of—the knowledge of pain. There is no growth without loss, even a rose bush must be trimmed to ensure beauty. I had been the buffer between her and the world. I see clearly that my love has crippled her in the same way that hers has maimed me. I never allowed her to grow as a person. If I have always defined myself as her big sister, it is easy to conclude that I have defined her as my little one as well. For all these years, I have shielded her from the things that build character, the things that shape us. Knowing this does not make it easier.

I cursed myself a thousand times today, no matter how far she had driven the wedge between us, and I couldn't shake the urge to hug her. To hold her when I knew she was hurting, because I could see that she was. My little sister, my twin, the person whom I carried for as long as I have lived, needed me. I know now that even when I thought her to be the strong one it was me who gave her strength. It is easy to climb the tight rope when there is a net there to catch you. So she had not been the brave one after all, she had just counted on my catching her, and that made her seem, and it is not her fault because I am sure even she believed that she was, fearless. She had no way of knowing that she was not until today.

She has once again done something that cannot be undone. Something that I could not fix for her, and just as much as I wanted to fix her hurt I wanted to stop mine. That has been my responsibility, when we were younger, my mother never reminded me to be careful, and instead it was always look after your sister. Maybe she knew that I was the protector, or that I didn't need someone to look out for me. It is what I'd like to believe now. Then it just seemed as if, my sister was her only concern, and therefore should be mine as well.

How different we have become. There was a time when I would push aside my wants, just as soon as I knew what they were, for her to avoid any sense of want. I would have given in to her at the slightest hint of her discomfort. Today was different, not because my love for her had stopped, but because it had changed. For the first time, I question if I still love her more than myself. I had, for all these years, been programmed to do so. I have loved her more than Lance as well and more than our aunt, who had given us anything and everything we could ask. I even loved her more than I loved my parents. Now I understand why.

I have no right to blame her for this; honestly it was all my doing. She just played the hand she was dealt. For so long we made her the center of our universe, and now she is lost, not just to her, but to me.

Lynette

The clock in the waiting room continues to tick loudly, making me aware to the fact that I have not only wasted time but am continuing to do so. I am sitting here waiting for someone to show me that there is such a thing as compassion, and if I am lucky, I will know not just that, but companionship too, which sadly is what my life has come to. There is a fine line between being alone and lonely, and I have found myself standing behind the wrong side too many times. I am now tired with it all. *Fatigued* would be much better a description. I am done cleaning up after someone else while sweeping myself aside.

I am aching in places that have no name. It would be hard to pinpoint exactly where my soul is located, and my temperature is not elevated, though my blood pressure may be. I do not have a cough or chills, but something is not right. My heart is broken, and I am counting on my friend to help me fix it, to set it the same way I have watched him set broken bones. Luckily there is never a need for me to explain my emergency appointments to the receptionist. How do I tell her that nothing is ailing me physically? Instead it is my heart and soul that needs the attention of my doctor.

Eugene Flowers is the kindest man I know, and I am blessed to say I have known him for more than half my life. I have learned a million things at my age. Some lessons were forgotten almost immediately; others stick simply because the lesson is ever changing, taking shape as if to fit the need. I have learned that friends are few and far between and that every once in a while it is okay to put myself first—selfish I was never raised to be, but there are no rules against self-preservation. I wish I could take credit for learning these things myself, but I cannot. They have been taught to me by a man that is more patient and generous than time has been.

Both of those lessons brought me here today. I didn't know which of my girls to call first, but I knew neither of them was considering reaching out to me, so I ran to the first person I knew would not just think of me or reach out but would hold me and console me until this burden seemed a tad lighter.

It would not take a lifetime for this man to tire of me. Even now as I sit here waiting for my friend, I am afraid to see him. He looks at me as if I am still the size six that walked into his office thirty-some odd years and a few too many pounds ago, and that makes me feel good. His eyes have always shown me the sides of Lynette that I liked to believe were real. I was always young, desirable, and unattainable. Today I fear they will show me for just what I am, a very old lady who has out lasted her usefulness to him and them. He will be upset that I have not come sooner, that I did not allow him to be a friend to me, this one time, which may be the time I need him most. That is my hope; I pray that he is only upset. My fear is that he will be disappointed because the only family that he has known has fallen apart under my watch. My beautiful friend who has meant more to me than that simple word can contain will see me as a fraud and will be disillusioned. Without him, I would have nowhere to turn.

Dr. Flowers had been there for me when I expected no one to be; he had carried me through the hardest moments in my life, and he had become the person that I could count on. I do not know where my life would be if I lost him, so I took the easy way out and decided we could never be together in the ways most people assumed we were.

He had never once let me down in anyway. It seemed that he defied the rules of what a friend should and could be. I would not allow myself to love this man, even though it broke my heart every time I saw the need in his eyes. It hurt me knowing that I would at some point hurt him if I gave him what he wanted, and hurting him in that way would be the equivalent of allowing little pieces of me to die, and there was nothing of me to spare since it had all been given to my girls. That is the true reason why I could not be with him. So we remained friends, despite his every objection.

He would not understand this, and it was not in me to explain. I made excuses because they were all I had to offer him, excuses for not being what he needed me to be when he was more than I deserved.

This man believed that the sun rose in my eyes and that the moon controlled the sway of my hips. I needed him to see me this way. The truth would be too ugly a price to pay. There was no way I would allow him to know the real me when the one he believed suited us both so much better. Eugene did not know the way my heart threatened to give out on me every time I visited my sister's grave. He would never believe that the woman he loved had once upon a time believed that she could do a better job than her sister at raising her girls or that I had admonished Jo a million times for the way she treated her husband. It was me who made them take that trip all those years ago. My sister wanted to leave her husband. I told her she could not. I told her to fight for what she had and, more importantly, what she could make of it.

When Jolene told me she wanted to leave Wayne and take my girls away with her back to Virginia, I told her she could not. I told her I would not be able to leave my job with such short notice, and I would never let my girls be more than a few minutes away from me.

I laughed at her. I let her know that she could never survive as a single mother with two small children and nothing but her fading looks to fall back on. She would be doing them more harm than good, and that was unacceptable. It was jealousy that spoke those words that day, not because I didn't love my sister because I did and still do, but I loved her daughters much more. I told her to pack a bag for her and Wayne and use my time-share in the Pocono's to get away and fix their marriage so that when they came back, everything would be in order. That was the last time I heard her voice. I ignored her tears, and even when it was her husband who brought their daughters to me that Friday night instead of her, I made peace with my decision, knowing that everything I told her was for the benefit of those innocent girls. How was I to know then that my decision to "fix" my sister's marriage would be what caused her to lose her life and my girls to lose the innocence that I wanted them to keep?

I look to the clock again, and even though this appointment had not been scheduled, it was unlike Eugene to keep me waiting this long. I refuse to ask his receptionist the reason for the delay since I have seen the looks she gives me when I come in and have not missed the tone she uses when I call. Sarena is not old enough to understand our relationship, and even though I would love to, for just a little while, go back to the time in my life before life actually showed up and knocked me on my ass, I find that I pity her more so than I envy her. I know that she has no idea what type of relationship I share with her employer, and I do not expect her to because there is no way she can understand the depths of love I have been privileged to know. I do not resent the stares or the whispers. Knowing that someday it will all make sense to her is security enough for now. It will happen suddenly, as if overnight, she will wake up one morning, and finally understand just how hard this life can be alone, and she will know that I have done right by finding someone to share it with, even if it is not in a conventional way. I am as sure of this as I am that one day her hair will gray, her beauty fade, and the world that she thinks she has figured out will turn upside down. Been there, survived that.

There is a comfort in reaching my age because there seems to be nothing more life can throw at you without you having the last laugh. That does not mean that the next regret won't hurt as much as the last or that every heart break won't seem crippling. It means that you learn to get up a little faster. When I stumble, the man who I have come to see today is my crutch.

If I wanted to or felt in the least compelled to explain, I cannot clarify to them just what Eugene has meant to me. I do not believe that anyone could. Explaining my love for him would be just as complicated as trying to explain why a mother's kiss can erase the pain of a skinned knee. He is to me a life raft in rough currents; she could not understand that, not now anyway. I do not understand it at times either. When I feel as if the next breath will carry me over the cliff, he pulls me back to safety.

Safety is what has brought me here to the one person who has seen past my faults and loved me in spite of myself and has become my version of home. Home is where you want to be when the storm hits, and there is a storm brewing.

Tonya

The building is nondescript; nothing but the address is displayed. Had we not Googled the directions, despite being very familiar with the area, I would have sworn we were lost. The number 218 is displayed on the glass doorway, announcing that we are in fact at the right location, with a few minutes to spare.

Nothing seems official about the structure at all. I expected more, considering what is done here. The address could use another coating of paint. Fragments of gold outlined in black had begun to fade in places and chip in others, yet there was a charm about the place. It was one of those buildings that would fit perfectly in any major city as if it could be hauled across state lines on a flat bed, and no one would be any the wiser wherever it was placed.

Ready, I was not. After standing there for a few seconds, Lance presses the buzzer and squeezes my hands as he does. My dress begins to stick to my back, and I am aware of the dampness as my body shivers slightly. My husband interprets this as a need to place his arm around me. I do not have the heart to tell him that that is not what I want right now.

We are greeted at the door by a smart-looking young lady. Her cheerful disposition is a little off-putting; it seems she is as confused as the building to the nature of business conducted here. Her smile is as out of place as laughter is at a funeral home. We follow behind her into the waiting room.

Moving closer to Lance on the sitting chair, I pray silently, reminding myself to not allow my lips to move. I ask God for a double dose of Lance's charm and request that I not appear too standoffish. In the midst of my prayer, the young lady reappears. This time I notice she is wearing reading glasses. They are too big for her face.

"Dr. Taylor will be ready for you in just a few minutes. Is there anything I can get the two of you?" Her too-big smile appears again, and I want to tell her exactly what she can get for me. Instead I shake my head no. I do not frown, but I refuse to return her smile.

She reacts as if no is not an answer she is accustomed to. No longer do I see her as smart, she too is part of a mirage. Slowly I am seeing past the image, and I am greeted by dry sand. Her talents seem to only include answering the buzzer and asking if anyone is in the mood for beverages. This is obvious by the way she pauses in front of us, unsure if she should move or not. We are saved by the parting of wooden doors. The receptionist's tension dissipates, and mine goes into over drive. She returns to her desk in the corner of the room.

I grab Lance's hand as we stand in unison.

"Mr. and Mrs. Lawson, thank you for waiting. I am Dr. Taylor. Please come in."

She steps aside, allowing us to walk in front of her. There are no sofas; instead, there are two chairs waiting for us. The office looked inviting enough, a subtle hint of orderly chaos. Apparently we had interrupted her lunch. I wish I could ask if we could reschedule, but I do not want to ask anything more from her assistant. The polite thing would be to apologize for the inconvenience.

Cowardly moments do creep in every so often, and admittedly I want to run. Subconsciously, that is why I chose to wear wedged sandals instead of the strapped yellow ones with the black heels I had originally chosen when I purchased this dress. I allow Lance to walk in first though he had motioned with his hands for me to. I wanted him in the chair closest to her; there was only about a centimeter of a difference, but it was enough for me.

We all take our places and wait for her to start.

"Have you ever done this before, spoken with a therapist?" She presses the button on a small tape recorder.

"Yes." We both answer in unison; however, my voice had been a little too loud for the size of the room.

"Couples or individual?"

"Couples," Lance responds.

"Both," I share.

"That can be a blessing and a curse." Dr. Taylor smiles as she says this. I wonder what the heck they are drinking here and regret my decision not to accept the refreshments offered. Whatever they are sipping appears to cause temporary memory loss. I am beginning to think that Lance and I are the only ones who know why we are here. "I do things a little different than most therapists. For example, I have the benefit of knowing what brings you here, so I like to skip the traditional question-and-answer section for our first meeting. Instead I'd like to try something a little different." She stands abruptly and walks over to her desk. She returns with her hands full.

"Tell me about yourself. Write down whatever you want me to know about you as an individual and as a couple. Take the whole session if you'd like. Think about what you need to say to me. Use this as an opportunity. I will tailor our meetings around the things you chose to share and, sometimes what is more important, the things you don't." She handed both of us a legal notepad and a pen. Our court-appointed therapist is asking us to sum our life up into a few paragraphs and asking as if it were not the most arduous task ever presented.

"Not prepared" is now an understatement. This is a challenge. We had rehearsed the question and answer portion, based upon our past experiences and a list of questions our attorney had come up with. Arnold agreed, we were charming, endearing, and most of all, we seemed credible during our many practice runs. Everything had been choreographed, down to when I would gently grab my husband's hand or when he would place his on my knee. Even the style of my hair had been designed to create a situation wherein he'd have to gently sweep it away from my face so that I could look deeply into his eyes as I profess how the situation had not been easy but we had still grown closer. *Deflated* is a very apt description of what I am feeling right now.

I do not think the written translation will be as charming as the verbal version. Instead, I am to write down these things, which will not flow without being prompted. Lance will not be able to teasingly interrupt when she asks how we met. Playful banter will not be an option as we "argue" about the color of my dress the night he proposed.

If I am writing these things down, Lance will not have the chance to kiss my hand when I get choked up at the mention of my sister's treachery. I need him to do that for me. Without him, I come across as bitter.

Our therapist is asking us to reveal ourselves to her completely; I do not understand the benefit in that, considering we were not looking for treatment. Admittedly she knows why we are here, and just like any other doctor, she enjoys playing the role of savior, something we are not in the market for. Revealing too much was not an option. Not sharing enough would be the equivalent of admitting there was something we had to hide. I shut down immediately. This was not what we planned, and I need consistency, or I will unravel.

Because I am angered by her decision to throw a wrench into my carefully constructed two-man play, I cannot bring myself to look at her directly. Dr. Taylor's peach-colored blouse becomes my focus. When I am confronted with something too difficult, I allow my mind to wander, one of my many coping mechanisms.

Focus, breathe, breathe, and focus, I remind myself over and over again in my head. I place both feet firmly on the ground, and I begin to take in air slowly through my nose, exhaling out of my mouth. I am trying to prevent a panic attack.

"I am not sure what you are asking us to do." Arnold told us we were required to have six sessions with this woman; he had pushed to make it ten. I am sure he thought this would benefit us, expecting that even I could eventually grow on anyone. Her decision would weigh heavily with the courts. I am not sure if I should be grateful for the extra time or resentful of it. Ten sessions totaled five hundred minutes. That wouldn't even be considered a good night's sleep. Definitely it is not enough time to determine if I am fit to do anything but stand under a microscope.

Tilting her head as if she were addressing a child, Dr. Taylor smiles. "I have done this a thousand times, and I can only imagine how you two must feel, having a complete stranger ask you to tell her the most intimate parts of your life without so much as an introduction. There is a method to my madness, if you will. I did not get here overnight. Trust me when I say anything that I ask is for your benefit. It is amazing to learn what you think of yourself when given the opportunity to write things down. Sometimes the revelations alone open floodgates, I think you'd be surprised." She leans forward, trying to minimize the intentional space I have placed between us while she was giving her speech. "I am not your enemy, and I hope that you do not see me that way." Her tone implies that the thought alone hurts her feelings.

Briefly I am saddened by the thought. It is easy to tell she has spent her life making friends; if we had met at a different time and place, I am sure I would have liked her. Maybe she would've liked me also.

"I am asking you to tell me whatever you want me to know about you. For example, tell me what you hope to gain from our sessions or any fears you may have about them as well. Tell me about the type of parents you want to be. No matter how prepared you are for it, there is always some apprehension. The decision is yours. Whatever you write will stay between us, so be as open as possible." This is lie number one, if we are to keep track. It is only fair to note that Dr. Taylor has told the first one. "Here's a trick that may make it easier. Think of me as a friend you haven't spoken to in a while. Catch me up on your life as you see it." The grin returns again as if she has said something inspirational. She is pleased with herself; her smile is easy, and surely she uses it often, which is an enigma, considering she mostly meets people at the worst times in their life. Had I not come prepared with a wall around me, she certainly would have gained some ground with her polite disposition alone, but the wall has been placed, and the line has been drawn with her standing on the opposite side.

I am not sure what I expected from this session or the doctor, but this is not it. In all fairness, Lance and I had done some research on her first. That is something my husband does, and not surprising at all, it is something he is wonderful at—researching. What makes this situation absurd is that I am rattled by the fact that Dr. Taylor wants me to reveal myself to her when I should be thankful that she has at least asked for permission to peek into my life, a courtesy Lance and I did not extend to her.

Sitting across from this woman, I feel guilty. Admittedly we pried into her life, without so much as a hesitation on our part, and I am frightened by the possibility of what she might find or not find in my words if I give her what she asks for. I stare at the pen as if it were a hot coal. She expects me to juggle, attributing it to my guilty conscience, since I know more about her than I think she could imagine; it is amazing what the Internet and the right investigator can find out about anyone.

Her name is Denise Marie Taylor. She is a few years younger than me, single, and is not a Philadelphia native. She interned in the city and fell in love with the culture shortly after graduating from college. She has worked for the state after quitting a lucrative private practice for almost five years now.

As a child, Denise was a classically trained dancer and had been considered a prodigy. Sadly her foot had been broken in a car accident caused by a drunk driver at the age of seventeen, changing her life in an instant. Her mother had blamed herself for the mishap, believing that her decision to leave at that very moment stripped her daughter of her only dream; ironically she began to drink heavily after.

I consider being honest or at least as honest as discretion allows. But I do not understand how this is designed to build trust when I know that anything shared here will be far from confidential; the reason for the meeting is to disclose her findings to the court.

Could she answer this question herself? I bite my tongue so that I don't ask her. Something is missing, though she seems completely at ease in her surroundings, and I can tell despite the countless accolades, she is still waiting for more. Misery does not necessarily love company, but it does recognize it when it appears. If I handed her a legal pad and a pen, expecting her to divulge her life story to me, I do not assume she would meet me with graciousness either.

A few minutes pass, and I have given no hint as to whether or not I am willing to complete her requested task. I am now wondering where she has hidden the timer since there are no clocks in here.

I should definitely include somewhere in there that I have found my "mean side." In the past few days, I have found it easier to lash out. This is the second stage of grief, the anger stage; I do not know how long it will last, considering the denial phase passed away so quickly. We should have stuck with the choreographed version for all our sakes.

Besides, she should know all of these things. There is nothing that I can write down that she has not read already. It would not surprise me if our file had been an inch thick. Arnold and Veronica had submitted facts already. Our educational backgrounds and the reports from child services on the safety of our homes were sure to be included as well.

This woman would be the one to make or break me, and she is asking that I write out all the reasons why she should hang or pardon us. It did not seem responsible on her part. Truthfully, I could tell her anything. It is not as if the pen or paper could prevent me from stretching or ignoring certain facts. Dr. Taylor seems more intelligent than this. It would be too easy to verify things, but she is not the courts. She does not need evidence. Most of what she does is based upon things that are not exactly concrete. There is no way to quantify someone's feelings or thoughts. No measurements have been designed to understand exactly why the human mind and heart react a certain way. So many things about her job are based upon speculations and surely impressions. Question and answer would be easier; again I curse her for not using standard methods.

I am taking too long to jot down these few sentences. How long does it take to reveal one's self to a stranger who has more control over your life than you do? More than likely, if I pick up the pen I have placed on the table, my paragraph would contain nothing but questions, most of which no one can answer.

Simply put, I want her to know that I am the best choice, the only choice. Listing my sister's faults would have been a better request; asking me why my husband would be the best father would have been easier. Instead she wants to know about me, and that is intimidating.

I would rather use a pencil, but judging by the various plaques on the wall, I am certain she chose to provide us with pens for a reason. Final, the words on this sheet of paper would be absolute. There is no option to erase and start over, even my mistakes will be left, written in blue ink, for her to decipher.

I pick up the pen and set it down almost immediately after as if it had burned me. I search her eyes. Dr. Taylor had paid more attention to me than my husband since we entered her office over twelve minutes ago now. She is searching me as well, waiting for my response to this task. Certainly my hesitation will be noted, but I do not want to rush into anything either. Whatever I choose to write, I will have to commit myself to. My hands are back in my lap, and I use my thumb to turn my engagement ring around my finger. Nervous energy has to be radiating from me; Lance is oblivious to it as he continues to write.

"Tell me what you're feeling right now." This is directed toward me, and without giving much thought, I shrug my shoulders like a sullen child. "Why are you apprehensive?" She has picked up a pen of her own, opened her notepad, and leaned closer all in one swift motion as she waits for my response. My husband pauses, and for the first time, he notices I have not written anything. He stares at the blank page and then at me.

"I'm just not sure what you expect me to write." Are the words that come out of my mouth replacing my original thought to ask her what it is she wanted me to say? If she told me what she wanted, I would give it to her. I would write it in the elegant scroll I had been praised for my entire life. If she doesn't, I am afraid I will throw a tantrum. *Give me direction* is what I want to scream at her. *Tell me what you are looking for, and I will become that if I am not already.*

"I want you to tell me the truth about you." The doctor says this as if it will make things easier. Truth. A five-letter word that holds more implication then she intended it to. The truth is I should not be here. The truth is that I know she is already forming her opinions about me, and I am powerless to change her mind, which is comical considering the truth is that I am not sure exactly who I am, though she must certainly have her own ideas. I could tell her who I was a few months ago. That would be easy. She wants to know who I am today, sitting in this office, and who I will be if ever given the opportunity to walk out of the courtroom with my child in my arms.

Justification is what she is looking for, a piece of paper she can pull out later and claim this is the reason she voted either way. My mind keeps coming back to that one tricky word, *truth*. Is there such a thing? My truths may be different from someone else's, but that is not her concern. She is expecting my version of it about myself.

"I was not prepared for this. We've gone through marriage counseling, and my sister and I were forced into grief counseling as children. I have never been asked about myself, more so told what I must be feeling, or how I should be feeling. I'm sorry you didn't ask me about my feelings did you, you asked me about myself."

She is now concerned. I have seen this look before. It is a look given when a stranger is not certain of exactly how to interpret your words.

"May I have some water and a few minutes please?" Round one is definitely not looking too good for us.

"Tonya, I will not patronize you by saying I understand what you must be going through. What I can say is that heartbreak, disappointments, and setbacks are experienced by all of us. I know this for a fact. I have experienced these things too."

Comparing her desire to be a dancer with my need to be a mother is a testament to how unforgiving life could be. For seventeen years she had dedicated herself to music; for a lifetime I have dedicated myself to the idea that I would be able to love another human being in the way that only a mother could know. Options had presented themselves to her; for me there were no more options. This was my last chance. She had a fallback plan; for me there isn't one.

She could pretend if she needed, and I would see past all of it because I know her truth more than I know my own. No other option will ever be right for me. I could never fathom loving another or opening my heart so freely to anyone but my daughter.

There is nothing to say, and I wait for her to continue. "Life can be hard, and to be honest, for some people, it is much harder than others, but those experiences are what make the journey. You can never have a true understanding of what makes something sweet until you've tasted bitter. That is the irony and the beauty of life. There is an opposite to any and every thing. Even the pain you must be feeling right now. But I will let you in on a little secret about life: no matter how hard it may be for some or how easy it appears for others, none of us make it out alive."

That causes Lance to chuckle a little. The sound should put me at ease, but it does not. He is obviously comfortable with her.

She clears her throat to see if I am paying attention. Just as she has, I have made my decision on the outcome of our sessions. There is no way this woman will ever understand me, and I will pretend to be what she wants me to be. Now it is my turn to smile and nod politely as if her speech had somehow given me the epiphany I had been waiting for. This pleases her.

"In regards to you and your husband, my goal is to help you get through this no matter what the judge decides. I am not just working in the capacity of the court. I have devoted the whole of my adult life to ensuring that families stay together, that children are protected, and that the best possible results are reached."

Lance reaches for my hand; apparently he has had his fill of the Kool-Aid and decided that I too should have my portion of it. His finished paragraph has taken up three quarters of the first page. I am unable to read what he has written. This was done purposefully considering the angle he placed his notepad on the table. I am not sure if I want to know. I feel betrayed because this was easy for him. He did not understand that this was a game, and we will either play or be played.

"This is hard for me. I may be overthinking it. I often make things harder than necessary." Now they are both looking at me with concern.

"There is nothing wrong with feeling. God wouldn't have given them to us if he didn't want us to use them." She hands me a tissue for the tears I did not know were there until the moment she squeezes my hand. Dr. Taylor now looks at my husband as if he will have the answer.

"Lance, would you like to help her. I would assume you are the one person who knows her best. Tell me something about your wife, anything at all." Again Dr. Taylor hands me the pen and pad.

"No," I say with more assertiveness than I intended. My husband will not be forced to lie for me. "I can do this. I will do this." My stomach tumbles as I speak these words.

Another few minutes pass by, the pen is still in my hand. I have done what was asked of me. I rambled, which is much more attractive when spoken aloud. Some sentences injured me more as I wrote them, yet others seemed like a breath of fresh air.

This was therapeutic, and I understand why it was necessary. Life for me is not as well-ordered as it may have been when I set upon this journey so long ago. There were snags and missteps, but I am finding my footing, and it has taken me on a trip that I never imagined.

I did not see life this way before; I did not see the beauty in the promise of the next day, or the sweetness in the memories of yesterday. I am angry yes, but I am not bitter. Anger is just another emotion I will work my way through. These revelations are too much for a paragraph or two, so I keep them for myself.

I place the notepad on the coffee table in front of me and lay the pen on top of it. I pick up my purse and walk out of the room. I am not sure if it is customary. I do not care at all. There is nothing more I can gain today, nothing more I can give. There is always the next session.

When I finally reach the parking garage, Lance has made his way to my side. I am sure he made excuses enough to last a lifetime for me. I do not want to know. I do not care what he thought to say. I reach for his hand; it is waiting for mine. This time, I squeeze, letting him know I am okay.

Then he kisses my hand, sweetly, while no one is looking, and I am glad we did not have to pretend in front of a stranger. This is what my marriage is about, the quiet moments shared between best friends. I am sure the doctor read my thoughts first. I do not know how much insight she will gain from my words, and I do not care either way.

I am sure by now she has picked up the pad I wonder how she will view me after reading my words.

> If you asked me for my truth a few months, maybe even a few weeks ago, it would be much different. I no longer know what is true or what is not. I have lost touch with so much of myself, but I'd be lying if I said I hadn't discovered pieces along the way. I will start with the basics.
>
> I am a twin, though that concept seems foreign to me now, and I am afraid of this. I have always been identified as the other one, or Toya's sister. That is a part of me that

has been misplaced, and strangely it is not as missed as I would have thought. Our parents died when we were nine, and I believe that is when the first part of me went missing along with them. Maybe they took it into the next life; that thought comforts me since I have never considered it before. I miss them every single day with my entire heart. I was never their favorite, and I did not need to be. My sister did. She has always needed to be first, it was enough for me to know that they loved me. I have resigned myself to this simply because there is nothing else I can do about it. We were raised by our aunt, who has loved us for our whole life. As I write I am conscious of the amount of times I say we or our or even us. My life has been a constant strand of "we," "our "and "us." I know that does not make sense, but it doesn't stop it from being true for as long as I can remember.

I went straight from my aunts home to my husband's. I have never had to be alone, though I have often felt lonely. I have been lucky enough to marry my first and, up until a few weeks ago, my only love. Marriage has not been easy, and I have made my mistakes, but never have I stopped loving him. It would be easier for me to stop breathing purposefully than to stop loving this man. He has taught me so much about myself just by loving me endlessly. It is an amazing feeling, overwhelming at times, but amazing. If there were a rule book on the way a man should love his wife, Lance would be the one to write it. If I could be some of what he sees in me, then I must be remarkable.

I have a daughter. I am blessed to say those words because I never thought I would be able to. I have a daughter whose heartbeat I feel inside of me stronger than my own. Even though I have never carried her there physically, I have carried her inside of my spirit from the moment I heard her heartbeat in the doctor's office. It was so fast, incredible, and I fell head over heels in love with her that very moment. I can still close my eyes and hear the tiny *thump*, *thump* that would be my call to motherhood. It was like a ritualistic drum, and I knew I would be powerless to run from it. Her heart calls out to mine with every beat, and my every breath is a response. She is the person I am living for. I have a daughter. This is the truth that is holding me together like a string, and my sister wants to take that from me. She wants to unravel my life in the way one does an old frayed sweater, removing the hanging thread that seems so inconsequential at first. One firm tug will be my undoing.

I am sure you want to know how that makes me feel, where my truth is in that. I want to hate her. I think it would be easier for me to actually do so, but it is hard. She is nowhere to be found, and I cry for her at night as much as I cry for myself. I am the only one who knows just how fragile she is, and I am the one she is pushing away. She is distraught too, and this has been done by her own hand. I do not know how she could ever find peace in that, how she will reconcile herself to the fact that she has been her own undoing. When she finally does, I do not trust I will have the strength to help her put her life back together again. In the briefest of moments, I do allow myself to feel sorry for her, but I cannot hate her. I do not have the energy to do so. I am reminded that this joy that I have found in the tiny hands, the smoothest skin, and the sweetest-smelling breath of my daughter is possible because my sister said yes.

That one yes should outweigh any other no. It does not erase them though. My heart is torn; she has apologized for hurting me, which is laughable. Hurt is too small of a word. It is tiny in comparison to what she has actually done. She has damaged me.

Sometimes I feel like there is nothing left of me. All that I was born to give has been used up, and I am wasted. I am empty.

At those times, I remember that I am someone's mother, and I am the example she will look to when she is older. We all reach a certain age, and we make a choice.

It is subconscious, but a decision is made. We decide as women whether we will be like our mother or not. I want to be the woman my daughter wants to be, so when I feel empty, I reach down for more of myself, when I want to give up, I find strength from places I didn't know I had. I love without fear of being hurt again, and I give freely of myself.

That is all I can say about myself. Every day before life gets too hectic and I am pulled in a thousand directions, I pray that God makes me a woman that my daughter would be proud to call her mother. I ask that she finds something in me that makes her want to be better someday as well because she has restored me in ways I cannot begin to say.

The woman I was weeks ago would not recognize the one sitting here today. She would be outraged by a few things but proud of me all the same. She will wonder how it is that I have not completely lost my faith. I would tell her one thing simply. My faith has been my foundation. I will not turn my back on a Creator that saw it fit to make a place in this world for my daughter, and if it is his will that I not see tomorrow, today was sweet because I know she is here.

Toya

I hate running late for things I deem important. I am always on time. This meeting is very important, and I could kick myself for not being more punctual. Ronnie's at fault. She called me thirteen times this morning alone. I stopped answering after the fourth call. Thinking my attorney had my best interest at heart has afforded her quite a few passes in the way I have let her speak to me. Now I am exasperated; she addresses me as if I am a spoiled child that she has lost patience with.

"It is essential that you seem in control yet receptive. Maintain good eye contact, but do not stare. Do not minimize what hurt you have caused Mrs. Lawson, but emphasize your willingness to meet your sister halfway." That was her last voice message though she had said those same things countless times before. Also, I hate the way she references my sister as Mrs. Lawson, as if she has no other identity. She is either my sister or Lance's wife. Ronnie was the queen of minimization.

My attorney makes me nervous. She is the only person I have ever met that made me second guess myself. I have been doing too much of that lately. My reaction time has slowed, and I hope

I do carry this with me into the operating room when I decide to go back to work. I have taken a brief hiatus until this custody battle has been resolved. I do not have the ability to juggle the situation with my sister and the stress of the job. I needed my other half to keep me balanced.

Being a surgeon has spoiled me in certain aspects. I do not claim to be God, but I do believe while I am operating that His hand guides me. That is one of the things that separates me from my peers. I am not overly religious. Outside of the operating room, I find it hard to pray, not because I don't want to, but because I never know what to ask. There, in that room, with others surrounding me, waiting for me to perform some type of miracle, I humble myself. I ask God to guide me, and I believe he does. There I never second guess myself. There I am at peace with every decision because I know they are not mine. As every surgeon does, I always go in with a plan; things change, and I am never frightened when they do. That is the way I lived my life. I plan to improvise. But as of late, that strategy has failed me.

For example, my morning had been planned out. Shower, breakfast, feed McKenzie, dress, do something with my hair, which is now in that horrible in-between stage, and then head out the door to this meeting. There was just enough time to spare for me to grab a cup of coffee from the shop around the corner, leaving a few minutes to get here and seem refreshed.

There is a difference between sleeplessness and the "new mommy" restless nights. Tonya and Lance are still making their nightly visits, and I am unable to sleep through them. I wish things were easier.

Not so long ago, I would be out of it before my head ever even hit the pillow. I would fall asleep in whatever manner I made it to my bedroom. More often than not, I'd wake in my scrubs sometimes, with one or both shoes on. Once or twice, I had slept with no pants even though I was still wearing my sneakers, having no idea how I had managed to get them off without undoing my footwear. No matter what state of dress I woke in, I always felt reinvigorated. I used to sleep for more than twelve hours straight, but now I find that I am only afforded a few hours at a time, and those are far from relaxing.

This morning I woke startled. I knew there was something I had to do and some place I had to be, but I could not place my finger on it at first. There is always a feeling of immediate panic when my alarm goes off, and it seems to take longer for the cloudiness in my head to dissipate. Ronnie had woken me up a full half an hour before my alarm clock was due to go off, causing me to hit the snooze button one too many times.

The coffee that I refused to do without is now seeping its way under my white blouse. I was trying to go for a more casual look since I am certain my sister went for the conservative one. I wanted to paint the differences between us for the doctor. Instead I have managed to arrive not just late but also covered in a sticky morning beverage.

I reach into my black Birkin bag and pull out wipes. I'd rather be late than on time but appearing disheveled. Settling for a plain white camisole, a black jacket, pastel pink dress pants, and black Christian Loubouton's, I look the part—chic, timeless, and most importantly, motherly, or my version of it. Surprisingly enough, this outfit had been approved by my attorney.

"If you feel comfortable in your clothes, you will come across as comfortable in your skin."

We had spent the day going over exactly what I would wear, what I would say, and more importantly, how I would say those things.

Tonya had the advantage of meeting Dr. Taylor first. I had drawn the short end of the stick, I am sure. When she arrived at my home last night, I wanted to ask her what she had already discussed about me. Using her first hour to throw dirt would have been the smart thing to do. Definitely my approach. Now, that would be impossible. I would come across as hostile and jealous if I tried to bad-mouth my sister this late in the game. LaTonya has a helplessness about her that is not just endearing at times, but it can also be her strongest card. Thankfully for me, she has no idea how to play it.

Twin lacked the killer instinct; she would rather sit politely on the sidelines, avoiding any possibility of getting dirty. I had mastered the art of slinging mud and always coming out clean on the other side. Some things just can't be taught. Now it would be impossible not to picture her belittling me in front of this stranger. I have given her more than a fair share of dirt to throw.

Speaking of which, the baby wipe is doing little to remove the stain from my blouse. I passed an Old Navy on my way; I walk back in the direction I came. I couldn't afford to be any later, but my pride would not allow me to show up unkempt either. I figured it would take me about eight minutes round trip and approximately five in the store if I'm lucky. In all, I should be no more than twenty minutes late.

Pulling out my cell, I dial the therapist's number.

"Doctor Taylor's office, how may I help you?"

I pull the phone back from my ear; the voice on the other end was a tad too loud for my liking.

"Yes, my name is Dr. LaToya Garrett, and I had, um I mean I have a nine o'clock appointment. I am running a little late. I am stuck in traffic, but I should be there in the next few minutes." As if on cue, someone honks their horn and yells out an obscenity at the driver in front of them. Thankfully there are still impatient people in this world.

"That shouldn't be a problem. I will let the doctor know. Please give us a call back if you do not think you will be able to make it."

"I certainly will."

That was easy enough. I am in and out of the store with very little hassle. Within a few minutes, I am back where I started, having enough sense to hand my coffee to the woman at the register for her to toss away.

I rinse my hands again on yet another baby wipe and then ring the bell. Before my finger has even left the buzzer, I am greeted by a young lady. I open my mouth to apologize; she is not going to allow me to.

"Would you like anything to drink?" she asks while rushing me forward. "We have coffee, tea, or water." I know she would prefer that I answer as quickly as she is speaking to me, so I do not think about it, and I ask for bottled water. I did not want her to fumble over the questions that come along with any coffee order—cream, sugar, or sweetener. I am already late, and I can tell by the haste in her step that the question is more of a courtesy than a concern.

"Dr. Garrett, hello, I am Dr. Taylor. It is nice to meet you. Please come in. We have so little time, and this session is one of the most important." Dr. Taylor smiles at me, and I cannot tell if she is at all upset about my being late.

"I apologize. The traffic was horrendous." I try to match her reassuring smile.

"It's understandable. We will try to schedule our sessions at a later time. That way we can avoid the inconvenience." Obviously she is annoyed with my tardiness.

"It should not be a problem in the future." I take my seat, and before I can say anything else, the secretary enters with my water. She closes the door behind her, and I wonder how much privacy the sliding doors offer. Her assistant may know more secrets than what she lets on. I do not think I would have the resolve not to eavesdrop as well. I take a polite sip of the water and place it on top of the coffee table.

"I will try to speed through this since we are already at a disadvantage when it comes to time. I am told you have entered counseling before, is that correct?" Was she allowed to tell me that? She didn't say she had read it; instead, she was told. I would assume that is something my sister revealed to her.

"I am sorry, I am wondering why that would matter."

The therapist is taken off guard by my comment. *Shit.* That is not the way I wanted to start off. First I was late, and now I am being offensive.

"I mean yes, I have been in therapy before." The smile is back, but this time it is not genuine.

"I did not ask to offend. Normally I would give a speech letting you know that I do things a little differently, but we no longer have the luxury of time. So I will get the ball rolling." She hands me a fresh legal pad and a pen. "I'd like to start by asking you to write down whatever it is you'd like me to know about you. I will tailor our sessions around the things you choose to share and the things you may overlook. I'd like you to sum your life up into one paragraph."

"How long can it be?" I ask while searching my bag. Superstitious, I would not consider myself, though I do have a few quirks. I am looking for *my* pen; I usually carry one with me wherever I go. My penmanship has always been awful; my sister had joked when I finished medical school that I already had the horrible handwriting that it took most doctors years to master. I relied on certain ink to mask my terrible scribble; truthfully I wrote with as much skill as a serial killer. It would be better if I just cut out newspaper clippings to get my point across.

"I'm sorry, I prefer to use a certain pen, and I am sure I have one in here. This bag is huge, and it doubles as a diaper bag at times as well." I am searching for some form of levity and missing the mark. The therapist starts to write something down onto her own legal pad.

"I am not trying to avoid the question," I say into my bag, which now seems like a bottomless pit. Rummaging around inside of it, I am sure I look like a lunatic. What is wrong with me? More importantly, how many times will I have to ask myself this question?

"Just one minute, and I will start, I promise." Now the panic sets in. I am not sure if I'm more concerned by the way I must appear or by the way the doctor is not interjecting. If she just said the pen was trivial and that it did not matter, I would stop searching for it, but she is allowing me to do so. Now it seems impossible for me to stop looking. I want her to know that there is in fact a pen in my purse, and I am not using this as a stall tactic.

Pulling out lipstick, mascara, and other minor things, I begin to feel claustrophobic. Knowing that something is unimportant does not stop me from making it significant in my mind. I place the located items next to me in my chair. I lean forward and place the bag on the table, hoping to give myself a better vantage point while simultaneously knocking my water over.

Great, not only was I late, I am searching for a pen, which may not exist, and now I have managed to spill water on my therapist.

"I am so sorry." This time I reach in my bag for something that will be of use and pull out a tightly folded cloth diaper. The swift tug causes all the contents of the bag to fall onto the floor, but I ignore this and rush over to the doctor to remove the liquid from the bottom of her pants. I am reminded of patients vomiting on my scrubs. It is an occupational hazard, and the patients always seem so embarrassed, which makes it all the more uncomfortable for me. I know I am causing the same discomfort for Dr. Taylor, but I am powerless to stop myself from trying to correct the mistake.

"That is not necessary. Things happen, and it is just water." She tries to remove my hand from her leg, and I back away, falling into a bookcase. This is what my life has boiled down to: sitting in a room with a complete stranger, unable to stop myself from coming undone. Reminding myself that this is not the time or the place causes more anxiety. I wish I just canceled.

There I sit on my behind afraid that one more movement might just bring the whole place down, and I know it is coming. Usually I have the ability to stop these things, but I can't, not this time. Blaming the hormones in my head while whispering profanities, I begin to sob uncontrollably.

Now it is the doctor's turn to come to my rescue.

"You are a lot like that bag you're carrying around, aren't you?" Instead of waiting for me to answer, I think we are both aware I would be unable to, she continues. "You, like your bag, are well put together on the outside, functional, fashionable, not a stitch out of place, but still a mess inside." This makes me cry harder.

"Do you want to take a break? It is okay to ask for space sometime. I won't force you to do anything you don't want to." Dr. Taylor says as she places another tissue into my shaking hands.

"No, but I don't think I can write anything right now. Is it all right if I just talk?" It takes me longer to say those words than it should have. In between sobbing, I manage to spit them out.

"Take a second. I will get you another bottle of water, and we can talk while I help you put your purse back together." With that, she exits the room. Thankfully she gives me another minute or so before she returns.

"Where should I start?" This time I do not open the bottle of water that has been handed to me.

"Next session I will ask you to write about you. This session I will allow you to start wherever you feel necessary." She smiles a reassuring smile that places me at ease. For some reason I believe that she wants to help.

"I didn't plan on hurting my sister." I pause, waiting for her to pass judgment. When there is no response, I continue. "There was always something missing. I have never felt at home anywhere except for the operating room. I have never felt like I had a friend besides my twin. She was always the one person who loved me in spite of everything I have ever done. There is no way I can explain to her why I did it because she can't understand."

This time the doctor does say something. "Why do you think she won't understand? You may need to explain it to her just as much as she may need you to."

"I wish I could. I wish she could understand, but she won't be able to."

"Do you think it is fair of you to make the assumption? You of course would know your sister better than I. But everyone wants an explanation when they are hurt. Most people call it closure. Even when we ask for an explanation, no one ever truly understands why someone hurt them. It is the fact that you are willing to offer an answer that sometimes make the hurt easier to bare. Does that make sense?"

I nod my head yes because in some small way I do understand how it can hurt more not to know the reason why, but I also understand that the why in this case will not be enough for my sister.

"Tell me what you would want to tell Tonya. Even if you do not choose to share your reasons with her, it may offer you some comfort if you walk yourself through it."

"I never planned on doing this. I have said that a million times, and it is losing effect if it was ever believed, but I had no intentions of betraying my sister. She has been for me everything, and I have never told her that, but it is without any hesitation the one thing I can say with sincerity. When she asked me to be her surrogate, I wanted to say no for various reasons, and mostly I did not want to be the one to tell her it didn't work. I didn't want to be the one who would possibly give her bad news, worse yet, the person she could blame if it did not work. She wouldn't have said anything to me directly because that was never her style. Instead she would have blamed me in secret, and it would have killed me to cause her anymore pain. It sounds ridiculous, I know, but it is true. After a few agonizing days, I promised her I would do it. This was the one time where I put her first, and I am thankful every single day that I did. In some way, I wanted to vindicate myself; for all the things I took from her, I wanted to give her the thing she wanted most in life. So I agreed to put my life on hold; nine months seemed such a short time when compared to a lifetime."

"The day we went to the doctors, she was so nervous, she was shaking, and I wanted to comfort her. I remember thinking how beautiful she was, how striking, even if she didn't know it. She had been through so much, and still she could smile at me and believe that life would get better. I loved that I was a part of that for her because all I have ever wanted was for my sister to have everything she deserves. Lance chauffeured us to the appointment. We sat in the back of the car giggling at all the possibilities. We guessed what the sex would be, where he or she would go to college, whether it would be a doctor like me or a lawyer like Lance. We wanted so much for a baby that was nothing more at that point than a possibility. She promised me that I would be more than an aunt, that she expected me to be there for everything. That was the first time she mentioned me coming to live with them.

"I said yes to anything she asked. At that time everything was for them. I listened as my sister told me her fears and her hopes, and I prayed that she would be right, that the insemination would take, and finally she would be whole. I knew that feeling. I understood her emptiness, and for a brief moment, I wished that I could have been enough for her because she had been for me since our parents died. I quickly pushed those thoughts aside. It was easier then, simply because I knew if there was ever anything that meant as much to me, Tonya would have given it to me, even if it meant killing herself to do so.

"Tonya and Lance stayed in the room while the doctor released the sperm, and I reached for her hand the moment the doctor told me to take a deep breath, and she reached for mine as well. We laughed because that was the most familiar thing in the world to us. She always knew when I needed her hand, and I had always known when she wanted mine.

"Her hand was so cool, and I held onto her as if both of our lives depended on it. I know there are people who claim they know right away when they conceive, and I never ever thought it was possible. Then it happened to me, I felt inside my heart that it worked, that it would work for them. I told her so right then before the doctor had left the room. I told her we were having a baby, and just like I knew it, she did as well. Without warning we both began to cry. When she pulled her other hand away from Lance to place it on my cheek and kiss me, I realized then how warm she was. It was comforting but wrong, if that makes any sense at all.

"The other hand that was still in mine was cool, not as cold as it was at first, but much cooler than the one she was using to wipe away my tears forgetting about her own, and I felt hollow again. She had someone in this world, someone who was hers, and I knew then I would never have what she had. I wasn't jealous, I was saddened by it. The realization took my breath away. She was no longer the other half of me. I was blinded to this truth for so long. I guess I ignored Lance's place in her life. I love my brother-in-law. I love him for what he was for my sister and who he has been in our family. I never really gave him credit. To me he was a distraction—I guess that would be harsh—instead I will say he was a replacement for when I was unavailable, and I accepted that. In fact, I welcome it. My sister needed someone to hold her hand when it wasn't feasible for me to be there. I loved him for holding my place for me because that is how I viewed him, a placeholder. Then it seemed crystal clear that he was her completion, and I would remain pieces of a whole for the rest of my life.

"My sister had someone who loved her in the same way she loved me, in a way that I could never give back. I saw it for the first time that day. She would always love me for what I did for her. I knew that was true, but part of me felt her slipping away right there as she held my hand. There would be no place for me. She would have the family she always wanted, she found what was missing, and I wanted to give it to her, but I was apprehensive about the day I would have to because that would be the same day she would be whole, and I would be obsolete to her.

"I know it sounds selfish, and I do not take any pleasure in my sister's pain, but admittedly, I do miss the time when I was for her what she has always been for me. There is no name for it, no way to explain or describe what being a twin means. It goes beyond a sibling. We share more than DNA, we share more than memories. She was the center of my world. She gave me balance. She was not just my twin, she was part of me. I know I am a part of her as well, but that day, I felt that part shrinking.

"Exactly two weeks later, we were given the good news, though I already knew I was pregnant. Once again we all cried, but this time the distance between us was more pronounced, and I fought it as much as I could. I felt amazing. There was someone growing inside of me, and that feeling surpasses all human understanding. Inside of me I was carrying the future, a sentiment I am sure is shared by millions, and we all believe our child will grow up to somehow save the world, but it was greater than that for me. I knew that the possibilities for this child were endless. I have never felt more alive or stronger or brilliant in my own right. I finally felt whole, like the piece that was missing since my parents died had finally been placed back where it belonged.

"Still I did not think of betraying my sister. Instead I focused on the miraculous task placed before me. I changed my whole life. I ate better, exercised, slept regularly, and began to read the same books my sister had. I wanted to give that child every advantage before she was born. I had even began to read to her at night even when I knew she could not hear. The routine was more so for me than anything, but it made me feel a part of something—no, not something, *someone*. I was connected to someone again.

"When my daughter moved for the first time, I couldn't tell anyone. I kept it to myself. My sister had read every book on expecting, and she called me every single day on the hour during the sixteenth week to find out if I had felt him or her, and I lied, I couldn't bring myself to share it with her. She blamed herself, as is her norm, and decided then that I was to come live with them. She said it was her way of keeping my life as stress-free as possible. She demanded that I cut back at work, and that I never be alone. My twin had never demanded anything of or from me, but this time I was not able to tell her no. Shortly after, I found out the sex of the baby, and it was another delicious secret I had, one that was acceptable not to share. Our baby girl, even now when I say it I smile. I talked to my daughter like she was my best friend, and I loved the way my skin stretched in response to her every move. I giggled when she had hiccups and laughed at the way she moved in response to Lance or Tonya's voice. I was still doing it for them even then. I told her how wonderful her parents were, and I begged her not to forget me. I needed her to remember that for the first parts of her life I was the only one who knew her, that it was my heartbeat that soothed her to sleep and my body that held her. The thought that those things would be forgotten created a bigger hole inside of my heart.

"When I went into labor, I was so afraid, not because I thought anything would go wrong, but because I knew I would be lonely once again. I knew the emptiness would come back, and I dreaded it. Then something went wrong, and I knew at that moment, I would never be able to replace my daughter, I would never have those feelings again, and I decided to keep her.

"I wasn't doing it to hurt my sister. I was doing it to save myself. My everyday life consists of loss, most of which is senseless. Not many people know the pain associated with telling a mother, brother, sister, husband, or son that no matter how hard you tried, their loved one didn't survive. We all want to feel we belong to someone. My sister wants to take that from me, and I cannot bring myself to give it to her.

"She will never understand this. I don't blame her, I don't think anyone would be able to unless they have held a child inside their womb for nine months. Yes, she knows what it means to love another person more than herself. When that person is a part of you in the way that my daughter is a part of me, there is no comparison. McKenzie is the best of me manifested. She is my hopes, my dreams, and I cannot let her go, not even for my sister."

Lance

"How did Tonya react to my request for a private session?" Dr. Taylor asks as she turns on the now ever-present tape recorder with a smile. She is a very attractive woman, though I would never look at her in any way that is not professional. Tonya had asked her once why she was single; instead of taking the offense, she simply replied she was waiting for her earth to move. I understood what she meant. Tonya was that for me. She made my world shift with just one glance, and it is something that everyone should experience at least once in life. It is a shame though that the doctor who has spent now a few weeks with us trying to make sure our relationship remained intact did not have someone to share her days with.

This saddens me. Everyone deserves someone who makes their life just a little easier, who makes them smile when there is absolutely every reason not to. I am sure she is in need of more than a few reasons to smile. She reminds me of LaToya, in this matter only. Both of them seem to walk into someone's life when it is falling apart, and neither have someone to hold them together.

Tonya liked her, more than even I thought she would. It makes me uneasy to think of how she would react if the doctor chose her sister instead of her at the upcoming hearing. It is now less than a week away.

Dr. Taylor asks her question again. It appears I have not answered fast enough for her liking. She wants to know if Tonya approved of this private session.

"Both of us were apprehensive. We are not sure why you wanted to meet with me separately." That was certainly putting Tonya's reaction mildly. She was more than irritated at the idea that I might say something that would jeopardize the rapport she had with the doctor. I tried to assure her that this was all part of the process and convinced an even more baffled Arnold to play along.

I have no idea why I am here or what she expects to gain from our conference. The doctor has met with all of us, a few times at this point, and I am sure her mind has been made up. There is no way I will allow her or anyone else to justify the decision to take my daughter away from us. Surely she knows that by now. Tonya does not see how she could possibly ask the judge to consider placing McKenzie with Toya. I always agree because it is the polite thing to do; however, I am more than aware of the way people change when they swear to tell the whole truth. Witnesses are often unstable, and no amount of coaching can assure anyone of another person's testimony once they are inside of a polished witness box. Added to the fact that Ronnie is very accomplished at cross examination, she could twist the doctor's words so that even Denise would not be certain of her original choice. Ronnie is good, but I am better. This time is different. I am trusting Arnold to know when to pounce or be lenient.

I look at Dr. Taylor, and for a split second, I am glad it will not be me asking her questions. I would certainly destroy her.

Once again I am sure my wife will fall apart if she has misjudged Denise. I will be upset as well. I have watched Tonya blossom under her influence.

"How is Tonya?" Denise asks with the reassuring smile.

"She is doing fine, better than fine actually."

"I am happy for her." She takes a sip from her mug, which was obviously designed by a child. There is a simple handprint on it with multicolored fingers. She seemed more concerned with not breaking the mug; I can tell by the way she always places it down with such care, then scolding herself with the hot beverage inside. I wonder if it was a gift from one of her patients; there are no pictures of children in her office, and I know she doesn't have any of her own. I would assume whoever gave her that coffee cup means a great deal to her. I have learned what women find irreplaceable; in some case, it may seem irrational. But it does not make the item less special for them. My mother kept every one of my baby teeth, my first blanket, and every single Mother's Day card I have ever made or purchased for her in a keepsake box. My father referred to these things she collected as "life's baseball cards." Whenever I gave her anything, they'd both say in unison, "Go get the box," and we'd laugh.

Tonya has started her own collection as well, and I find this comforts me. She had McKenzie's "first day" home outfit dry cleaned, though she had only worn it for a few minutes, preserved and placed in a frame that now hangs above her crib in the nursery. The pink bloomers with the white lace ruffles are placed next to the dress, and above them is the hair band that caused such a commotion in the nursery. I did not expect for such a small thing to bring a man like me to tears and make me understand the need for such sentimental reminders. A few months after my father passed away, and I had finally found the will to clean out his office, I found his "baseball card" collection as well inside of a very large tackle box. He had also kept every single Father's Day card, and there were pictures I have forgotten all about. I cried when I went through them all one by one. Truthfully I have never felt more loved.

"I think it is time we addressed the elephant in the room. I have put it off for as long as possible, partly because I am not sure what Tonya's reaction would be. I have never said or implied in anyway which side I am leaning towards, not wanting that to be the focus of any of our sessions. If I presented this question in front of your wife, I am sure she would assume I have already made up my mind, which could not be farther from the truth at this time. It seems no matter what the court decides in this custody case, you will have the advantage of being a father." I know that Denise is saying this as delicately as possible; however, I can no longer sit still as she speaks of the fate of my family in this manner. My abrupt need to stand startles her, but she continues while I look around her office. "Your wife or sister-in-law will be designated as an aunt, which I do not see either of them being happy with. This knowledge could not have escaped you, and I am sure you are dealing with it, but I want to know just how well you are dealing with it."

"No, the knowledge has not escaped me. Either way, I will be the man my daughter knows as her father. It is the one thing I have wanted for longer than even I knew. But I need more than just the acknowledgment of being called Dad."

"How so, for the entirety of our meetings, I was certain that was all you wanted?" I can tell my answer intrigues Denise. She would make a horrible poker player since she has so many "tells". I decide it would be best to sit down for this.

"I want to spend every day with my daughter, and as a father, that is not too much to ask. Since the moment she was born, I have thought of nothing else but being there for her in all the ways my dad was there for me. I want what is best for my daughter, and I know that what is best for her is to be with her father and her mother. Tonya is that in all the ways that no one seems to understand. From the very first day we found out her sister was carrying our daughter, Tonya was the one who worried, the one who sacrificed, the one who planned. She has devoted her life to becoming the one thing that everyone wants to deny her, the opportunity to be a mother. Without any doubts, I can say she will be wonderful at it. She will exceed in this in the ways that she never allowed herself to excel in anything before.

"We all want our version of what we think is best for McKenzie. We are all fighting for what we think will benefit her the most, and it seems that they are only considering the now. I am thinking about the long term."

"You don't think that Mrs. Lawson and Dr. Garrett are concerned with your daughter's future?" This she writes down into her notepad.

"I am referring to what comes next. The decisions we make now will affect our daughter for the rest of her life." I frown because I am the only person who knows when I say "our," I am speaking of the three of us. McKenzie belongs to us all, but she belongs with my wife and me.

"Please explain this to me, Lance." She is now pushing her hair behind her ear while writing, so much for my streak.

"Tonya does not want to acknowledge that Toya is McKenzie's biological mother, and I understand why, but that does not mean I think she is right. At some point, McKenzie deserves the truth. Growing up, it didn't matter to me that my parents weren't my biological mother and father. Truthfully I had no idea until I went to kindergarten and another student told me my parents were white. I asked them why we were different, and they explained that it was God's design that they were supposed to be my parents. At five years old, I knew that made me special, and it didn't matter what other people saw when they looked at us. What mattered was that the most amazing people I have ever had the pleasure of knowing chose to love me. They gave me more than I think my real parents could have. I have never wanted to know anything or anyone else but my parents, and I know it sounds inconsiderate, but it is not. As a parent now, I'd like to believe that my biological mother loved me enough to do what was best for me, and that meant to let someone else raise me. I do not hate them for giving me up. There is no desire to know them or their reasoning either." My throat becomes dry reaching for my bottled water I momentarily wished I had something stronger to drink.

"My parents never lied to me. They respected me enough to tell me the truth. For my eighteenth birthday, my mother handed me my adoption records. She wanted to give me the opportunity to know where I came from, and I told her the same thing I have told my wife or anyone else who cared to ask. I knew where I come from. Daniel and Joann Lawson are the only parents I care to know. I am a product of their love, even if it is not in the conventional way, the love they had for each other was too much not to share, and they decided to share it with me, and I have never wanted for anything or felt like I was missing something. They were more than enough.

"McKenzie deserves to know, eventually, that we wanted her so badly and tried for so long that we asked Toya to carry her for us. She needs to know what we went through to have her in our life. She deserves to know how much she has meant to us from the very thought of her. Toya deserves for her niece to understand what she has sacrificed as well to bring her into this world. Though the thought pains my wife very much and admittedly her sister has caused hurt, she deserves some admiration for her part in this. There is no better way for either of us to repay her than to acknowledge her sacrifice. She will never be able to bear another child, and I feel for her in a way her sister refuses to, but I do not forgive her for her choices."

I wait for the doctors response, the pause assures me that she has considered what I said before responding. "I understand your desire to tell McKenzie the truth. Certainly it is a result of your own childhood experiences. A wise lady once told me we all decide at some point what we want to be like as adults. We chose what type of parents or spouses we want to be. We draw those perceptions from our parents. We decide what worked with us and what did not, and we think we can improve upon their techniques. I do not think it is ever in the best interest of any child to lie to them, but I do not think it is realistic to believe that your child will have the same experiences you did. Have you told Tonya how you feel about this?"

I look at the doctor, and she laughs. I can tell she has read my facial expression correctly. My wife is not the only one who has built up a rapport.

"The twins," Lance said, gesturing the air quotes, "are each other's best defenders, as well as worse enemies. Saying that one has done something wrong is the equivalent of accusing them both. Yet defending one is like condemning the other. If I told my wife I thought she was wrong, she'd accuse me of favoring her sister, and that would not be conducive to a happy home. Yet I do not think it is fair to my daughter to agree with my wife simply because she needs me to."

"How happy can you be if you do not feel you can be open with your spouse? Trust should be one of the foundations of any marriage. You have to trust her to respect your opinion even if she doesn't agree."

"No offense, Doctor, but that is easier to say when you are not married. I understand that what should be and what is are often very different things. I trust my wife, please make no mistake about it. I do not trust myself to articulate what I mean in a way she will understand." Even as I speak I am not sure I understand how to explain this to my wife. I shift in my seat again trying to find my place.

"That is a fair statement. I am not married, but I have counseled enough couples to know what makes or breaks any relationship. One thing I know for sure, if you cannot trust someone to love you at your worst, you can never trust that they truly love you at your best. You have to give her the chance to understand, and even if she doesn't, you have to trust that she will love you enough to try." Dr. Taylor says this as if I have not considered these things prior.

"I take my vows very seriously, and when I said for better or worse, I meant it with everything that I have to give. Tonya is and will always be the better in my life. If that means I have to bite my tongue at times, it is a small sacrifice."

"We will come back to that at another time. For now tell me about Toya. What are your concerns? From what I have gathered from you both, there is a mutual love and respect there, do you think you will be able to co-parent with her?"

"Yes, I will. There is nothing that can come between my child and me. Not even Toya, no matter how stubborn she can be. I have grown to love her as my sister-in-law. I respect her. She is one of the most driven woman I have ever known. In her own weird way, she is very protective of her own but as long as she does not have to sacrifice herself in anyway. LaToya and LaTonya are so incredibly different. The twins are the complete opposite of each other, and it is hard to believe that the two of them grew up in the same zip code, let alone share DNA.

"Whatever the outcome, I will make sure that I am the father my daughter deserves. I just wonder how we will explain to McKenzie I am her father. As a child, she will accept it without any thought. All children grow up, and one day she is going to want to know how her father is her uncle or her aunt's husband. Is it fair for us to minimize Tonya as her aunt, or will she be considered her stepmother? There is no book on how to explain that to her. We live in the era of daytime television, but that does not mean I want my daughter's life to mimic what people see on soap operas every day. I do not want her to feel in any way she has something to be ashamed of."

"Your concerns are valid, and I am sure that when and if the time comes, all of you will have a way to cope with your family dynamic. Before you say anything, I am not a mother either, but I have spoken with enough children to know, all they want is for their parents to be honest with them. They want to be treated with love, and they need to know that they are the most important thing in your life. Anything else after that is just filler in your story." Denise takes another satisfactory sip from her mug.

"I could argue that the filler is what makes the story."

"Yes, as an attorney, I am sure you could argue anything." With this she gives me another smile.

"Making a living from arguing facts often has disadvantages. I have argued both sides for the past few months, and no matter how this works out, I feel my daughter will be the one who suffers. This kills me because it is my job as her father to prevent as much hurt as possible. How do you protect your child from her family?"

"You often refer to what a father is supposed to do or be, and it seems you have most of it figured out, but I would like to hear from you what type of father do you think you will be?"

"I want to be like my father. I want to be the type of man my daughter looks up to."

"That is a very vague description. Tell me about your father. He has obviously made an impact on the type of man you are." Her tone has changed, and it seems that I am not the only one who has found some measure of comfort in our conversation.

"My dad was the type of man anyone would want to know. Growing up, I honestly believed there was nothing he could not do. There was never a single moment when I did not believe that his family was the most important thing in his life. I was always a priority. He helped with homework even when he worked late. He'd call home almost the moment I walked in and ask, 'What do we have today?' I'd read my math problems to him. I could tell he was writing them down. Even though he already knew the answer, he'd wait while I solved it and asked how I came to my answer, whether right or wrong.

"He was there at every single sporting event since peewee league. He coached a few of my teams as well, but he never played favorites. Some of the other parents would ask him to give me more time. I was always a great athlete, just to ensure a win. After we lost one of our championship games, I was upset with him. Told him he should have put me in the game more. He responded by telling me he hoped his son would understand it means more to lose as a team than to win as an individual. I didn't understand it then, but I do now. That is what he did. He taught me how to be a man, he cheered when I needed it, he corrected me when I was wrong, and more importantly, he stood by me through everything."

"When I brought Tonya home to meet my parents she became an instant part of our family. I admit now I was nervous about it at first." I chuckle at the memory of that night.

"My mother loved everyone, that is the type of woman she was, but it seemed as if Tonya had been the daughter she was waiting for. My father was no different. Their love for her made it easier for me to picture a life with LaTonya."

"That is the type of man my father was and the type of man I have tried to be. He was an amazing father and father-in-law. I need the chance to make my daughter as proud of me as I am of him."

"He sounds like a very wise and caring man. I have no doubt that you will make him proud as well."

Toya

A single sheet of paper can change someone's life, and as I stare at the packet in front of me, I am reminded just how much so. I have never really given so much consideration to this fact up until now. Every single milestone in life or history has been written down, signed, and imprinted with a seal, just like the legal documents sprawled across my desk.

These papers are verifying the one thing I have known to be true since the moment I declared I was keeping McKenzie. I am being sued for full custody by my sister and her husband. I expected them, but it does not make the reality of it any easier. I trace her signature with my pointer finger, and I can feel the desperation and agony in each beautifully crafted letter of her name.

Certainly she cried, knowing that it has come to this. Despite Ronnie's pleas, I would not be the first to file the necessary paperwork. I had set the ball in motion, but I refused to be the one to finalize anything.

This is my Dear John letter, with all the confusing legal jargon. My sister has officially broken up with me. A piece of paper has caused a shift in my life. This is no different from a birth certificate or a marriage license. No, it is instead the equivalent of a death certificate, announcing that my relationship with Tonya has been ended.

This week had gone by smoothly, though I would not say perfectly. We have been making this work, and for some reason, I assumed that Lance and Tonya would see just how well we were all doing. The routine was not without fault; eventually I am sure both of them would get tired of sleeping on such a small bed, but at some point, I expected them to see we were handling this joint custody arrangement very well.

The details had been ironed out in my head. I would let Tonya and Lance have her while I worked, and on my days off, she would stay with me. I am sure we could arrange some type of agreement for the holidays, and we spent every holiday together anyway. McKenzie would grow up with two loving homes. I was certain we could have made it work if given enough time to do so. Visitation was not an option, which is the one thing we have all been able to agree upon. Ronnie verified this for and with me countless times, but I still held out hope that joint custody could be the compromise we were all looking for.

Full custody is what they were requesting. Once again I look at the petition as if I missed something. I search in between the lines for any hidden messages. In less than ten days, I will have to sit in a courtroom and watch as Ronnie destroys what little part of the relationship between my sister and I that can be salvaged. I wish there was another way to make this right, but the alternative does not suit me any better.

The last time I saw my sister was a few days ago, a few feet away in my kitchen. I had woken from my sleep, not sure exactly why, and could not fall back into it. When we were kids, my mother would make us a glass of warm milk, and I decided that was exactly what I needed. I am not sure why it was that night in particular, considering I have woken countless nights since my return from the hospital.

I made my way down the steps, careful not to make any noises. I avoided the one creaky step and walked on tiptoes like a cat burglar. Making my way to the kitchen without any noise, conscious of every floorboard, I assumed everyone in the house was asleep. There Tonya was humming one of her songs with McKenzie in her arms. Everything about them seemed so right, and for a few seconds, I watched her as she heated the bottle on the stove, the old-fashioned way. She had refused to use a bottle warmer or the microwave even. Leave it to her to never take the easy way out. I watched as she tested the temperature on her wrist, and I had no doubts that she had somehow managed to calculate exactly how much time was needed to warm the refrigerated bottle to the exact temperature on the stove. She was wonderful at things like that. She develops countless skills that were out of place in the real world, ones that had no marketable value whatsoever. That was one of the beautiful things about my twin. She was more concerned with making things right for everyone else than for herself.

She shifted McKenzie in her arms, and within seconds she was feeding her. It happened so fast, I assumed I missed something. I do not know how she managed to make everything look so effortless. I was jealous of them both. I missed the calm of my sister's whispered songs of comfort. She was the one I called on nights like that, when sleep seemed to evade me and there was no one to talk to. I'd call her, never conscious of the time or what she could have been doing, and she'd answer, always on the first ring, as if she were expecting my call, and she'd ask if I needed her. It did not matter to her why, and we both knew if I asked, she'd leave the warmth of her bed and come to my rescue. There are still so many things I need to be rescued from, but she will no longer be the one to save me. That is why I could not sleep. Or maybe I was the reason she could not as well.

This was the role she was meant to play, and as I watched a content McKenzie doze off in her arms, I choked up. That was what I have wanted for my sister for so long. Up until recently, I didn't believe I could have it for myself. It pained me to see that they were so perfect together. McKenzie fit and looked better in her arms than she did in mine, and I am sure they both knew it as well.

"You couldn't sleep either?" she asked, and I knew she was speaking to me, even though I am not sure exactly how she knew I was there.

"No," I whispered ashamed that she had caught me spying on her.

"Sit down. I'll make you some sweet milk." She had not looked at me yet. I needed her to, but I also couldn't stand the thought of her doing so all at the same time. I wanted to watch her and, just like I had with the nursery, try my best to mimic her. Some people were made for things as ordinary as that—feeding a baby in the middle of the night and doing it as if it were the only thing that mattered in the world.

She moved around my kitchen as if it were hers. She knew exactly where everything was when even I would have to stop to think where I had placed something. Tonya looked at home, and I could only imagine how uncomfortable it must have been for her, considering I did not feel welcome in my own kitchen. The baby gave her balance; anyone would have been able to see it. McKenzie was the one thing that erased everything, and it was obvious that with her in my twin's arm, she would have seemed at ease in a den of lions.

Twin managed to pour the milk into the pot with McKenzie in her arms, all the while positioning herself so that the infant was as far away from the heat of the stove as possible. *This I would never be able to do*, I thought while I watched her. She was mesmerizing. It is amazing to watch someone in their element. This was what she was created to do.

I am not certain how long it took since I was so absorbed in the choreography of the dance my sister and my daughter were performing in front of me. She walked McKenzie through every step as she prepared my mother's secret recipe. Tonya explained how to stir carefully from the moment you pour in the milk to prevent it from burning and sticking to the pot. She told her when to add the sugar and cinnamon, and it was then that I noticed she was not speaking as softly as before. This lesson was for me as well. I was uneasy with it all. I felt like there was something I was missing, and then I understood it. The tone Tonya used when explaining the ingredients was not one of a teacher, but instead of someone who was afraid they would not be around to teach their student when the lesson was mandatory.

It is the same tone my patients use before surgery. I had walked into a few dozen home videos, one where a father tried to explain to a son who could not yet walk how to throw a curve ball. I once listened to a mother, who was a florist, explain to her five-year-old daughter how to pin a boutonniere on her prom date when the time came. All their voices, no matter the lesson, were the same. I listened as they explained to their loved ones, all the things they thought were important enough to not leave this earth without teaching. In my mind, they all ran together. Each voice undecipherable from the rest, each lesson the same.

Listening to Tonya made me wonder how old must she have been when my mother taught her how to make sweet milk and where I was when the lesson was being taught. I doubt my parents would have wasted their time with something as minor as how to stir a pot of milk, but what could they have said? I am sure they would have asked that we take care of each other.

Immediately I felt hollow at the thought. If Tonya was not saying this for McKenzie, who would obviously not remember, but for my benefit, this was indeed her way of saying good-bye. I would not be able to call her during my sleepless nights nor would she be there to help me when bad dreams keep McKenzie awake. She was the woman in Solomon's court. She would not split our daughter in half; instead, she would want all or nothing, and to have nothing would certainly kill her.

Tonya poured the warm milk into an oversized mug. She handed it to me on her way out of the kitchen. The smell had been so alluring. It brought back memories that I didn't know I had. My mother had done this for us dozens of times, and just as Tonya was doing moments before, she did share with us how to do it exactly right. I had taken her for granted. I never paid attention because I was certain there would always be sweet milk during sleepless nights.

She still did not look at me, and I could not bring myself to look up at her as well. I sat at the breakfast table and cried. I do not know if she heard me, but for once in our life, I can say that I finally heard her.

Lynette

LaToya looks so helpless sitting on that bench alone. My heart breaks for her. This was the ugly side of betrayal, abandonment, and desertion, and she has no one to blame but herself. During their adolescence, she had been the one with all the friends, I do not remember a period when she was not surrounded by admirers. Time has managed to change so many things and leave others very much the same.

Tonya was flanked on either side, guarded like royalty, and she was glowing, her sister had no other choice but to look pathetic. LaTonya's appearance made it seem as if she had taken a misstep and ended up at the wrong place. There is nothing but tranquility surrounding her as if it was hidden underneath the camel-colored cashmere sweater she placed back over her shoulders, and for a brief second, I considered the possibility that Lance may have sedated her.

Her mother's lucky pearls, which had been the "something old" for her wedding, look stunning against her blouse, paired with her "something new" pearl earrings. I am reminded just how regal she can appear. She did not need to wear her sling backs today. Standing there she seemed taller than before, as if her resolve alone added a few inches. She looks formidable yet receiving, resilient but dainty. Her husband complements her very well. Their movements are so fluid, and I am sure they are aware of the way others are watching them.

Lance, though he may look at ease, is ready to pounce at the slightest hint of Tonya's distress. God could not have created a better man for my little girl. He will always protect her even if she doesn't know she needs it.

Her laugh fills the empty space as it reverberates across the walls. There is music in her mouth, and I am not the only one who hears it. She has always had a pretty voice, and it is the one thing she has ever taken pride in. Laughter in its purest form seems so out of place right now, and that is exactly why we need it. Tonya is not doing these things to agitate her sister. She is not the one to play with another's emotions. If the action had been perpetrated by the other I would have believed it was in fact a show. This is a side of her I have not seen in a while, and I miss it.

They barely look at each other. I want to blow a whistle in the same manner a referee would. Off sides, I want to yell at one or both of them. Again I wish I could lock them in their bedroom and order them to fix whatever they had broken between them, thus mending my broken heart as well.

Tonya smiles at me. She understood why I needed to be seated with her twin for those few moments, and I find that for what I wished was the only time my daughter knew better than me what was necessary. She has always been the mature one.

I watch them walk into the courtroom. Lance and Tonya enter first.

"I am glad you're still here. I thought I had the wrong room number." The voice I hear in my ear is the one I had no idea I needed until now. Eugene has come, and though part of me wished he hadn't, a larger part wants nothing more than to crawl into his arms until all the thoughtlessness is over with.

Eugene is beside me, and for the first time this morning, my soul finds peace. There are no illusions that he could somehow make any of this go away; however, there is the very real possibility that he will do the one thing I need him to do. Eugene will hold my hand.

"You just missed them. They have both gone in. I am sure they would have loved to see you." I take the time to adjust his tie even though his appearance is perfect. I need an excuse to touch him.

He smiles at this, even though we both know I am exaggerating. Dr. Flowers is here for me. He has always been here for me.

"I am sure we will get a chance to speak before the day is over. For now, what would you like to do?" *Run to the moon. Drown in the sea.* Either option seems better than the only one I have.

"They will call me as a witness, though I am told by Arnold it will most likely be later this afternoon. For now I have to wait, do you mind?" Eugene takes my hand leading me down the hall.

"Not in the least." We sit on the same bench, and this time, it seems more comfortable. I had my doubts, but now I am glad I shared this with Eugene.

"Tell me a story." I ask in a voice much quieter than I have used in some time.

He chuckles as I place my head on his shoulders. "Well, that is an unusual request."

"I know, and you are the first man I have ever asked since my father to do so."

"Is that a fact?" He asks while caressing my hand.

"Yes, it is." The stories would always start the same. It always started with, 'Did I ever tell you, girls, about the time I...' and we'd fall asleep to the rise and fall of his chest. In the morning, we'd wake in our bed not sure when or how we made it there. Throughout the day, we'd try to recall parts of the story to see which one of us had managed to stay awake the longest. We competed for everything, but never for our father. He belonged to us both, and neither would dare to take him away from the other. There was never a time when I felt safer than when I would sit on my father's lap. You remind me a lot of him. I knew it the first time I saw you. Your every mannerism reminded me of him, and it frightened me.

"Now I am sitting here with you, and I wish that I had the courage to love you all those years ago. I feel sick about it. You have always been a part of this family, and when we needed you, I shut you out. There were so many things I was afraid of, mostly of losing you. It was best for me not to have you than to lose you." My eyes have filled with tears that I beg not to escape. There have been so many reasons I've pushed this man away, and now I realize there were never enough reasons to justify it.

"We do not have to talk about that right now," Eugene says with his lips close enough to my skin that I can feel his warm breath as it escapes.

"That is what I mean. You being here scares me, but it is what I need. You always know what I need more than I do. You can't imagine how scary that is for a woman like me." I close my eyes tight not wanting him to see just how afraid I am.

"I know exactly what type of woman you are, and I love you for it. Even when you stubbornly push me away, I love you." I raise my head. I need to tell him that I love him also in the same way. We have said the words before, but this is different. "Lay your head back. You asked for a story, and I am going to tell you one." He playfully pulls me back to his chest. The little girl inside of me is overjoyed, the woman is frightened by exactly how good he feels.

"Did I ever tell you about the time I fell in love?" We both giggle at his first line. Within seconds, I am transformed into the little girl who found sanctuary in the words of the man in her life. I am no longer a woman on the edge of insanity fighting for her daughters.

"No, I don't think you have." I say with a giggle that belongs more to a school girl than a woman of my age.

"Well, I am not sure where to start, so I will begin at our beginning."

I listen as Eugene tells the story of us. The trip down memory lane is a well-needed distraction, and I am shocked at the attention this man has paid not just me but my girls. I am reminded that I have done nothing in life to deserve this type of love, and I cherish it all the more.

When he is done with his montage, I ask, "I thought you were going to tell me about the day you fell in love with me. I think you have managed to highlight the past thirty years."

"I did. I told you about the very first day I fell in love with you and every single day thereafter that I can remember falling more in love."

"Are you afraid?" I am not sure if I am prepared for his answer.

"Yes, and that is how I know that this is real. You are the first woman I have ever been afraid of. I am afraid that I could never stop loving you, afraid that I will not be able to show you just how much, and afraid to lose you. That is why I have never pushed."

"I am afraid that I won't be enough for you." There it is the truth in all of its ugliness. "I love the way you look at me, and I am not the woman you think I am. I am afraid that I will never be, and I am afraid to lose you as well. I'd rather imagine what we could have than live with what we will never be." My lips tremble with the truth.

"Lynette, I have loved you from the first time I laid eyes on you, and despite what you may think, I am a very intelligent man. I have learned a lot about love, and most of it from you. There is nothing that could make me stop loving you." He means these things and I lean further into him as if I am willing myself to fall completely.

"I want to be the person who knows all of your faults, everything that you hide from the world. I need to be the one you trust with your secrets. That is what love is. If it were just about the easy things, it wouldn't be worth a damn. Love is about the hard times, the knowing that even at your ugliest, your weakest, and your most unforgiving moments, someone will be there to see your beauty, your strength, and be willing to forgive. That is the way I love you. You will always be for me the person I need to give my all."

"I need you too," I whisper.

"Not now, not today." His words are not harsh but they are firm.

The tears fall, and I finally bring myself to look him in the eyes. This is what I was afraid of: when I was finally able to give myself to him, he would not want me back. I feel like a fool. I had resisted him for so long, and now sitting on this bench listening for God knows how long as he explained the way he loved me, he does not want me. I shouldn't have let him stay.

"Lynette, I have waited for you, and I am willing to wait as long as it takes. I won't take advantage. We both deserve better. When all of this is over and you wake up the next morning still needing me, I will be there. Don't want me because you feel as though you have no one else. You are a better woman than that, and I am a man with very little pride when it comes to you." Once again he cradles me.

"I will respect that, and I know that I will still need you after all of this because I have always needed you. I just didn't have the courage to admit it. You think I am saying this in a weak moment, and I understand how you can mistake it, but truthfully, I have never been this brave." I feel another smile cross his lips, and I am thankful for this day. God does work in mysterious ways.

"Did I ever tell you about the time I fell in love?" I ask into his chest.

"No, I don't think you have." We both laugh, and that seals the deal for me. I too begin to tell the story of us. As a music teacher, I searched for harmonies, and I have finally found mine. This time I will not let him go. This man has heard my heart's call each and every time, and when I pushed away, he waited for me. This is the type of love I want for my girls, and I will not deny myself it any longer.

Lynette

I take the stand as I search for Eugene. He is sitting in the back of the room on Tonya's side for now. We agreed to alternate so both of the girls feel supported. The older sister won the coin toss. I smile at him because I do not feel comfortable up here and I wish that I could have refused.

He will be my center, we agreed. It is something I remembered from the twin's birthing classes: when the pain seems unbearable, find one thing to focus on and breathe your way through it. The twins selected a photo of the two of them taken at a fair where their arms were wrapped so tightly around each other and the lights in the background formed a massive blur of colors around them, casting an angelic glow across their skin. It was one of those perfect days filled with funnel cake, cotton candy, and laughter, the type of day you wished could last forever. That picture had remained on my desk for years; now it has found a new home in McKenzie's nursery.

The Garrett sisters—there is no one without the other; their lives have been intertwined from the beginning, and as I sit on this very hard chair in this uncomfortably cold room, I am reminded that I am just as entangled in the outcome of all of this.

Suddenly my eyes filled with tears, and I want to run from this room, from the eyes waiting for me to pick a side, needing me to validate one or the other. That would be impossible for me to do. As I sit here in front of them both, I found it difficult to see one separated from the other. LaTonya is an extension of LaToya. I look up at the judge to gage whether or not he has put it together as well.

The gray hair would lead me to believe that he has countless years of experience. With his slack-jawed look of boredom, I am certain he has witnessed everything and will not be impressed by my words of praise for either.

I would be considered a character witness; the thought is absurd to me. The only character that will be tested is my own. There is no way I will say anything derogatory about either, and my fear is that I will be tricked into saying something I do not want to.

Placing my hand on the Bible, I swear to tell the truth the whole truth and nothing but, drawing strength from the words I know are inside. We have been promised from childhood that the truth is always the best option, and according to the good book, it will set you free. I have never doubted the word of God, and today will not be the day I start. I am just concerned that what I will be set free from may not be as bad as what I will be opening myself up to. There are things that are better left unsaid, an unkind word for example. As their mother, I am rightfully the keeper of secrets, those things I will not reveal.

Arnold approaches the stand, and I am pleasantly surprised that his smile puts me at ease. I am happy to see him. He has gained a few pounds and lost even more hair over the years, but he has always had such a boyish charm about him. I liked him immediately. Even though there are only a few years separating us in age, he has always referred to me as "ma'am" coupled with his subtle accent. He was certainly endearing.

"How are you this morning, Ms. Carter?" And there it is, the charm.

"I could be better, but I won't complain. All in all, I would still say I am blessed."

"I would certainly agree with that statement, Lynette. I'm sorry where are my manners? May I call you Lynette?" Arnold asks, and I know this is a show.

"As long as you don't intend to make it a habit, yes, you can." Most of the courtroom laughs at my statement. It is an uncomfortable one, but at least my sense of humor has not missed the mark.

"Thanks, I promise not to make it a habit, ma'am." He touches the box a few inches away from my hand, and I know for the sake of propriety he will keep this as professional as possible. "Lynette, right now I just want to ask you a few questions, is that all right with you?" I nod my head in response. "If there is anything I ask that you'd like me to rephrase for you, let me know."

"All right."

"How long have you known Mrs. Lawson and Dr. Garrett?" The question seemed a ridiculous one since everyone here knows the answer.

"I have known them all of their lives."

"They are both remarkable women, and you have played a major role and assuring that. Would you agree that you have been more of a mother to them than an aunt?" Again a question that does not need to be answered, but I trust there is a reason why I am being asked.

"Yes, I have thought of myself as their second mother, and I hope that is the way my girls have seen me as well." With this statement, I cannot bring myself to look at either. Instead I concentrate on Arnold's tie.

"Your girls, is that the way you always refer to them?"

"Yes, they have always been and will always be my girls." There is sadness in my voice that I wish I could erase. Tonya notices, as she always has, that there is something wrong. The little girl that I had comforted is gone. She has been replaced with the woman who no longer needs me to console her. Her look is not defiant nor submissive; she is instead searching to make sure that I am all right. She has now taken on the role of protector, and I can remember the same resolve build in me almost immediately after they were born.

"Even though you did not birth either of them, you have loved them in the same way a mother loves her children."

"Is that a statement or a question? Yes, I have loved them both as much as I think any mother could."

"I will try to make myself clearer next time." Arnold smiles teasingly at me. "Do you think you could have loved your girls more if they were biologically yours?"

"That wouldn't have made a difference to me. From the moment they were born, I loved them as my own." That question angered me, and I am sure Arnold felt the brunt of my response.

"Please do not take offense," Arnold says this as if it were at all possible. "I am just trying to establish a family dynamic. I think we would all agree that birth doesn't make someone a mother. You are an exceptional example of that. Can you explain briefly how you came to be their custodial parent? I don't want to drag up unpleasant memories, just the facts please."

There is no way to answer his question without bringing up the unpleasant memories. It appears the southern gentleman I had met countless times was a rouse. I do not wish to discuss the loss of my sister, and even after all these years, it has not become easier. Twenty-seven years is a long time, and I may need twenty more to make my peace with it.

"My sister and her husband died in a car accident before the twins' tenth birthday. Since I am their next of kin, I was awarded custody."

"I am sure that was a tragic experience for all of you."

"Tragic is putting it mildly. It was crippling." With that said, I have nothing more to add. I give Arnold a look that lets him know exactly how I am feeling at this moment, and I believe he may have shrunk an inch or two.

"Sorry, Lynette, I do not mean in any way to minimize your loss. Losing a sibling can be devastating, and I can only imagine how hard it must have been for your girls to lose their mother. How did their mother's death affect them?"

"I do not know how you want me to answer that question."

"I would assume that there would have been drastic changes in their personalities after losing their parents at such a young age. Some people become more responsible, others reckless. I am wondering what side if any your girls fell into."

"Objection," Ronnie interjects, and even though she has saved me, I still want to tell her to wait her turn.

"Sustained." The judge does not seem any more interested in what is going on than he did prior. His response seemed more a reflex than anything else.

"After their parents' death, Toya was described by some as reckless, and Tonya became the opposite, would you agree?"

"LaToya was more active than most kids her age, I agree to that. I wouldn't say she was reckless. Tonya became more responsible, but she was always that way."

"Tonya became responsible, and Toya was 'active,'" he reiterated, using the appropriate air quotes. I feel like I am being mocked, and I do not like it at all. "That is an interesting take on it. Would you describe Dr. Garrett's behavior as irresponsible in some instances?"

"No, I would say she is more of a flower child. She was born in the wrong decade, I'd like to believe."

"That's interesting. A flower child, I think that is the perfect description. Has Dr. Garrett ever used drugs?"

"Not that I am aware of." My defenses are up now. I fold my arms across my chest to let Arnold know we are no longer on friendly terms.

"Were you aware that your daughter was charged with possession of marijuana her sophomore year in college?"

"I am certainly not aware of it."

Arnold returns to his table and shifts through papers. I have never wished harm on anyone, and I hope my Lord forgives me for wishing a paper cut at the least on Arnold.

"I have a document from campus police stating they were called to break up a party, one in which Toya was found in possession of marijuana. She was allowed to make a phone call— oh wait, I am sorry, it says right here, her sister was called." For some reason I do not believe this is the first time Arnold realized this. "I also have a copy of the canceled check for the fine. It appears her sister paid it." Tonya always kept meticulous records; I would not be surprised if she had the receipt from the first pack of gum she ever purchased. "Would you like to see them?"

"No, I believe the forms you have say what you claim they do." I instead wanted to tell him exactly what he could do with his files. The harm wished upon him has been upgraded from paper cut to something much worse.

"So you are not shocked to know that LaToya was fined and that my client was the one who had to clean up her mess?"

"What I meant to say is that I do not believe you would lie, but I am sure there is an explanation."

"Is it normal for LaTonya to clean up after her sister?"

"They have always taken care of each other."

"In what way do they take care of each other?"

"The things sisters do."

"I'm sorry I need you to spell it out for me. I don't have any sisters."

"Well, Tonya makes sure that her sister's bills are paid, she does her laundry, stocks her refrigerator, and cleans her home. Once, Toya was in an accident and she severely damaged her lower back. Tonya took care of her. She stayed with her for a few weeks until she was back to normal. She drove her to all of the appointments. She wouldn't let us hire a private nurse. I think she did a better job than anyone else could have. Things like that, the things that sisters do."

"It sound like LaTonya has been a wonderful nurturer. Would you use that word to describe her as well?"

"Yes, she is the most caring woman I know."

"You said they take care of each other. What does Dr. Garrett do for her sister?"

"Well, I don't know everything she has done. Toya is always busy, but she does things for her sister also."

"Can you give me an example?"

"Not off the top of my head, I can't. You put me on the spot."

"I agree, I did put you on the spot, but you didn't have a problem listing all of the things Tonya has done. Let's switch topics for a second, and I will give you some time to think about that question. How would you describe the Lawson's marriage?"

"They are a very loving and happy couple. I love them both very much."

"Would you consider them to be stable?"

"Yes."

"Would you agree that stability is something that all children need?"

"Yes, stability is important."

"When was LaToya's last stable relationship?"

"Toya is very private. She tends to keep her relationships to herself."

"So you've never met any of her male acquaintances?"

"Yes, I have met a few."

"How many have you met?"

"I don't know," I say between clenched teeth. He is making my baby out to be a drug-using floosy, and Ronnie hasn't said one word to stop him.

"Can you guess? Let's narrow it down some. In the past five years, how many men has your younger daughter dated?"

"I wouldn't be able to answer that."

"According to your older daughter and her husband, it has been about seven men in the past five years. Does that seem about right?"

"Again, I wouldn't know."

"Do you think my clients would lie about it?"

"No, I don't think either of them would lie. If they said seven, than maybe it was seven."

"So we can agree to seven."

"If you need a number, I guess we can agree to that."

"Does that seem stable to you?"

"I think Toya is searching for the right person to share her life with. She is single, and there is no law against a single woman dating whomever she wants. She has no one to answer to."

"Sorry, I beg to differ. She certainly does have someone to answer to now. Do you think that it is ideal for a child to grow up in a two-parent home?"

"Yes, ideal."

"So we have what you would consider an ideal situation, a stable one as well. And I am sorry, but I must ask if you had to make the choice. If everything rested on your decision, who would you choose to raise sweet innocent McKenzie?"

"I would choose a medium where everyone plays a part. I cannot pick one side over the other."

"Fair enough. Back to the question I asked you earlier. What has Dr. Garrett done for her sister?"

"She gave her a baby. There is nothing greater than that. You can try to make her a monster if you need to, but she did that for her sister, and that is the only thing Tonya has ever wanted." The tears are falling, and I want to defend Toya. We know she has taken from all of us and never thought to give back. But she has done some good also. It is unfair for anyone to minimize that.

"Did she give her sister a baby, Lynette? The one thing you said she has always wanted, after always giving so selflessly of herself—did her sister give it to her?" There is a long pause, and I cannot bring myself to answer.

"I have nothing further." Arnold hands me a tissue and sits back down next to his clients. Tonya's eyes are filled with tears as well. I am not sure if it is because of my hurt or her own.

"Ms. Carter, would you like a minute or something to drink?" the judge asks.

"No, we can continue." Just keep pulling the Band-Aid off no matter how hard I scream. It is for the best.

"Lynette, I will only ask you a few questions. Are you sure you are up to it? We can take a five-minute recess if you need." Veronica is in front of me this time, and despite the sincerity in her voice, I know she is the same woman who tore my daughter apart years ago and, just now, allowed me to do the same to the other.

"No, I am ready now." If I left this bench, there is no one here on earth that could get me back onto it.

"You said that the Lawsons have, in your opinion, a stable marriage. Is that correct?"

"Yes."

"What in your opinion makes them stable?"

"They both love each other very much, and after everything they have gone through, they have stayed together."

"Everything they have gone through—are you referring to the miscarriages?"

"Yes," I stutter over such a simple word.

"Is there anything else you'd care to add?"

"No, I meant the miscarriages and this situation as well."

"How did Tonya react after her miscarriages? I understand the experience can be quite traumatizing. There is often blame placed on either or both parties, and in their case, there were quite a few losses."

"I don't believe either blamed the other. It was just not in God's plan, and they accepted it."

"That seems like a hard pill to swallow. You're saying that a couple was able to justify losing six—I think it was six, right?—six pregnancies as the will of God."

"Yes."

"Do you think it made either of them bitter?"

"No, I think it made them stronger."

"So strong that they had to seek marriage counseling for years. Does that seem like something a stable couple would need?"

"I am not a married woman. I have never been, and I cannot testify as to why a couple would say they need counseling or why a couple would decide to split for instance."

"As Arnold said, you raised two remarkable women, and you just admitted that you did that alone. Do you think it is necessary to have a father in a child's life?"

"No, I do not believe it is necessary, but I do believe when the option is present, it is in the best interest of the child."

"What if the father's involvement somehow posed a threat to the well-being of the child? What do you say then?"

"I say that is not a concern here."

"Hypothetically, if it were the case, what would you say?"

"Then I would say that the child may be better off without a parent who poses a risk."

"I won't ask you to make a choice right now. I think that is unfair. Instead, I will ask that you be patient with me. There are a few things I will present, and I hope that we can again talk about the issue of stability, is that fair?" She doesn't wait for a response. "Nothing further, Your Honor." Ronnie makes her way back to her side of the courtroom, and now I can finally breathe. She was not as bad as I thought she would be. For a few seconds, I wait for her to turn around and attack me. I had been prepared for it.

"Am I done?" I ask the judge.

"Yes, you can step down now." After leaving the box, I decide to leave the courtroom as well. I need the time to regroup; I would never have guessed that it would be Arnold to bring me to tears. Arnold is apparently the wolf in sheep's clothing.

Tonya

It is now my turn to speak. We agreed to let Lance hold the rear as if this was a long-distance marathon. In some ways, I guess we could classify it as such. We have gone over what Arnold is supposed to ask, and I feel confident that I will do well with him. Ronnie is another story entirely.

She was too nice to Lynette, we all agreed during the brief recess. I have been warned to watch myself and my temper when she questions me. Considering Ronnie's kindness most likely ended with my aunt and I am familiar with her venomous tongue, I understand the warning more than my attorney or husband could.

I am asked to place my hand on the Bible just as every other witness before me, and then I state my full name and address for the record. Then Arnold stands up. He buttons his jacket, letting me know he is ready to start.

Even though he is on my side, my stomach sinks. This is what we have been working for, and I am afraid that I will undo it all with just a few words.

"Mrs. Lawson, I have a few questions for you, and it is late in the day, so I will make this as quick and easy as possible."

"Thank you."

"Can you tell me briefly why you want to be a mother?"

"I have always wanted to be a mom. Since I held my first baby doll in my arms, I knew it was what I was meant to be. There is nothing I could do that would mean more to me than giving a child all of my love. In my opinion, there is nothing better a person can do with their lives than to ensure the physical and mental well-being of child."

"How long have you tried to conceive the conventional way?"

"It's been about four years now."

"Did you get pregnant?" We have walked through this, and I promised to get past this part without tears.

"Yes, six times, and we lost them all."

"Did this fuel your desire more?"

"Yes, I think each miscarriage has reinforced for me that I am supposed to be a mother. No one puts themselves through all of that if they don't want it more than anything else in life."

"Did you consider adoption?"

"No, not at first, we didn't."

"When did you consider it?"

"We considered it as an option if Toya refused to be our surrogate."

"Is adoption an option for you now?"

"No, and I honestly wish that it was." This is the truth I promised to tell. "There is no way I can love another child in the way I love my daughter. I have cried a thousand tears for this reason alone. I do not care to admit it, but I will if I must. There is no other option but McKenzie for me. No one else can fill that void, and a life without her would be just that void. After McKenzie was born things changed for Lance and me. He was an advocate for adoption since he was adopted as a newborn. We both formed such an attachment to McKenzie that it would be impossible to give up on having her in our lives."

"Can you tell me what led you to ask your sister to be your surrogate?"

"Lance and I thought we were not going to have a baby the traditional way. We looked into adoption and surrogacy. There are a million happy endings, but there are also a few not-so-happy ones. I couldn't bear the thought of someone changing their minds and denying us the child during the adoption waiting period. As far as surrogacy, I didn't want to place the future of my child in the hands of a stranger."

"To avoid the possibility of a stranger changing their mind, you asked your sister, is that correct?"

"I wanted this to bring us closer. I have never wanted anything more than a child of my own. My sister knew this. We have been through so much, and through all of those things, we have been together. It never crossed my mind that she would change hers."

"When you asked her to be your surrogate, did she know how much being a mother has meant to you?"

"Yes, she knows how much this means to me."

"And did she know about the six miscarriages?"

"Yes, she had been there for the first three. After those, she sent flowers when we lost a child. Well, Lynette sent them on her behalf, but she was aware."

"Okay, I am trying to paint a picture here, more so that I can understand correctly. You both lost your parents at a young age. You chose to help put your sister through college. When she gets into trouble, you are the person who is called upon to clean things up for her. Your twin knew exactly how much being a mother has meant to you even though she could only bother herself to console you on three of the six occasions you suffered loss, and yet she still chose to keep your child."

"Yes."

"Were you surprised?"

"Of course, no matter how selfish Toya has been, I did not expect this from her."

"Did she give you a reason?"

"No, she did not give us any reason. I am not sure what her reason could be or if she even had one, but I would have liked to know."

"Did she ever express any interest prior to this in starting a family of her own?"

"No, Toya enjoys her independence. Her schedule leaves little time for a family anyway."

"Do you think your sister would make a good mother?"

"I think my sister is talented, and she has always excelled in everything, but I do not believe she is what is best for McKenzie."

"What do you think is best for McKenzie?"

"My husband and I are best for McKenzie."

"Why do you feel that way?"

"Lance and I have devoted our lives to the idea of being parents. We can offer a child a home with stability. Our schedule would allow for extracurricular activities. I would like to believe I have more patience and experience when it comes to small children. My husband and I have more than enough love to give to a child. We want the opportunity to do so."

"Let's talk about your marriage. How long have you and Mr. Lawson been together?"

"We have been a couple for eighteen years, married for sixteen of them."

"Do you think your husband will make a great father?"

"I think he will be more than great."

"I promised to make this quick, and I only have one last question. Do you forgive your sister?" This was not one of our rehearsed questions, and I am more than caught off guard.

"Yes." With the answer, I cannot pick my eyes up off the ground.

"Yes, you have forgiven her. Can you tell me how, better yet, why?"

Don't do this to me, Arnold. If I answer this question, I can either make myself look like a saint or a fraud.

"I am sorry, Mrs. Lawson, we are waiting for an answer."

"Because I can't help it, because I have loved her for as long as I have known who she was or I for that matter. We learned to swing together, to do cartwheels in our aunt's back yard together, I learned how to braid hair by practicing on her. There is no easy way to explain it. She taught me how to tie my shoes, and I taught her how to swim. She knows why I am afraid of the dark, and I remember why sunflowers are her favorite. There is no memory that I have she is not a part of. You can't walk away from that, no matter how much you want to, no matter how hard it is to stay. My whole life has revolved around her, and I loved her every single heartbeat in between. I cannot erase that.

"Yes, I want to hold on to this hurt. I want to keep it in my heart so that I do not feel hers breaking also. I want to ignore her pain and pretend that she is not so much a piece of me that I have no idea who I am without her, but I can't. To forget her would be the equivalent of losing me. I have to forgive her because I can't stop loving her." My sister ignores my eyes; I can see my words have brought her to tears as well.

I want to run to her, to hold her and comfort her, but I am afraid that it would be just as easy for me to unleash the type of fury no heart should know. Did she forget all those things? How could she not remember countless nights under makeshift tents planning a future that would never be for either of us? It would be impossible not to remember the knees I have bandaged for her or the tears she has wiped for me. Arnold hands me tissues and walks back to Lance. I look to him now since my sister has offered me nothing.

My husband's eyes are clouded as well, but not with any form of sentiment. This is anger, and in the moment, I had forgotten how he considers every tear cried of mine as a personal cross to bear. For now I want to tell him he will have to love me a little less to make it through this.

"As Arnold said, Mrs. Lawson, it is late in the day, and I hope that we can wrap this up as soon as possible." Ronnie is in front of me. Her presence brings everything into focus.

"You said you love your sister, is that correct?"

"Yes, I do love my sister."

"Despite everything, you don't feel any resentment?"

"No, I do not."

"So after all of this, her keeping what you have deemed your child, her using all of your savings for school without any regards for you, and for being as what was quite evident as your aunt's favorite, you have no feelings of resentment."

"I would have to disagree with that."

"What part—she wants to keep *your* child. she did in fact spend both of your college funds, or as was evident, when your aunt was on the stand she is in fact her favorite?"

"I would say that I offered her the college fund, that she believes McKenzie is her child as much as I believe she is mine, and that our aunt did not have a favorite."

"After all that you and your attorney have done to paint you as your twin's savior, your aunt agreed that you have both given as much without a shred of proof on your sister's behalf even still you do not consider her a favorite?"

"I do not see how that has anything to do with this."

"As Arnold said and please forgive me for stealing this line, 'I am trying to paint a picture here.' You are either a very good liar or a martyr."

"Was that a question?"

"I could rephrase it for you if you'd like."

"Objection." In the few seconds it take the judge to rule in Arnold's favor, I have regained my composure.

"You said and everyone here has stated you and Mr. Lawson have a very stable marriage. Why have you two been in couple's counseling for the past few years?"

"That is a private matter."

"You're correct, and unfortunately at this point, we have forfeited every right to privacy. Do you need me to repeat my question?"

"We were dealing with the loss of our pregnancies."

"Why were you prescribed antidepressants?"

"Excuse me?"

"Objection." This time the judge does not rule in our favor.

"I have been prescribed antianxiety medication in the past."

"Are you currently taking them?"

"No."

"When is the last time you filled that prescription?"

"Before LaToya agreed to be our surrogate."

"You've filled the same prescription monthly for years, during pregnancies as well. Do you believe the medication could have played a role in your miscarriages?"

Once again Arnold objects and loses.

"No, I am certain it played no role whatsoever."

"You are certain. I think I could call an expert to testify differently."

"I am sure you could, but as I stated, I am certain filling those prescriptions played no role at all."

"I find it hard to believe that a woman who claims she wanted nothing more than to be a mother would take such a risk. Even after loss after loss, you faithfully filled that prescription, and you expect us to believe that being a mother was important to you?"

"Being a mother means more to me than you or anyone else could ever know."

"Yet you still took that risk."

"There was no risk."

"If you are not awarded custody, do you believe you will need them again?"

"No." Once again I find myself looking at my twin, wishing she would stop this.

"I am not an expert, but I would think it is not as easy as waking up one morning and deciding you no longer need medication. What if you were to experience more loss, do you think then you will need to rely on drugs to cope with everyday life?"

"No, and I do not believe the use of medication in anyway constitutes weakness. It takes a great deal of strength to admit that help is needed."

"That is a very strong argument. You're right, the use of medication does not mean someone is weak. I admire tenacity, someone who refuses to give up, wouldn't you agree?" I nod my head in agreement. Though I am certain the question was rhetorical. "Mrs. Lawson, have you ever been hospitalized for anything?""

"No."

"So you are the picture-perfect version of health, besides the miscarriages and the anxiety, is that correct?"

"I wouldn't say that, but I have never been hospitalized."

Ronnie returns to her table and produces a file.

"Fall of 1995, did you seek medical attention for an apparent overdose on acetaminophen?"

"Objection." I wait patiently while Arnold and Veronica debate the merits of my medical history. Lance is as clueless about this as everyone else in the courtroom, and I can tell he is hurt. I watch as he tries to compose himself. Anger flashes across his face, pity follows, and finally his poise is restored.

Lynette is in tears, and I wish Uncle Eugene could make his way to her. We all know what Ronnie is trying to say. She wants everyone to believe that I had been weak enough once to try and end my life. There would be no way to explain to any of them what I know now. At twenty years old, there was no concept of the rest of your life. There was no way to measure the possibility of what there is to gain. Once I had viewed suicide as cowardly. After that day, I understand how much someone can hurt and how the desire to no longer feel can be overwhelming and pain too consuming.

"Mrs. Lawson, did you try to kill yourself?"

"No." Even as I spoke, I can tell no one is at all convinced.

"It says here you took over twenty pills. Is that correct?"

"If that is what your form says, I will have to agree."

"According to the documentation, you had a headache and decided to swallow those pills with half a bottle of vodka. That must have been quite some headache, or was there something more going on?"

"I used to suffer from frequent migraines."

"So why this particular night? Did you feel the need to swallow over half a bottle of medication?"

"I was in a lot of pain."

"Was that pain physical or mental?"

"I've already answered that question. It was a headache."

"A headache so severe you wanted to end your life?"

"No. It was a headache so severe I wanted to end the pain."

"Have you had a headache so severe since?" *Stop it, stop it.* She is turning this into something it is not, or worse yet, turning me into someone I am not.

"I do not believe so."

"What if you did? Are we supposed to trust that you would not risk the same behavior again?"

"No—I mean, yes. What I mean is that there is nothing to be concerned about." My body language demands she stops her line of questioning right here, but my tone does not have the same authority. I search again for Lynette; she is crying the tears I cannot cry even though she is sitting behind my sister. I know she would rather be right here by my side. My husband whispers to Arnold, and I see him shake his head. Apparently there is little either of them can do, and I will have to endure.

"Has your husband ever had an affair?" The question seems preposterous, and it takes everything in me to remember that I am a lady and not jump across the stand. The only other woman I have believed my husband to love. The woman who threatened to take him from me without any hesitation or remorse was the same woman who is questioning me now. I will not give her the satisfaction of having me admit that here and now.

"No."

"Would you be surprised if I told you that Mr. Lawson has been unfaithful to you?" With that question, there is a unanimous outburst from our side of the courtroom. Both Lance and Arnold are standing while I am trying to process what has been asked.

"What?"

"If I were to produce evidence of your husband's infidelity, would you be surprised?"

"No, I wouldn't be surprised by anything you would produce. I would, however, consider you a liar." The judge bangs his gavel at my last statement.

"No further questions, Your Honor." Ronnie saunters back to her side. The judge instructs me to step down. I stumble blindly down the two stairs; now I allow the tears to fall. It is Lance's turn. I am praying that he is able to recover the ground that has been lost.

Lance

Taking care of my wife is my job and not one I take very lightly. I am reminded today that I have failed. Despite giving everything to her, it had not been enough; knowing this can drive any man over the edge. She looked so fragile compared to Ronnie, and I blame myself for that. I knew better. I knew the moment Ronnie took this case there was no line she would not be willing to cross. My warnings had gone unheeded. Tonya did not understand them. One minute she is the lion, the next the lamb, and no one will ever slaughter the first.

I cannot blame her. It would be too easy to say, "I told you so." Tonya is a constant reminder that there is such a thing as grace in the face of cruelty, but that is not what is needed now. I am finding it harder to balance my need to protect my wife with my desire to destroy her sister, the latter not being an option in Tonya's mind.

As for now, I am trying to figure out where I missed the signs, whether I ignored them to protect myself—or had my wife been that good at deceiving me? I have never witnessed her take anything more than a vitamin since we have been together. Now

I am expected to believe she was addicted to a medication I had never even heard of. Worse yet, that she had attempted to end her life without any concern for how it would affect me.

Ronnie is not the type to throw stones unless she knows exactly where they will land, and this afternoon, she has taken to throwing boulders, each anchoring against the foundation of my marriage, thus my soul. Tonya is my weakness, I have said it thousands of times, and the statement is nothing short of an undeniable truth. Now I have learned I have been the very same thing for her, and I am not in the least pleased with it; instead, I am sickened.

The "incident" happened years ago, after we had ended things—and I take some solace in that—but that is not enough. A world without her would not be one I'd care to live in either, but I would. I would go on, devastated and crushed, and I am certain less of a man than I had been before, but I would continue. I am not flattered by this revelation; it makes me feel sorry for her. Every nerve of mine has been exposed, and I sit on this stand raw with emotion.

I want to hold and scold my wife, to tell her how foolish she is for thinking a man like me worthy enough to end it all for, but I also want to hold her in my arms and explain just how much I understand.

The bailiff interrupts my thoughts. I am asked to tell the truth, and I find that is all that I want to do. Arnold approaches me, and the friend in him sees just what is happening inside. He is the one person at the firm who has taken time to know me, and I am thankful for that now, though years ago I found him intrusive. He knows now is not the time to play with words, and I am thankful that he sticks to the rehearsed questions only. I have done well, but we are both unaware if that will be enough. Arnold whispers a few words to Tonya when he returns to his seat, and I know they have not registered because her eyes have not left mine. Yes, it is truly a curse to love such a beautiful woman, but a blessing all the same.

Ronnie approaches, and my guard is back up. She is not the woman I knew, and if I have played any part in creating this version of her, I will surely have to answer for that someday. I want to ask for a sidebar. I need to know just when she became the person standing in front of me. I need her to know this was not my intention, and if there was a way to do things over or undo whatever I had done, I would. No one deserves to reside in the past.

Trying to remember a time when I did love her seems impossible now. She is not just the lesser of two evils. She is the only one.

"Mr. Lawson"—my jaws clench at the sound of my name escaping her lips—"forgive me for my abruptness, but it would appear that time is no longer afforded to us, so I will make this as quick as possible. Who is Nina Hart?" And now it all makes sense. I had assumed, silly of me, that she had mistaken the names of my assistants. Now I know exactly where she was headed, and I know this will be a bumpy road.

"She is a previous assistant of mine and a family friend."

"Do you often fire friends?"

"Not often, but then very few of my friends work for me."

"How long had you and Ms. Hart had an affair?" There is an immediate reaction from all sides of the courtroom. The judge bangs his gavel, and Arnold is out of his seat in objection. The judge agrees that the question is allowed, and Ronnie is once again in front of me. I look to my wife. She had been more adamant on the stand about my fidelity than her sanity, but I can tell the name shakes her.

"I have never had an affair with Nina. She was my assistant and a friend. That is all."

"Why did you terminate her employment?" Another objection. The question was a loaded one, and Arnold knew exactly why. Neither of us had missed the rumors, and we both knew how many had floated around about my alleged affair. In our firm, it was not just expected but accepted for fraternization to occur between partners and assistants. Often a more tenured attorney would advise the younger ones on just whom was open to participate and who would be worth the effort. Ironically there were never any suits filed against us. It appeared the women benefited as much from the arrangements as the men had.

I did not want that for Nina. She deserved better. I let the rumors circulate that we were seeing each other, only to prevent someone else from taking advantage of her. Her future was bright, and when I realized that her interest went beyond pretending, there was nothing left to do but to let her go. I cannot say that here, not in front of my wife.

No one would understand that a man could be denied any type of affection from his wife and then have a very steamy but very bogus relationship with a twenty-something who looked more like a playboy bunny than a secretary. Arnold was the first and only one to figure out that the relationship was a fantasy one. It appeared that I had taken my assistant on a romantic vacation the same weekend he and I spent on a case right outside of Scranton. There is no way to disprove this now; it is my word against what my word was then.

"Nina agreed that our firm was not the right fit for her. She had other responsibilities, and the workload proved too much."

"After almost three years?"

"Yes, I suppose."

"How much did you offer her in severance?"

"I am not sure of the particulars, but all packages are reviewed by our human resources department, and I can assure you they found nothing wrong with it."

"Generally when an employee is terminated from your firm for anything other than a blatant violation of company policy, they are offered two weeks' severance for every year they have been employed, is that correct?"

"That is something you would need to verify with our HR department."

"I have verified it. Why was Nina offered three months' severance?"

"She was a great assistant, I was sorry to see her leave, but it was for the best."

"Is she the reason why you and your wife entered counseling?"

"No."

"So it's just a coincidence that you and your wife entered counseling a month before she was terminated and that she received such a hefty package from your firm, one that you approved?"

"Yes, it was a coincidence. We entered therapy after we lost our second pregnancy. It was our way of ensuring that we did not lose each other as well. I love my wife enough to make sure of that."

"Were you at all aware of your wife's attempted suicide?"

"No, and I am not sure that is what it was." I wished I did not have to place my hand on that Bible. I am praying that God forgives me for telling that lie. Surely there had to be a greater sin.

"Did you know about her prescription abuse?"

"You provided proof of prescriptions being filled, never did you provide proof of abuse."

"Is that a no?"

"No, I was not aware that my wife filled the prescriptions you mentioned."

"Is it customary for the two of you to keep secrets like that from each other?"

"I would like to believe everyone deserves privacy, which does not make it a secret."

"Your wife obviously took advantage of that belief as well." There is another objection, and this one, we win.

"Did you blame your wife for the miscarriages?"

"No, I did not."

"Even now after you have been made aware of her use of prescription drugs, you do not find her at fault?" Ronnie asks sarcastically.

"No."

"She continued to use medication that could be considered dangerous to the development of a fetus, and I could give you a long list of birth defects that could have been attributed to their use as well, yet you still do not blame her?"

"No, I do not believe my wife would do anything to jeopardize our family. This means too much to the both of us."

"Having a family means a lot to you, doesn't it, Lance, so much so that you are willing to ignore that the person you counted on to give you just that may in fact have played a part in denying you the very thing?"

"Having a family means everything to my wife and I."

"Then why haven't you left her?" I can tell this was not a question she intended on asking, and before Arnold can rise to object, I lift my hand to let him know he does not need to.

"I have not and would not leave my wife because she is the only woman I have ever loved, and without her, there is no such thing as family. I do not want to hold a child in my arms if my wife is not by my side while I do so, nor do I want to attend a recital or a soccer game or a parent-and-teacher conference without her being the one to hold my hand. She is my family. She is the reason why I am here." I have evened the playing field. It required another lie on my part, but I wanted to sting her in the same way she had done to both of us. She knows I have loved another, and unfortunately for us all, that woman loved me back as well, and still does.

"If you were to win this custody case, what would Dr. Garrett's place be in McKenzie's Life?"

"We would love her to play a part. Through everything, my wife and I are thankful for her sacrifice."

"Do you acknowledge that biologically she is McKenzie's mother? Do you think it fair she be delegated as an aunt only?"

"Biologically she is McKenzie's mother, but it takes more than a biological connection to be a parent. As far as we are concerned, my wife is McKenzie's mother and has been from the moment she was conceived. I do not want to diminish LaToya or the role she has played. I pray every day that my heart is softened towards her because she is the reason we have such a perfect gift. There will come a day when I hope we can all sit down and tell our daughter exactly how she was brought into this world, to explain that she was loved and wanted so very much by three people. I want nothing but the best for her as any parent would, and if I thought for just one second that was my sister-in-law, we would not be here."

"You want the best for your daughter as any good parent would, and I can assure you that the court feels the same way. You have done a great job of painting you and your wife as a loving, stable, and happy couple, but we have seen here that is just not the case."

"Is there a question, Counselor?" Arnold asks, though I can tell he is hoping there will be no more. We are all spent, and in the grand scheme of things, Ronnie has been gentle. I do not wish to encourage anything more.

"If you had to make the choice between one or the other—your daughter or your wife—which would it be?"

"I do not have to make that choice."

"Please instruct the witness to answer the question." Ronnie is addressing the judge.

"Please answer the question," the judge addresses me. The courtroom is silenced waiting for my response. I know what I am expected to say and what everyone wants me to.

"My daughter," I whisper the words as I stare into my wife's eyes. She would have answered the same, but it would have been acceptable for her to do so. This is the one thing I will not lie about, my redemption. I will be accountable for quite a few things in this life, but I will not, I cannot leave any room for doubt when it comes to the love I have for my child.

"No further questions, Your Honor." My testimony will be the last of the day. Now we are expected to go home and pretend as if none of this happened.

Tonya

I want to place my hand over Lance's mouth and shush him like a small child. There are too many things I need to consider, and his constant chatter is confusing me. This is a rare sight; still I have no tolerance for it, especially not today. It is not his fault; Lance is used to getting his own way. Admittedly, he is behaving badly; however, he manages to look amazing while doing so. I wonder how many men there are across the country throwing similar temper tantrums dressed in their own Armani suits. Instead of placing my hands on his face, I gently wipe something imaginary from his lapel. I am hoping my proximity calms him some; it has done little up until now. Yesterday had been damaging, and today had not been what we expected either.

"We'll appeal." Lance has uttered this statement more times than I can count; a few times it may even have been for my benefit. The case has not been lost, and we are no better or worse off than we had been yesterday.

I should be more upset. I want to be, but I am not. I had prepared myself for worse. Lance had underestimated my twin, something I had always known never to do.

Toya is charming; there is no other word to use. Even when you do not like her, you cannot help but want her to like you. Whatever she sold Denise had bought, and now she is deadlocked on her decision. Joint custody—that was the only thing she found agreeable, or as she put it, the one choice that "allowed her to sleep at night." The last comment caused Lance to snort in derision.

Blaming Denise is easy—weak, if I am frank. There was no way for her to decide; silly of us to think she could. The number of sessions did not matter. I listen as Arnold and Lance weigh the pros and cons of his decision to increase them. I do not care to interject, partially because my reasoning will not matter to either. I do not like the way they have taken to bad-mouthing our therapist. It would seem childish of me to remind my husband that he had trouble choosing between my twin and I at one point as well, so I bite my tongue.

Excusing myself from the conversation I am not a part of, I run to the bathroom. Within seconds, I am watching my breakfast circle the drain before it ever had the chance to settle completely in my stomach. I know exactly what this is, and I am ashamed to admit, I do not know how I feel about it.

The plus sign appeared seven weeks and three days ago, and according to my gynecologist, I am further along than I have ever been prior. Reminding myself that morning sickness is a sign of a healthy pregnancy, I flush again. It is, as my doctor describes it, a miracle. The one thing I have been waiting for and counting on, and I am unsure of how to feel. My doubt seems like blasphemy. My prayers have been answered, and with them comes the guilt of asking for too much.

Lance does not know. Part of me is upset that he had not noticed the moment I did. I tell myself that I am not keeping it from him; instead I am waiting for him to come to the realization on his own. I have used up all the creatively cute ways of announcing my pregnancies to him; the first time, I had presented him with a watch engraved with the approximate due date; the second I took him to a dinner at our favorite restaurant where the chef, an old friend of ours, presented us with deserts in the shape of baby booties.

He had been just as romantic. To match the watch, he had given me a tennis bracelet comprised of mine and the baby's birthstones. For the second, we had driven to the gynecologist in what I was told was a rental car to later discover was in fact my gift. There were no bows or gifts after that. This time will be no different. Part of me knows that it should be because it is very different from all the others. Fifteen weeks out of the woods, as they would say, but I will not force myself to see it that way. That is frightening. I may just get everything I have asked for, twice over.

The future has never been more terrifying. How do I ask God who has given me so much more than I have ever deserved the moment he blessed me with McKenzie to help me love another like I love her? I am ashamed to admit I do not think I could love them equally. More upsetting to me is the knowledge that Lance might not as well. If I could not love them the same, it would be acceptable, but not for him. I would forever look at her as my sister's child, my husband's favorite. Instead of finding joy when he would smile at her, it would be a dagger in my heart. He had admitted openly that if given the choice, he would take McKenzie. It was not as if I expected anything different. The choice would have been the same for me, but it does not make it easier to swallow. My child will be second. I do not trust him with the news. I do not trust myself enough to share it.

Then there is LaToya. I cannot bring myself to admit what I am taking from her. She may never have the chance to love her own child in the way that I would, and I am unwilling to let go.

I will have the privilege of loving not just one but two of Lance's children. It seems so unfair. I wish I could speak with

Denise and have her walk me through this. I want to tell her what I have been unable to tell anyone else. I want to cry and scream and shout that God has not forsaken me and that instead, I have been privy to a miracle of biblical proportions. That may be a bit dramatic or grandiose, but it is how I feel. And I have learned from our time together that I am never again to minimize my feelings for the sake of others.

But I am also afraid that life will be just as cruel as it has always been. Somehow my secret will come out, and when it does, the judge will grant my sister custody because that only seems just. Then it will happen the way it always has: I will lose this baby too and be left with nothing. For the first time in my life, I am willing to gamble with Toya's happiness to ensure a small piece of it for myself.

I return to find Lance and Lynette speaking. His posture tells me right away that this conversation is not one he finds at all pleasant. Lynette was the only one who seemed to favor Denise's opinion. I wish it were as simple as that. For the briefest of time while she testified, I considered it. I wondered what it would be like to share her than to risk not having our child at all.

I watched her speak, and I could not bring myself to be angry with her. I did not expect her to understand. Truthfully there is something broken inside of her as well. I am reminded of the old childhood taunt that it takes one to know one. I had been so wrapped up in my own self that I had not noticed it prior.

She was looking for something also.

Denise knew that neither of us would survive the loss of McKenzie, but I am not certain she grasped the gravity of it. In our sessions, I was asked who I am, or was. She never asked who I would be without my daughter. That would have been a better place for her to start. How else would she understand just how heartbreakingly and soul crushingly in love I am with my child? She did not know the nights I spent watching her sleep, admiring the sweet curve of her lips or the subtle movement of her chest as she took one breath after another. It would be too hard to explain to her in words the way that I could spend an entire day trying to count every single hair on my child's head and never get bored. How was she to understand me without first understanding this?

My twin and I are more alike than I care to admit. It would seem that I am the crueler of the two. She had made her choice when everything was so brand-new, when none of us truly understood what a life with McKenzie meant. Now I know love, and I am doing to her exactly what she did to me, but I am hiding behind the belief that I have the moral high ground. There is a name for this. It's called hedging my bet at whatever cost I am assuring myself a win as much as can be assured.

This recess has ended, and it is now Toya's turn to take the stand. I have avoided her not just because of what she has done but because of my actions as well. I am afraid she will be able to see right through me as she always has. There was a time when she knew I had a secret before I had even decided to keep one from her, a time when I could hide nothing from her.

Toya

Unlike my sister and her husband, I have very few character witnesses. Actually, I have none. Ronnie pretended to be surprised though I am sure she wasn't. At my age, it is inexcusable to have no friends or even a few colleagues who were willing to say nice things about you. There were a couple of sorority sisters I could have asked, and I am certain due to the code of sisterhood they would have responded. Part of me is ashamed. How do I call a figurative sister to help me hurt my biological one?

Once I am sworn in, I take my seat. My attorney has prepared me for the worst, or so she thinks.

"When did you decide you wanted to be a mother?" Ronnie ask.

"Once the doctors told me I could never have another baby, it felt like the right thing to do. I never planned on starting a family by destroying one, but I love my daughter more than anything." The courtroom is silent and frightening.

"You had not planned on keeping McKenzie prior?"

"No, the thought never crossed my mind before I was given the bad news."

Ronnie advised me to play up my own tragedy. It was unfair to compare my sister's loss with my own, but it was one of the few things I had working in my favor.

"How did you feel when you were told that you would never be able to have another child?"

"I felt an emptiness that I could not describe. I have loved McKenzie from the moment she was conceived. It was not the love that someone feels for a niece even though I tried to convince myself it was. When I was given the diagnosis, I knew I could never give her up. I knew she was meant to be with me."

"You have been painted as a selfish and flighty person. What is your response to that?"

"I can't defend myself against someone else's opinion of me. All that I can say is that I have devoted my life to helping others. It may not be in the way my sister has. If I had been flighty at some point, I would like to believe my daughter has grounded me."

There were quite a few other questions, and I answered each in the way we had practiced. Ronnie was a professional, and for the first time, I believed that we had a chance.

"Just one more question. Your sister admitted that she forgave you for what she thinks you have done. How does that make you feel?"

"It has been the hardest thing to deal with. I am thankful that she has forgiven me as she put it, but it still hurts to know that she believes I have done something wrong. I didn't do this on purpose. I had no way of knowing what would happen when I went into labor. Suddenly everything just made sense. McKenzie belongs to me. I did not mean to hurt Tonya. She has always been the best part of every day for me, even when I didn't want her to know, even when I couldn't let her know it. If I could change anything, I am not sure that I would. That has nothing to do with my love for my twin. She has other options. I do not."

"Thank you. I have nothing further, Your Honor."

Tonya had been my anchor for so long it was hard to picture her as anything but. I am certain that what I said was not as eloquent as her words, and that was part of the design. Ronnie advised me to stick to the facts. If I allowed myself to ramble and the judge did not believe me to be authentic, it would not serve me well in the long run.

Ronnie smiles before she walks away from me. A smile that even I can tell is not trustworthy. The gesture does not put me at ease.

Arnold is ready. I can tell by the way he struts toward the witness stand. He wore his arrogance, and in another situation, I might find it attractive.

"Dr. Garrett, what were you wearing the moment you decided to keep McKenzie?"

Ronnie is back on her feet before she is able to get comfortable in her chair. It is clear his strategy will be shock and awe.

"I'm sorry. Let me explain the question," Arnold says after losing the objection. "There a very few times in our lives where we as people are changed. You are describing your epiphany to keep McKenzie as such. For example, I can tell you where I was standing, wearing, and even drinking the moment my wife told me she was expecting our first child, and I can also tell you what I was wearing the day that child was born, what he and my wife wore home from the hospital, etcetera. Life-changing moments seem to etch themselves into our memory, so I am asking you, what you were doing the moment you decided to change three lives forever on a whim."

"I am not sure. I can't remember."

"Let me try to help you here. You woke up. I am sure you ate breakfast, but then again, hospital food is not all that memorable. I'd try to forget that as well." Arnold chuckles, apparently he is the type to laugh at his own jokes. "Let's see, you brushed your teeth, perhaps combed your hair, and somewhere between breakfast and lunch you decided to betray your sister. It couldn't have been an easy decision. Most would have wrestled with that one for hours, days, yet you can't remember the specifics?"

"No."

"That doesn't seem life-altering at all, does it?"

"Objection."

"I'm sorry, I don't mean to make light of the decision. I am sure it must have been hard for you to consider keeping your sister's child. Why did you?"

"Because the doctor said I wouldn't be able to have another child on my own."

"Did you want children before McKenzie?"

"No."

"So you didn't want to have any children before the doctor told you, that you could not, is that correct?"

"I guess you could say that."

"No, it's not about what I say here. It is about what you say. Your sister has wanted to be a mother for how long would you say?"

"All of our lives."

"And how long have you wanted to be a mother?"

"Since my daughter was born."

"Your sister has given up almost anything to make you happy. Do you think it fair that you could not give her this one thing she asked for?"

"I do not think a child is comparable to roller skates."

"A child you didn't want until you were told you could not have another. Even though you just admitted you wanted her since she was born, not after the doctor told you. If you did not receive bad news that day, if you were perfectly healthy and could go on to create your own family, would we be here?"

"I am not sure." There was a trap in those words. I could smell it, but I could not see it. This scared me.

"You never wanted to betray your sister, and you could not fathom not being able to be a mother when faced with it. Now you are saying you are not sure if that is what actually changed your mind. Which is it?"

"I didn't plan this."

"That's hard to believe now, Dr. Garrett. Would you have kept McKenzie if you could have other children?"

"I don't know."

"Truthfully, when did the thought first cross your mind to keep your sister's child?"

"I don't know, I can't remember."

"You can't, or you don't want to?"

"I can't remember."

"Was it before you went into labor?"

"It may have been." Suddenly I feel light-headed, and I just want this all to be over

"Was it the first time you felt the baby move?"

"I said I don't know."

"How about when you found out you were pregnant or maybe before that even, the day your sister asked you to be her surrogate. Is that when you decided to betray her in the most intimate way possible?"

"No," I said more adamantly than anything prior.

"When did you decide to tear your family apart? When did the idea first cross your mind?"

"I don't know, this time was different." I didn't want to admit to this, especially not in front of my family. I am ashamed by it. I wanted to believe that this had not been done on purpose, that I had not willingly duped my sister, but I had. Every time she rubbed my stomach, a small part of me wanted to tell her that I could not give my child up, but I didn't. When I watched her cry tears of joy and cried along with her, truthfully, I was mourning.

The doctor's diagnoses had not given me reason. It had given me validation. Arnold hands me a few tissues, all the while smirking. We both know that he has won; it is only fair that I concede graciously.

"Dr. Garrett, what did you mean by 'this time was different'?"

"Sorry." I clear my throat as I continue to wipe away tears. I look to Ronnie, and the look on her face says it all. She caught the slip too and is not amused. I am on my own.

"You said, 'This time was different.' Do I need to have the transcript read back to you?" I shake my head no while reaching for my glass of water.

"What did you mean?"

"I am not sure. I was confused."

"I doubt that. An intellectual woman such as you, confused by a few questions. Have you ever been pregnant before Dr. Garrett?" Lynette gasps in surprise. I look to Uncle Eugene, and before I can make eye contact, he is by her side. He is the only one who knows this secret, and he has faithfully kept it for all of these years.

"Yes." The entire room is in an uproar.

"What happened?"

"I lost the baby."

"When did this happen?"

Ronnie finally comes to my rescue, but it is a halfhearted objection at best. The judge knows this as well, and he does not rule in our favor.

"It happened when I was fourteen." With this acknowledgement, Lynette's sobs can be heard, the judge bangs his gavel yet again, and we are all advised to gather ourselves or our things and go.

"That must have been hard, and I am sorry for your loss."

"Thank you." I am sure his apology is sincere.

"Losing a child at any age can be devastating, especially when you are a child yourself. Did you confide in anyone?"

"Yes."

"We have spoken in great length on why your sister chose you to be her surrogate, and the loss was never mentioned. Did she know?"

"No, she did not."

"Who did you confide in?"

"My doctor at the time." The realization sets in almost immediately. I watch as Lynette shifts away from Uncle Eugene. It is not his fault, I want to tell her this. It was no one's fault. She has blamed herself for years for allowing me to go off on my own that day, punishing herself for something that was beyond her control, and I let her do just that. I am the monster. I could not deal with the pain on my own, so I inflicted it on her as well.

She turned a blind eye when I became belligerent, blatantly disregarded curfew even though she cringed every time I walked out the door. I did not ask to be raped, and she played no part in it either, but it was easier to share the pain than to deal with it alone.

I didn't come here for this; instead of cowering, I straighten my back. I will not play the victim. I refused that role years ago. I took control of my body. I gave it before it could be taken away ever again, but I refused to give my heart. I knew how easily that could be broken as well. This I will not explain. Tonya manages to get Arnold's attention, and for the first time since I took the stand, she looks at me.

She whispers something to him, and I can read her lips. She is telling him that I have had enough. She does not wish that he go any further, but Arnold is a shark, and he has smelled blood in the water. It would go against his nature to walk away now. In the end, he will succumb to what he is, and we will all suffer through it. I am not angry with him because there is a part of me that knows exactly how sweet it is to prey on the weak.

I do not mean to be callous or cold, but I threw my shoulders back, letting my sister know what must be done will be done.

She has fought to protect me for so long. Even as she took the stand, she never once broke that promise. I smile at her, which causes her to cry more. She thinks I am foolish, and I want to tell her that I am no longer the girl who jumped into the deep end just to see if I could touch the bottom. There is no more need for her protection. I do not deserve it. She knows that what I have done may not have been planned, but it wasn't exactly unintentional either.

"Why, I would think it would have brought you two closer. At the least, it could have explained your actions. Did you not respect her enough to share this with her?'

"I respected her too much to tell her. There was no comparison, no common link. She had lost children that she wanted with a man she loved. That had not been the case for me." I had been violated. My sister, loved. I was broken. She was and is cared for. Then it had been shame that caused me to hide this from her. As we grew, it became regret.

"What had been the case for you?"

Ronnie objects again. Though she does not know the details, she can tell the answer will not serve either of us well. The judge orders Arnold to go in another direction.

"You said this time was different. Does that mean you did not want your previous pregnancy?"

"No, I did not."

"Even though you did not want your previous pregnancy, I am sure the loss was unsettling for someone that young. How did you cope with it, since it appears to have been a secret?"

My defiant posture is taking its toll. My neck begins to hurt, but I refuse to let it go. "I am not sure what you mean."

"You admitted the only person who knew about your loss was your physician. Did he or she recommend counseling?"

"Yes." Uncle Eugene recommended so many things; truthfully I owe him more than I have admitted.

"Is that how you coped, counseling?"

"No."

"There are, I am sure, lingering effects from trauma at such a young age. You lost both of your parents suddenly before you were out of elementary school, and you suffered a tragic injustice a few short years later. I am wondering now if it is possible that we are risking placing a small child in the custody of a woman who may be more fragile than we all thought. Again, Dr. Garrett, I am asking how you coped with such loss."

"I am not sure."

"You're not sure, as unsure as you were about not knowing when you decided to stab your sister in the back?"

"That's not fair." I look to Veronica, hoping she will come to my aid even if it is just a stall tactic; I need a moment to breathe to think of what was next. I should have told her about this, that way she would have prepared me. The look on her face tells me she feels the same. I will sink or swim without her, and I am sure either way she will not be waiting for me back at shore.

"No one is that strong, and we would never expect you to be. Is that why you turned to drugs?"

He is bating me, and I know it, but I cannot help but bite.

"At first yes, and when that did not work, I tried other things." The tears were back, but this time they do not fall.

"What things did you try?" Arnold assumed he had me backed into a corner; that could not be further from the truth— not now anyway. There were no corners, no wrongs, not when it came to my daughter. She is my perfection, my redemption from all the wrongs I have done. Suddenly it all makes sense.

"I tried to end my life when the pain became unbearable," I said it as casually as if Arnold had asked what I ordered for lunch.

"Excuse me?" I can tell he didn't expect me to make it easy for him. Once again Ronnie is on her feet. If looks could kill, I would be dead. She objects, and I hold my hand up, letting her know I have had enough.

"They rushed me to the hospital after I had swallowed a bottle of pills. The EMTs asked me my name, and I all I could think of was my twin. I needed her there. I have always needed her there."

"I said LaTonya Garrett so many times they thought it was my name. When she got there in the midst of all the confusion, neither of us thought to correct the mistake. The next morning, the doctor came in with a few prescriptions for antianxiety and antidepressant meds. Tonya knew there was no way I could take them and hope to be a surgeon. She told me then that if I promised to never miss a dose, she would allow me to use her name. I had never seen her cry that hard before, not even after our parents had died."

"She sat on this stand and allowed you all to believe it was her, and I said nothing. I did nothing. She risked losing our daughter to protect me, and I just went along with it. She doesn't deserve it, and I don't deserve her."

My attorney objects again.

"Please let me finish now, while I have the strength to do so. I'm sorry, Twin." The look in her eyes says it all. Once again, I am forgiven, and I am reminded that she will always be better than me.

"My whole life I was told I was extraordinary and that I deserved anything I wanted. When McKenzie was born, I knew she was just as extraordinary, and what I really wanted was every day ordinary with her. I wanted to live the life that was denied me so long ago, but she is not mine. She is my sister's."

"I am the broken twin, the weaker one, and Tonya is what is best for her. LaTonya will be the better mother she has proven herself even after I have let her down again."

"No further questions." Arnold walks away.

The judge asks Veronica if she has anything further to say. She shakes her head no.

"What happens now? Tell me how to undo this." I ask the judge. I am ordered to confer with my counsel; I do not believe Ronnie would consider herself that any longer.

"Wait." Tonya stands. She is looking at me now, and I know she understands all the things I could never bring myself to say. Her tear-stained face is a testament to this. "I have something to say."